MERLIN'S LEGACY

BOOK 1

A SEED REBORN

By
P.J.PERROTTI

PublishAmerica
Baltimore

ISBN: 1-4241-2034-9
PUBLISHED BY PUBLISHAMERICA, LLLP
www.publishamerica.com
Baltimore

Printed in the United States of America

Dedication

This book is dedicated to my mother, Helen B. Adduci,
She is gone but never forgotten

It is also dedicated to all my grandchildren;
Andrew, Joshua, Marli, Elisabeth, Benjamin, Sierra, Kimberly,
Joeli, Abigail, Taylor, Nicholas, Julie, Amber.
But especially to my 'Kimmy' who has been such a joy.
I thank God everyday for putting her into my life,
I don't know what I would do without her.

CHAPTER 1

The golden shaft of light gleamed down on the face of the sleeping boy. He stirred, his brow wrinkling with a sign of a frown as he tried to cling onto the peaceful existence of his dream world. But it was too great a battle for such a small knight. He sat up slowly, letting the warm summer sun awaken his body. Looking at him anyone would have taken him for young Prince Allon. His hair and eyes were as black as the night. There was a kingly pride in the way he now held his head as he looked around the room. But he was not Prince Allon, son of Viviane of Larkwood. He was Ambrosius Myrddhin, whom all in the Lady Viviane's court called Amber. He was a child *'born to no woman and sired by no man'*. He had been told this often enough for now those words were burned into his brain and were the reason for his unyielding arrogance.

Amber was a boy of eleven years, playmate and companion of Prince Allon. He was also the prince's scapegoat, for whenever anything was amiss it was always Amber who was to blame. He didn't mind though, for Allon was his only friend. The other children of the household and in the nearby village of Larkwood were too frightened of the tales of his birth. They came just close enough to repeat the painful remarks they heard bandied about by their elders. At first, when Amber was old enough to understand, he would spend the hours away from Allon hiding in the old abandoned stone tower that stood outside the walls of Lady Vivian's house.

It was said the tower was built by Merlin, the Enchanter, to keep Lady Viviane a prisoner, but King Lot of Orkney freed her. The tower had but two rooms at the top of the winding stone steps. One was where Merlin's prisoner was kept. It was a small room with a few chairs and a pallet with a woolen coverlet on it. There was thick dust of time all over the room. Except, that is, on the pallet for this is where Amber would curl up and cry. The other room was across the stone casement, which stood at the middle of the tower. This room was guarded by a large oak door with symbols burned deep into its wood. It had a sinister look about it, which kept out even the bravest adventurers.

Once, Amber had mustered up enough courage to approach the door. As his hand reached for the brass handle, a fine mist settle around him. Beads of sweat formed on his brow. Blood pounded in his head and fear stalked his heart as he felt a prickly sensation creep up his spine and settle on the back of his neck. Out of the mist he heard words spoken in a deep whisper, *not yet, Ambrosius Myrddhin, not yet.* Then as quickly as it had appeared, the mist disappeared. That was the last time Amber had attempted to enter the room.

Now, in the light of a new day, thoughts of this frightening experience filled his mind. As he dressed, he could almost hear that cold voice, *not yet*. Amber quickly washed his face in the cold water that was left for him. The sounds of footsteps in the hall told him he would soon be sought after by Allon. He was just turning around when the door opened.

"Are you going to stay in your bed like a woman lying in?" Called out a familiar voice.

Amber's face flushed as he greeted Allon. His friend stood with his hand still on the latch, looking every bit the prince he was. His hair and eyes, like Amber's, were jet-black. But where Amber's skin was almost a bronze color, Allon's was lily white. Even this could not take away from his broad strong body. If anything it gave him the bearing of a king. He was the same age as Amber yet seemed to be the taller of the two.

Maybe it's the way he stands so straight. Thought Amber as he stared at the sight before him.

Allon's mother, Lady Viviane, was the second wife of King Lot of Orkney. Lot's first wife had been Morgana, King Arthur's sister. After Morgana's death Lot had joined his son, Sir Gawain, in his quest for the Holy Grail. It was while he was returning home that he came upon Lady Viviane locked in Merlin's tower. After her rescue, Lot became enchanted with her beauty and fell madly in love with her. Allon was their only child. Not only would he inherit his mother's house and surrounding lands, but because Sir Gawain was slain in Dover fighting the Saxons beside King Arthur, Allon would also receive Lot's lands and castle in Orkney.

Ah but to be born in such high graces. Thought Amber, *Were it but I instead......*

"I know I am a striking figure of young manhood," Allon broke into Amber's dream, "but I cannot stand here all day while you flatter me with your gaze. Come, Mored has set out cheese and new bread for us to eat before we go out on our adventure."

"It is silly," said Amber as he walked down the hall with his friend. "No one has been in that tower since your father took Lady Viviane from Merlin's grasp. It is said in the village the soul of the enchanter still walks the stone steps to the top, mourning the loss of his lady love."

"Now who is being silly?" laughed Allon, "and besides, how do you know what is said in the village? You never talk to anyone there."

"Just the same, if your mother finds out, I will be the one to get the strap." Amber replied, "It will be said the wicked Ambrosius Myrddhin, with his evil parentage, lured poor saintly Prince Allon astray again."

It was not the whipping, or even the whispers, that made Amber try to talk his friend out of going to the tower. Amber didn't want Allon to find out the tower was his retreat from all the cruelties he had to suffer. More frightening was the thought of meeting the voice in the mist.

While Amber ate the cheese and bread Mored put before them, he tried to think of a better reason to keep Allon out of the tower. He knew the prince would not be afraid to go against his mother's wishes. He was just about to feign illness for lack of a better excuse, when Uldin, the head house servant, came hurrying into the kitchen.

"Young master," he gasped breathlessly, "my Lady sent me to make haste in preparing you for a royal visitor. You are to go to the main hall at once. My Lady and your Kingly father await your presence."

All this was said as the short stumpy Uldin shuffled the prince out of his chair and down the hall toward the muffled noise that was stirring across the courtyard. Allon's thoughts of the tower were now lost in the excitement of who the royal visitor could be.

Amber's thoughts were also on this mystery, but he would have to wait until his friend could slip away and tell him. There was little doubt in his mind that he would not be called to the main hall. Mored was now clearing the cheese and left over bread from the table, giving him her well-known scowl. She only used this when the prince was not around, for Allon would not tolerate any of the servants being cruel to his friend. Amber moved to help her but the look in her eyes gave him second thoughts so he started to leave through the same door Uldin had just hurried the prince out of.

"Mind you stay clear of the main hall. There's no need for the likes of you there." Mored called after him. "Why my Lady ever took in a child of your birth is beyond me, even if she has the kindest heart of......"

Amber didn't wait to hear the rest of her little speech. Changing his choice of exits, the young lad turned to the outside door. For some reason he could not explain, he had to get out of that stuffy kitchen. In the courtyard he paused as he felt his heart quicken its beat. Unexpectedly he started to move like in a dream. He was aware of walking out of the courtyard and into the garden. By the time he reached the gate in the wall he had beads of sweat forming on his brow and a prickly sensation was creeping up his spine to the back of his neck.

Suddenly Amber felt stone steps beneath his feet. He tried to turn and run out of the tower, for that is where he was, but his body did not respond to his mind. Now it was too late for there before him stood the oak door with its half moons, stars, and suns staring at him. There was no mist but from all around him he could hear that deep whisper.

"Now, Ambrosius Myrddhin. Now is the time." As the words were spoken the latch lifted and the oak door creaked slightly open.

Sun, shining in a window hidden by the door, lit up the room and Amber could make out a few pieces of furniture. He pushed the door all the way open and was surprised to see the room was large. His fear gone and in its place curiosity, Amber walked over to the bookshelf that was standing against one wall. He had never in his young life seen so many books. Some had symbols like those on the door, while others had words he had seen before. A few of the books he thought he had seen in Lady Viviane's room when he had been called there to take a beating for Allon. He remembered she had called them books of Medicine. He moved away from the books and looked around the room.

To one side there was a table with a chair. Beneath the only window, which was large, was a bed. Not a pallet like in the small room across the stone casement, but a bed made with wooden slats across blocks of wood. The mattress was made of straw and there was a fur coverlet at its foot. Smaller chairs sat by the bookshelf and on the far wall, next to a stone hearth that was cut into the wall, stood a large wooden chest. When Amber opened one of the doors he found tunics hanging as if they were waiting to be worn.

The realization that this room was free of any dust suddenly hit Amber. As he sat down in the chair by the table trying to think things out, his hand touched a book lying there. It was open and the letters jumped out at him; *"Merlin; Myrddhin Ambrosius."*

"How can this be?" he said, "It is my name. Backwards maybe, but still MY NAME!"

The question fell on the emptiness of the room around him, while his thoughts wandered to the day he had first heard the words; *'born of no woman, sired by no man'*. In tears he had made the mistake of going to Lady Viviane. She had not taken him into her arms to comfort him as she did Allon. To the contrary, she was cold and stern when she heard the reason for his weeping.

"You are going to have to get use to this sort of thing Ambrosius." she had said, "After all it is the truth. My servants found you in that horrible tower the day I had my lying in with Allon. They say you were on the straw pallet in the room where I spent my confinement with that sinister prince of darkness, Merlin. They heard your cries and brought you into my house without my knowledge. You were taken care of by the same wet-nurse as Allon. When I was up out of bed Mored told me of the finding. She said the words 'Ambrosius Myrddhin' were written in the dust on the floor of that awful room, so that is what they named you.

"As much as I hate that tower, when I laid eyes upon you, I had not the heart to put you out. So I have kept you as a playmate for my

Allon. When you have grown out of your usefulness to him you will have to leave. Till then be happy you have a roof over your head and food in your stomach."

That was the last time Amber had gone to the Lady Viviane of his own free will.

Now, in this room, he felt he was close to the answer of his birth. He turned the pages of the book with a shaking hand. One by one he looked at them but could understand nothing, for the words were in a strange language.

Suddenly the logs in the hearth caught fire. Flames leaped about the stone sides in colors of yellow, red and blue. Smoke came out into the room in blue green curls bringing with it a pungent smell. Amber was aware of the smoke all around him but was not afraid. There was warmth deep in his soul and he felt he would be told what to do.

"You are not afraid Ambrosius, that is good. Listen carefully and do not ask questions." Said the now familiar voice. It was no longer a whisper, but spoke to him like it had substance. "You must leave this place at once as it is no longer safe here. Allon will be going to the court of Arthur and the Lady Viviane has no good plans for you. The royal visitor in the main hall is Votan, half brother to King Bolta of the lands in the south of Brittany. Bolta is building a fortress to protect his lands against Saxon raids. Each time his engineers lay the foundation, it cracks before they can raise the walls. His high priest has told him the foolish lie that the stones need the blood of the 'son of no birth'. Stories of your strange origin have reached Bolta and he sent Votan to bring you to his court."

Amber could not believe the Lady Viviane would agree to such a thing. She had told him he would be free to go when Allon no longer needed him.

"The Lady Viviane will do anything that has the right price on it." Said the voice as if it could read the young boy's mind. "There is a pony tied to the apple tree at the far side of the wall. Go there quickly and wait. You will know when to leave. Then do so with haste, not waiting to see if anyone pursues you I promise, there will be no one."

"Where am I to go?" Amber asked.

"To the north. You will know what road to take when the time comes. Go now and have no fear, I will be watching over you." The answer came.

"But who are you?" Amber cried as the smoke retreated into the hearth and the fire started to fade.

"Go now, before it is too late!" Came back the voice in a whisper. The fire gave a loud crack as the flames died out.

Amber ran down the stairs and out of the tower. The sun was low in the sky and for the first time he was aware of how long he had been in the room. Dusk was just settling around the house and, as he crept past the gate, Amber could see Votan's horses were still tied by the stables. Quickly, like a shadow, he moved to the far side of the wall. There by the apple tree was the pony, all black except for the white star on her rump. Amber went to her and ran his hand over her velvet like hair. There was an instant bonding between boy and animal.

Suddenly Amber realized that he still had the book in his hand. As he put it into the leather bag that hung from the pony's saddle, he had no time to think about anything, for in the direction of the tower there came a loud sinister rumble. Then the sky opened up and let large flashes of light out. They crackled as they hit the tip of the tower. The noise was so loud that it shook the ground under the boy's feet.

Quicker than the flashes in the sky, Amber was up on the pony's back and racing toward the north field. No one noticed the young figure, black against the sky, fleeing in the night. They were all too busy looking at the pile of rocks in the place where, just a moment ago, a tower had stood.

"That is something I should have done a long time ago." Said Lady Viviane, "Well no matter now, the gods have done it for me. Come Votan, let us have some wine and conclude our little bargain." She took his arm as they walked toward the house.

The only thing left to see was the smoke rising from the tumbled rocks and the young boy racing with the wind, if anyone would have looked.

CHAPTER 2

Amber sat with the sun to his back, watching two rabbits hopping around a nearby bush, a goat skin of wine by his side. There on the horizon were rolling green hills spotted here and there with clumps of trees. Just in front of the bush where the rabbits played, the ground fell away in a sharp slope. It made one side of a narrow, winding valley. At the foot, tumbling down its rocky bed, was the river Thames. After the river the other valley wall rose gradually to the top of the next hill.

About half way up the rise Amber could see the village of Calleve. He sat quietly for some time, deep in thought, staring at this little town. It looked so peaceful sitting there in the distance. To one side was a stone inn with horses tied in front. The young lad leaned forward, straining his eyes. There was something familiar about those horses, but he was too far away to see what it was. He lay back down on the soft grass, thinking about the last two days.

The night he had left Larkwood was spent in the woods, just outside a small village. Amber had rode fast and hard, not stopping until his pony could go no further. He came to a crop of trees with a little stream flowing through and fell breathlessly from the pony into it. Drinking with the cup of his hands, Amber slowly felt the numbness leaving his tired body. He raised himself off the ground and found he was not hurt. The pony was standing nearby, white foam streaming from her mouth, her nostrils dilated as she tried to catch her breath.

"Poor beast." said Amber as he led the pony to the stream. "I gave no thought to your well being, just of my desperate flight. Come, drink, not too fast." He talked to her gently as he held her bridle.

Tying the pony securely to the branch of a tree, Amber curled under a bush and pulled the leaves over him. In no time at all the boy was fast asleep, blotting out the days trials and tribulations.

When morning came he made his way cautiously into the village where he saw the keeper of the inn, splitting logs for the breakfast fire. Waldon was no longer a young man and the job was hard and tedious for him. As Amber approached the innkeeper, the man looked up.

"Well, well, what do we have here?" Waldon sat down his ax and smiled at the disheveled young boy coming towards him.

"I wonder if there is some work I can do in exchange for a good breakfast?" asked Amber.

"You think you can finish this wood for me?" As Amber nodded yes, the innkeeper handed him the ax. "When you finish, bring it in and stack it near the hearth. I will have my wife get some bread and cheese ready for you. Maybe if the job is done real good, she will find you some mutton and wine too." With this Waldon went off towards the inn.

Amber chopped and stacked the wood, then ate a hardy breakfast. Alicae, the innkeeper's wife, buzzed around him like a mother hen. He had finished eating and was helping her clean up the table when some men came into the inn. Amber was soon busy serving the hungry customers. As he gave them the mugs of ale and wine, he over heard them talking about the crumbling tower at Larkwood.

"The tower at Larkwood?" Asked Waldon; "is that not the place of the Enchanter?"

"Yes," said one of the travelers, "we came through there this morning. The town is all excited. It seems a boy of Lady Vivian's household was playing in that old tower. They thought he had gotten into some of Merlin's magic and blew up the tower and himself as well. Later when the servant Uldin searched through the stone rubble, he could not find any trace of the boy. There is talk that he left this earth the same way he came in. His name was Ambrosius Myrddhin and they say he was *'a child of no birth'*."

"Ah, yes," said the innkeeper, "I have heard that story myself but never put much faith in it."

"I think the Lady Viviane has the same feelings, for I heard she set Votan, half brother of King Bolta, and his men in search of the missing boy."

"Be careful, boy!" Cried Waldon sharply at Amber who, on hearing the last words of the traveler, had upset a mug of ale. "These young lads always have their mind on things other than work." The innkeeper explained to his guests. Amber wiped up the ale and moved away from the men. Still listening he heard Waldon continue the talk.

"Votan you say. And what brings him across the channel from Brittany?" the innkeeper asked.

"King Bolta is building a fortress to keep out the Saxons." The man answered. "His priest has told him, to keep the evil spirits out of the foundation; the blood of a *'son of no birth'* was needed. Hearing the stories of Prince Allon's companion, he sent Votan to strike a deal with Lady Viviane."

"And what of Prince Allon? I have heard he is very close to the boy and would let no one abuse him." Waldon pressed for more information.

"The lady made sure the prince would not know of her plan. Shortly after Votan arrived, Allon was whisked off to the court of King Arthur with the story that his luggage and servants, along with his companion, would follow shortly. She is also offering a reward for the boy's safe return. So she can send him to Prince Allon, she says, but you and I know differently." The traveler broke into a loud vulgar laugh.

The innkeeper laughed with him, but his eyes were on Amber. They were not mean and hard as the other men, and Amber met them with understanding. He could no longer stay for it would not be long before someone would recognize him.

"Boy," Waldon called to him, "the fire wood is getting low. Alicae's bread will not taste so good if the fire is not hot. Take the cart and go off into the woods. Bring back enough logs for tomorrow too." He smiled at the traveler, "That should keep him out of trouble until sundown." He laughed. To Amber he sent a sly wink.

Amber slipped the harness over the innkeepers brown horse. He was glad to be getting away from those men. He smiled, remembering what the one had said about Allon. He was glad his friend was not in on his planned death. Waldon and his wife asked no questions when he came back with the logs. They were waiting in the barn with his pony saddled. The innkeeper was putting sweet bread into the pouch and Alicae was tying a goat skin of wine onto the saddle horn. She gave Amber a hug then sniffling a little she left the barn.

Suddenly Amber jumped to his feet shaking off the memories of last night. In their place the realization of where he had seen those horses before. To be sure, he strained his eyes to see if they were still tied in front of the inn, down the valley in Calleve. They were, but now the owners were mounting to leave the village. He was right, it was Votan and his men. As the group rode off, heading east following the river, Amber could see three horses left behind. From the colors on them he knew they too belonged to Votan's men. There was no place for him to go now but west.

Amber looked around for the quickest way out of there. He could not go down the path in front of him for he would be seen before he could get to the river. The only way left was over the sharp slope. Walking to it and looking over the side he could see it was not as steep as it seemed. There was loose sand all the way to the bottom so he would have to be very careful. One slip and Bolta would have all the blood he wanted. Amber took the reins of his pony and wrapped them around his hand twice. Then he led her cautiously to the crest of the slope making his way down easier than he had thought he would. Boy and pony, both small, were able to lean into the cliff. A larger man and horse would surely have fallen head first into the valley below.

Once at the bottom, there were enough trees to cover his flight. Amber lost no time racing through the woods. Turning west he followed the river while still hidden by the trees. He rode fast and hard until he was sure a good distance had been put between him and Votan. He then slowed his pony to a trot not wanting to tire her. Besides he had no idea where he was going and the woods were ending bringing him out into the open.

Amber stopped to get a better look of the land around him. The river flowed past the open field then disappeared between the sharp cliffs of two mountains. The boy knew he would not be able to climb the mountain before him, both pony and rider being tired. It took him but a few minutes to decide to keep near the river by riding through the two mountains with it. Nudging his pony with his knees he hurried across the field. Arriving at the river he dismounted and led her by the reins into the water. It was shallow, going just to the boy's mid-leg, and cold, but felt soothing on his tired limbs.

It was a beautiful place and Amber was filled with a feeling of contentment. The high walls of the mountains were like the sheltering sides of a fortress. At their tops he could see the branches of trees reaching out over the side as if they were trying to grasp each other. For the first time in his life he felt an inner peace. His life was in danger, he knew neither who he was nor where he was going, and yet he had the feeling that all would be right.

Coming out of the mountains, Amber stopped short not believing his eyes. If he thought his walk through the cliffs was beautiful he had no words to describe the scene before him. The river was wider and on the right were the tallest pine trees he had ever seen, stretching as far as the eye could view. On the left there was a clearing with tall pine trees sitting behind it. In the clearing, closest to him, were yellow flowers. The smell reaching Amber's nose was sweeter than anything he had ever smelled. Past the field of flowers were what looked like little houses. Instead of being made of stone or wood, they were made of straw with roofs of pine needles. There were women by the river washing what looked like clothes, their children laughing and playing in the water. Men were sitting on the ground by the huts.

As Amber came out of the river the women stopped their washing, the children ran to their mothers to hide and the men came slowly forward. The clothing these people had on were not tunics but some kind of animal hides that were brown in color. All the men had long bushy black hair that covered head and face. Some of the children, no longer afraid, were now around Amber jabbering away in a language he could not understand.

As the men came closer Amber noticed they had an odor about them that was not very pleasant. They had spears made of long shafts with pointed stones tied on the ends by leather thongs and poked

19

them at Amber indicating they wanted him to move away from the river and go towards the huts. As he moved in that direction the young lad saw a huge man standing in front of the middle and largest hut. Before he knew what was happening, someone took his pony and the huge man took him by the arm.

"Not to worry, we not harm, come." He said speaking slowly as he ushered Amber into the hut.

The area they walked into was one large room. In the center of this room was a large circle of stones with charred wood. There were no tables or chairs, only mats placed around the dirt floor. In one corner was a pile of straw with hides on it. Hides, to keep the elements out were also covering the windows. These were tied up now to let the sun in. Against one wall were some spears and bowls which seemed to be made of wood. A woman came in and put two heavy mats down while behind her a boy put some wood in the stone circle.

"Come, sit." Said the man. He pointed to one of the mats while he sat down on the other. "Yata!" He said pointing to himself. "You?" he turned the pointing finger at Amber.

"Ambrosius Myrddhin." he said then changed it to "Amber" when he saw Yata's confused look. The name was probably too hard for him to understand.

"Ambrosius Myrddhin?" Yata said the two words like he was tasting newly made wine. "You Ambrosius Myrddhin?" he asked in a whisper.

"Yes," Amber said, "but you can call me Amber, all my friends do." then he added, "Well, one friend anyway."

Yata got up and said something to the woman in his own tongue. Then, turning to Amber, he said, "She Lila. She get you food. Stay, eat." Mumbling to himself "Myrddhin, Myrddhin." he left.

"Where is he going?" Amber asked Lila. But she just gave him a blank look and he realized she could not understand him. He was worried. What if word had come to this village about the reward? *Maybe Yata is going to turn me over to Votan.* he thought, and then felt very silly for thinking that. As he looked around the room he could see that money meant nothing to these people.

Lila set down another mat in front of Amber. On this she put a bowl with what looked like yellow meal in it, a cup with liquid and another larger bowl with meat. Looking at the food he realized he had not eaten a good meal since leaving Waldon's inn. Amber picked up the meat and took a bite. It was rabbit and tasted good. So did the yellow meal. But when the young lad sipped the liquid in the cup he almost threw up the food he had just eaten. The taste was so vile and sour that he could not help making an awful face. When Lila saw this she said something and left. Amber thought he had hurt her feelings and she was going to get one of the men to deal with him, until she came back into the hut alone. In her hand was the goat skin of wine Alicae had tied on his saddle horn. Thanking her with a smile, he drank long to get rid of the awful taste in his mouth.

Amber felt good after the emptiness in his stomach was filled with Lila's food. Rubbing the muscles in his aching limbs, he looked at the pile of straw and realized just how tired he was. Watching him, Lila could see what was on the young lad's mind. Taking him by the hand she led him to the corner. When he was settled comfortable on the straw, she covered him with the hides and then left the hut. As she went she pulled down another hide over the door way, leaving him to sleep. Amber never noticed the strong odor of the hides as he succumbed to the tiredness in his body. Soon he was sound asleep, safe and secure in his world of dreams.

CHAPTER 3

Amber stood with his back leaning against the rocky wall looking at the surrounding landscape. It was a warm sunny day and the sight before him took his breath away. He had come back to where the river split the mountains and climbed up the steep cliffs. He now had a better look at where he was. From this vantage point he could see the village below was isolated from the world around it in a secluded valley surrounded by mountains and trees.

Beyond the pine trees on both sides of the river, the mountain walls rose up and continued around forming a circle. The river flowed into this sanctuary between the pointed cliffs of the split mountain. It continued across the floor of the basin then vacated the valley by splitting the ring of mountains again. The land that held the forest of pines was not flat. Here and there in the distance, scattered hills and large boulders could be seen peeking out from between the rows of trees.

Amber strained his eyes looking at where the river vanished between the opposite cliffs. There seemed to be smoke coming out of the trees sheltering the side of the mountain. It was too far away for him to be sure. Rubbing his eyes the boy turned his attention to the valley below. The women were still in the field of flowers where he had left Lila. She had showed him earlier how they harvested the yellow pollen to be made into the meal they ate.

The young girl that had followed him from the field was sitting on a rock at the edge of the river. She looked elf like below him, legs dangling as she made rings in the water with her feet. Her brown hair was long and unruly, falling over her shoulders as she bent to watch the ripples. The sun shone on the features of her face; a small pointed nose, round full lips, and high protruding cheek bones.

"She's a pretty lass." Amber said to himself, "I would like to know her name."

She was waiting for him as he climbed down the rocks. Smiling at her Amber suddenly lost his footing. Before he knew it he slid down the slope on his back side and came to an abrupt stop at her feet. She bent over him chattering frantically as she tried to help him up. The embarrassed boy refused her assistance angry at his undignified descent.

"How stupid to be watching a girl instead of your feet." he shouted at himself. While he brushed his torn tunic, the girl moved away from him, hands behind her back and head down.

"Poor girl." he said walking to her side. "You do not know what I am saying so you think I am yelling at you." He put his hand on her chin. Lifting her head both sets of black eyes met. As Amber smiled at her she slowly smiled back then quickly lowered her eyes again in shyness.

Lila was now coming through the thicket from the field. She saw the state of Amber's clothing and gave out a small cry. Talking to the girl in her own tongue she went over to him and started to feel his arms and legs. When the girl answered, pointing to the mountain Amber had just slid down, Lila gasped. He smiled and tried to show them he was not hurt by dancing around. Both Lila and the girl began to giggle.

"Well, I know I have never danced at the court of King Arthur but that is no reason to make fun of me." he said joining them in their laughter.

Back at the village Lila took Amber by the hand and led him into the hut where he had spent the night. Rummaging around in a bunch of hides she pulled some out and handed them to him. He stood looking at them, uncertain what to do with them. Lila made a grunting noise while moving her hands over her body showing they were for him to put on.

"Oh," said Amber, "they are clothes to replace my torn tunic." Lila smiled knowing she had communicated with him. As she left to go the girl tried to slip into the hut, but Lila caught her arm and led her out the door.

When Amber had finished dressing, he went outside. The girl, seeing him, quickly fell into step behind him as he walked to where some men were sitting. They were making spears and as Amber stopped to watch, one of them motioned for the boy to sit beside him. Making sure he could see what was being done, the man picked up a long reed that was smooth on the outside and hollow on the inside. It was as long as the boy was tall and as thick as the tallow candles Lady Viviane used to light her house. On one end of the reed, the man made two cuts with a sharp stone. He then placed a flat thin pointed stone into the indentation. Holding this in place he took a small piece of hide, which had been soaking in water, and wrapped it around both stone and reed. To finish, a long thong was used to tie tightly around the hide. When this was all done, the man stood, weighing the newly made spear in his hand. Giving a quick move, he threw it at a tree about a hundred paces from where they were standing. It struck half way up the trunk with a loud thud. The man looked pleased with his work and Amber smiled, happy that the man seemed to accept his presence in the village.

Is this the life I am meant to have? the young boy thought. *I could be happy here and yet I cannot help feeling I was born for more than just existing day to day.*

He wondered, too, where Yata had disappeared to. "Where could he have gone?" Amber questioned the air. "Why did my name seem to scare him? If he knew the stories of my birth, I do not think I would have been treated so nicely."

His thoughts went to the book with his name so boldly written on its pages. He was glad he had put it in the saddle bag. Suddenly he jumped to his feet, startling the girl sitting beside him. He had just remembered his pony and began looking around the village for her.

Not finding her anywhere he came to the conclusion that Yata must have taken her with him. "Well the only thing I can do now," he mused, "is wait until he comes back" He went back to where the men were still working, determined to learn more about spear making. The young girl still trailing behind.

The next day, Amber decided he needed a wash badly. The man who taught him spear making was starting to smell good. Following the river away from the village, he had found a little inlet. It was surrounded by bushes and private enough for him to bathe. Somehow he had been able to slip away from the girl to enjoy some time alone. It wasn't that he minded having her around but it would be better if he could talk with her.

"Maybe I can teach her some words." he said as he slipped into the pool. For now though, he was lost in feeling the cool water whirling over him.

She was waiting for him when he returned to the village. Taking her by the hand he led her down to the river. The day was sunny and warm causing Amber to wonder if it ever rained there. They came to some rocks nestled by the water where he sat her down and tried to teach her his language.

"How about my name to start with." Amber said. She looked at him with her eyebrows raised and such a funny look he had to laugh.

"Ammm-berrr." he mouthed the words, "Come now, try, Ammm-berrr."

She opened her mouth, trying to say the word. "Ahh-borrr." she said looking proud at her attempt.

"Not too bad." said Amber, "Let us try again. Ammm-berrr, Amber."

Her second attempt was just the same as her first, but after a few more times, she finally said it right, "Ammm-berrr, Amber."

"Good." he said, "Now let us see if you have a name. 'You'" he said pointing at her.

"Amber!" she answered smiling.

Amber laughed and shook his head. Pointing at himself he said 'Amber', then to her saying 'you?'. When she looked at him puzzled he repeated the procedure. After a few moments her eyes lit up with understanding.

"Ah, Ronya." she said proudly.

"Ronya." Amber repeated, liking it. He resolved he would spend the time waiting for Yata to return, teaching Ronya more words.

The days went by with Amber teaching the girl and helping to make spears. He wanted to go with the men hunting but Lila always stopped him. Ever since his fall down the cliff she was very protective of him. She did let him go to the river and learn how to spear fish. This took patience and a quick hand but it wasn't long before Amber was proudly bringing home fish for supper.

One morning Amber woke to the sound of voices. Sitting up on the pallet he had made for himself, he saw Yata near the fire talking with Lila.

"Yata, it is good to see you." said the boy getting up from the straw bed. He was looking at the man's face to see if he would still be friendly.

"Ambrosius, my friend. You look like men of village." he answered, seeing how Amber was dressed. He handed the boy a cup of the sour wine.

"Nooo..., thank you!!" said Amber.

Lila laughed and said something to Yata, then he too laughed. "Our drink does not please you?" he asked.

"Not exactly." the boy replied. "Just what is it?"

"You have seen field, yellow flowers? Drink made from stems. Have wetness in them. We crush with stone. Makes good drink. Man's drink." He smiled, took a drink of the wine, then asked, "You happy here?"

"Yes, everyone has been very nice to me. Lila, the man who makes spears, Ronya..." his face flushed as Lila again said something to Yata and they both started to laugh. "Where have you been?" Amber continued, trying to change the course the conversation was taking. "Why did you leave so suddenly the day I arrived?"

"You eat first, then we go." replied Yata.

"Where are we going?" asked Amber, but the man did not answer. He just set about the room gathering food and wrapping it in a hide, while Lila gave the boy his breakfast.

Amber did not ask Yata anymore questions as he watched the older man getting everything together. When he was through there were two bundles with rope loops, packed with food and extra hides. Yata went over to the corner where the spears were kept. Picking up two he handed one to Amber

"Come, we go." he said as he slipped one of the bundles onto his back. Amber had trouble with his pack so Lila helped him. With spear in hand he followed Yata out the door.

As they got to the edge of the village the boy looked around, disappointed that Ronya had not come to say good-bye. They took a well worn path into the woods that turned to the right and led up a hill. At the top Amber turned to take one last look at the village below. How peaceful it looked. Suddenly he was aware of Yata arguing with someone. Turning to see who it was, he lost his footing and fell, landing again at the feet of Ronya.

"Why is it I always seem to be so clumsy around you?" he asked as he picked himself off the ground.

Yata laughed, said something to the girl, and then continued down the path. Ronya walked passed Amber to her place behind him without looking at him.

"You look like a little warrior, pack on your back and spear in your hand." he said watching her.

"Women and children make no good warrior." grunted Yata. This was all he said for the rest of the trip.

From the general direction they were going Amber calculated they were heading towards the mountains where the river left the valley. During the day they walked at an even pace stopping only to eat. At night fall they always found shelter in caves that looked like they were cut into the sides of small hills.

"Someone must have dug them out for rest spots along the trail." Amber said to himself.

They went on like this for five days and nights. By the sixth day they were standing in a large clearing. It was late in the afternoon as most of the morning was spent climbing the side of the mountain above the end of the river. Amber could see it winding below as they made their way up the path but he was not prepared for what he found in the clearing. The area was large yet hidden from the valley by huge pine trees. There were little huts, made from stone, surrounding a large building that looked out of place in this environment.

Amber stopped short frozen to the ground as a memory flashed in his head. He saw himself standing in front of a painting in Lady Viviane's sitting room, and asking her what it was.

27

"That is a temple of the Druids." she had answered.

"Druids?" the little boy inquired. "What are they?"

"They are the priests of the Celts. Backward sort of people who lived in these parts before the Romans came. With the conquest, they were pushed into the mountains of Wales. The Romans stopped their religious goings on as they were a vicious race who held festivals to the gods. They would take innocent people and offer them up as a sacrifice."

The little boy's eyes widened and his body shook. Seeing this the malicious lady continued.

"This was performed by the high priest who wore white robes, and a crown of oak leaves. The victims were lain out on a slab of stone and stakes were driven into their hearts."

The boy started to cry as he tried to run away, but the spiteful lady held him fast.

"You have asked, you shall stay to hear it all. Sometimes the victims were put in great wicker cages and burned alive, others were......"

The small boy broke away from the lady's grip and ran sobbing from the room.

Amber's hands were wet with sweat as the tears in his eyes tried to wash away the burning memory that pierced his brain. Could this be, the village back by the river, the people called Celts? Is that why Yata had brought him here, to be a human sacrifice? All the time Amber was thinking this, they were walking towards the temple. He wanted to run but something pushed him on. When they reached the stairs of the temple, he looked up to see an old man standing at the top. He had a white neatly kept beard and wore a long black robe that was tied at the waist with a gold sash. Amber turned to ask Yata who the man was, only to find he was alone. Both his companions were gone.

"Do not worry about your friends." said the old man coming down the stairs. "They have work to do and we have much to talk about."

As the man's voice echoed in his ears, Amber felt a familiar experience. Beads of sweat formed upon his brow and a prickly sensation crept up his spine, settling on the back of his neck. While the old man led him up the stairs and into the small room in the temple, the blood pounded in the young boy's head and fear stalked his heart.

CHAPTER 4

"Well Ambrosius, are you hungry?" asked the old man as he cut some bread and cheese.

"Yes, a little." Amber answered, "What is your name?" he questioned the man.

"My name? Some say the 'Old one', but you may call me Dhin." he said. As he poured the wine Amber's eyes inspected the room.

It was small with a table, two chairs and a bed its only furniture. There was a fire in the hearth that gave the place a warm glow. The food had been brought in by a man dressed similar to the men of Yata's village. That was where the similarity ended for he had short brown hair, was free of any beard and smelled clean.

"Now," said Dhin taking up his goblet, "tell me how you stumbled into our secluded retreat?"

Amber looked up from his meal, "You mean that you do not know?" There was disappointment in his young voice.

"I only know that Yata came rushing up here a few weeks ago to tell me a young stranger had come out of the water like a god. He said his name was Ambrosius Myrddhin and that he wore odd clothing." He smiled at Amber, "I must say, you do look a bit odd."

"Lila gave me these when I tore my tunic." the boy explained, "But that is not what I meant about you knowing, I thought......" Amber hesitated. How could he tell this old man that he had thought it was Dhin's voice he had heard in the tower and that just maybe Dhin might know who his parents were.

"Oh well, it does not matter what I thought." he finally said and then went on to tell the 'Old one' all that had happened since he left Larkwood, leaving out the part about the voice in the tower. If Amber had bothered to look, he would have seen a gleam in the old man's eyes.

It was dark when they came out of the temple yet the clearing was brightly illuminated by torches. Dhin led Amber to one of the huts where he motioned for the boy to enter. Inside were three pallets of fresh straw, a table with a lamp on the top and some chairs. A hearth with a fire blazing in it was cut into one of the stone walls. Yata and Ronya were sitting on mats in front of the fire and jumped to their feet when Dhin came in. Yata hurried over to the table and pulled out a chair for the old man.

"I will not be staying." he said, "The boy is tired and needs sleep. Tomorrow we will start the lessons."

"Lessons?" Amber asked.

"Yes, I think it is about time you learned how to read and write the different languages of our land." came the answer.

Amber was too tired to even wonder how Dhin knew he never had that kind of learning and went right off to sleep on one of the pallets. The next morning he was finishing a breakfast of cheese and bread when Jasper, Dhin's personal servant, came into the hut.

"My Lord Dhin has sent me to accompany you to the main hall in the temple. He will give you your lessons until Gorganis arrives." he said.

"Who is Gorganis?" the young boy asked as he followed the servant.

"He is the master of the Temple of Dawn, which lies on the other side of the river and he will be your tutor." the man answered.

As they approached the center of the clearing, Amber looked up at the temple. "What is the name of this place?" he inquired.

"It is called the Temple of Dusk." Jasper replied as they climbed the stone steps.

Dhin was waiting for them in the main hall. This room was quite large, with furniture unrelated to its surroundings. Bookshelves covered one entire wall and the floor was void of any covering. A large hearth was cut deep into the wall next to the bookshelves. It appeared to be newly made as the stones were lighter in color than the rest of the wall. At the end of the room stood a sinister looking slab of stone with a white cloth and candles laying on top. It was in a large cove and seemed very much out of place. In front of the fire was a large oak table with chairs around it where Dhin was sitting waiting for Amber.

"We will start with a little history of this area and the people in it." Dhin spoke after Amber had settled in one of the large chairs. "Yata's ancestors came to this place when they were driven from their lands in the south eastern corner of Britain. The Saxons, after freeing the land from the barbarians, decided the island of Thenet was not large enough for them. they invaded that corner of our land and forced the people to either flee or stay and become slaves. Yata's people chose to be free and ran. They came upon this retreat, as you did, when the river was at its low point. Here they settled and have lived in peace these many years. When the river is at its high point the valley cannot be entered as the waters flow fast and would drown both horse and rider." Dhin paused allowing the boy to take in what he was saying.

"The village by the river are descendants of these Britons? They are not Celts?" Amber's eyes were wide with confusion. "This is not the temple of the Druids?"

"The Druids!" Dhin laughed, "What ever gave you that idea?"

"In Larkwood I had seen a drawing of a temple that looked just like this one. I was told it was a Druid house of worship where human sacrifices were performed at festivals to the gods." the boy answered in a soft voice.

"And you thought Yata had brought you here to be one of these sacrifices?" the old man looked sadly at the boy thinking how threatened he must have felt, being led into the temple the night before.

"Listen and I will tell you the story that is told of this temple." Dhin then said to Amber. "First of all the Druids escaped from the Romans into the mountains of Wales. We are still in Britain. Second, they are no longer vicious, nor do they practice the old religion. Now to get back to the origin of this temple.

"When the Romans came they brought their knowledge of the Greek gods with them. As the Druids were gone the people adopted this belief and began worshiping the different Roman gods, building temples to them. This one is to Diana the goddess of the Moon, hence the name 'Dusk'. She is also the protector of the youth of the world and mistress of the hunt. She is said to love the woodlands and all its creatures. In this temple, built over three hundred years ago, the young of Britain were sent to learn the arts of hunting. When the Romans left our land this practice stopped. Then Yata's people came with all the wisdom of the past in their books and in the heads of the elders of the village. Having nothing else to believe in they turned back to the Roman gods. This place and the temple of Dawn across the river are the only ones left in the whole of Britain. There are not many who know of their existence." Dhin stopped speaking to take a sip of wine.

"What is the temple of Dawn?" Amber asked, taking advantage of the old man's pause.

"That was built to Apollo, god of the sun." answered Dhin. "He was twin brother to Diana, so you see one temple could not be built without the other. Gorganis, your tutor, will bring with him the arts of medicine and healing." Dhin noticed Amber trying to cover up a yawn. "I think we will stop for now as you seem to be getting tired."

It was not that he was bored with what the old man was telling him, rather it was the stuffiness of the room. Once outside, Amber took a deep breath of air.

"You may do and go where it will please you till Jasper comes for you." said Dhin following the boy down the stairs. "But under no circumstances are you to take the path that leads out of the clearing behind the temple. That is the only place forbidden to everyone except myself." As they neared this path, Dhin turned to Amber and spoke once more, "You will get on well here, Ambrosius, if you learn your lessons adequately and obey all rules." He then disappeared into the woods.

Amber walked around the clearing which held nine small huts and the temple. There were no women or children to be seen. The area was large and bare with torches protruding out of the ground to give light during the dark hours. Off to one side was another path that led to a statue of a woman. From the majestic look Amber knew it had to be the goddess Diana. Flowers were growing all around her feet and the tree limbs above seemed to part for there was sun shining down on her head.

"When the moon is high in the heavens, the rays light up the goddess." Amber turned to see that the voice belonged to Jasper. "Have you eaten?" he asked the boy. When Amber shook his head no, the servant led him to the back door of the temple.

They came into a large kitchen. Even here there were no women, only men who were doing all the cooking. Jasper gathered some hot bread and pieces of cheese. Motioning for Amber to take the goat skin of wine sitting on the table, the man headed for the door.

"I know a place as peaceful as the shrine of Diana where we can eat." he said as they came into the sunlight.

Jasper led Amber to the edge of the clearing facing the side of the mountain and then walked on into the woods. There was no path yet he went as if there was one. Before long they came to the slope of the mountain. On the right trees continued down its side, while on the left was a sharp cliff with a ledge leading down its incline.

"Just look straight ahead and not down." instructed Jasper as he stepped out onto the shelf.

Amber took a deep breath and followed, remembering the time he had slid down another cliff. They had not gone far when a large rock suddenly appeared before them. Amber stopped short in amazement as he watched Jasper climb up stairs that had been cut into the side of the boulder. He then turned and waved for the boy to follow.

Once on top of the stone Amber sat speechless as he took in the panoramic view before him. From this position he could see the river winding along the valley floor. It was like he was still on the other side except now everything was in reverse. The village, off in the distance, was on the right, while the forest of pines was on the left.

"You are right, it is peaceful here. It gives a boy plenty of room to think." Amber said turning to Jasper.

"Or a man!" the servant answered. "Dhin has told me of your ordeal in escaping from Larkwood. It would take a man to survive all that you have."

"Thank you for those kind words." Amber smiled.

Time seemed to stand still as Amber sat looking out over the valley. The wind picked up and blew the low hanging clouds around him. He felt as light as the air and there was a roaring sound in his head. As the cloud vanished, his eyes were transfixed on the scene before him. There was the clatter of horse's hoofs and the shouting of men. He could see Lila held fast in the grips of a man dressed in armor.

"I know you have hidden him. Now tell me where he is or I will shake your very teeth from out your head." yelled the man as the frightened woman just stared blankly at him.

Amber tried to cry out that she could not understand his language, but he could neither speak nor move. When Lila did not answer the man threw her across the room. She fell on the straw bed and was very still as the man growled and stormed out of the hut. In the clearing in front of the village Amber could see the destruction these men had brought down on Yata's people. The field of yellow flowers was disappearing in a blaze of fire, as were most of the huts. Men, women and children were laying scattered around the area in pools of blood. As the smoke filled the scene Amber caught a glimpse of one face.

"*Votan*" he shouted.

"What did you say?" Jasper asked. He came over to the boy who had jumped to his feet and was standing there shaking. "Are you all right master Ambrosius?" he questioned.

With fear blazing in his eyes, Amber turned back to look out over the cliff. The land before him was as peaceful as when they had sat down to eat. "I do not understand." he spoke softly, "How could I see something that was not there?"

"Come, you are tired. I fear you have had too much sun." Jasper led him slowly down the stone stairs, across the ledge and back to the clearing. As Amber curled down on the straw pallet in his hut, the servant wrapped him in a warm coverlet and watched him fall asleep.

Upset by the boy's death like sleep Jasper ran to Dhin and told him of Amber's unconscious state. The 'Old one' ordered his servant to fetch the lad quickly and carry him to the small room in the temple. After Jasper laid the boy down on the pallet, Dhin gave the man samples of the plants he wanted from the forest. As Dhin waited for Jasper to return he sat in front of the fire peering into the flames as if he were looking for something.

Time passed and soon Amber was vaguely aware of the voices moving around the room. He tried to open his eyes but it was too great a task and he gave in to the hands of sleep pulling him into unconsciousness once again.

"Are you sure he is all right?" Jasper was asking, "When he jumped to his feet and yelled 'Votan', I thought he would leap right off the cliff. The fear in his eyes stood out in hues of red and yellow giving him the appearance of one not of this world. Then, as I led him to his hut, he spoke not another word and walked as though he was in shock."

"You are not to worry, just do as I say and he will be all right." Dhin said. He put the plants and some wine into a kettle and hung it over the fire. After boiling for a while, he poured just the wine into a goblet and turned to his servant. "For now he needs to sleep but the minute he awakes give him this warm mixture to drink. It is very important that he sips some as soon as he stirs." Setting the goblet on the hearths ledge to stay warm, the old man then left the room.

Jasper felt he had cause to worry for it had been two days since he had carried the unconscious boy into this room. Suddenly the boy moaned as he stirred on the bed. Jasper quickly brought the goblet of warm wine and forced some of it between Amber's lips. The lad choked a little as the first few drops reached his throat. Then, as his senses returned, he drank the rest of the wine eagerly. The servant set the empty goblet down and hurried from the room. Amber was looking around, trying to get his bearing, when the man returned with Dhin.

"Well Jasper," Dhin said coming over to the bed, "it seems we have not lost him after all. How do you feel my boy?" he asked.

Amber spoke, softly at first, "Better, I think, but my throat feels like it is on fire.

Dhin laughed, "That is from the wine. It is the best medicine for man or beast." Amber smiled and started to sit up, but when his head pounded like a warrior's drum, he settled back down. Dhin, motioning for Jasper to leave them, closed the door as he asked the boy, "Can you tell me what happened to you two days ago out on the cliff?"

"Two days ago!" Amber exclaimed, "I have been laying here that long?"

"Yes, and all that time you never moved or opened your eyes." Dhin moved closer to him. "Tell me, what did you see?"

Amber stared into the old man's black, glassy eyes. Speaking as though he was hypnotized the boy told all that had happened. When he was through, Dhin turned to the fire contemplating the flames.

"What does it all mean?" Amber asked breaking the silence. "How could I have seen something that was not there and why did I sleep for two days, not even knowing that time was passing?"

Dhin stared at the boy for a few moments before he answered, "It is the sight. Do you know what that word means?" When Amber shook his head no, the old man continued. "It is when you can see what is going to happen in the future like it is happening at the time you see it. In my youth I also had this power. Mine came in the flames of a fire, yours in the clouds of the air. It is nothing to be afraid of for utilized properly it can be a great and powerful advantage. I will teach you all you need to know but for now, sleep again Ambrosius Myrddhin. When you awake the pounding in your head will be gone."

As the 'Old one' left, Amber tried to put together all that had transpired but sleep came too quickly for any thoughts to shape.

CHAPTER 5

As Amber slept, Dhin sent Yata back to his home to fortify the valley. Three months later he returned and described the events that had occurred in the village. Men had been sent to the mountains where the river entered the area. They hid in the rocks and watched for Votan. From this advantage point they could see the river winding all the way back to the town of Calleve. It wasn't long before Votan and his men were spotted coming out of the woods on the other side of the field. By the time they were following the river through the mountain cliffs the people of Yata's village were hid deep in the forest. Votan, angry that his trip was unsuccessful, had his men burn all the huts.

"Yes!" exclaimed Amber as he excitedly cut into Yata's narration. "I remember seeing the black smoke from my lofty perch. I had just finished my noon meal and was hurrying off to my studies."

"It was good you did not stay out on your rock," said Dhin, "for you might have been seen by Votan as he followed the river out of the valley." Amber's eyes grew wide at the 'Old one's' words. "Do not worry Ambrosius," he continued, "Votan has left our quiet retreat to look elsewhere for his *'son of no birth'*. Think no more about that part of your life. Look only to the future." As Dhin moved towards the door of the hut, he turned to Amber, "Come," he said, "you have lessons to learn."

Time passed quickly for Amber as he studied the lessons put before him. Ten years to be exact. He went often to his rock yet had no more visions of things to come. Dhin told him this was not unusual, for the same thing happened to him after his first phantasm. Still Amber felt let down and every spare moment was spent on the rock trying. But soon spare moments became very scarce. During the day Gorganis would come to the hut with his arms full of books. There was a lot for the young man to master. Among the things he learned was how to make the mixture of wine and plants that Jasper had given him to drink after his apparition. In the evenings Amber would go to the temple's main hall where Dhin would be waiting with their night's meal. Afterward, while sitting in front of the fire, the old man taught him many languages. Soon the boy was conversing with Yata in the man's own tongue, which pleased him very much.

In this time of growing and learning Amber progressed not only in wisdom but in looks too. His body became strong and firm as Jasper taught him the art of fighting. Dhin frowned on this but the servant convinced him the boy needed to know how to defend himself. At first Amber didn't care much for this part of his schooling. Most of the time he was picking himself up off the ground. After a while he found he could avoid Jasper's attack and soon the servant was the one on the ground.

If Amber had grown to be a handsome, strong young man, Ronya had surely matured into a very beautiful woman. Even though the young man could feel no more love for her than that of a friend, he felt that she expected more. Telling Dhin, the old man chuckled at the growing boy's frustration.

"When the woman for you comes along, you will know." he said. Then his smile turned to a thoughtful frown as he continued. "Just remember to be wise for you must never betray yourself by giving too much of your wisdom to any woman, no matter how much your heart burns for love of her. Imprint these words upon your brain, Ambrosius, for they may some day save your life."

After this Amber managed to evade Ronya. At night he would wait until she was asleep before going into the hut. It wasn't long before she sensed his feelings and moved to one of the small rooms in the temple. This pleased Dhin for now Amber would be able to get back to his lessons without any distractions.

Now, ten years after Amber's arrival, Gorganis was telling Dhin that the young man had learned all he could teach him. "I must return to my duties at the Temple of Dawn," he said.

Dhin was very proud of Amber's progress and as a reward for learning his lessons well, he allowed the young man to accompany Yata and Gorganis across the river. Amber's excitement grew as they walked down the path to the valley below. The pack on his back was much lighter than when he had come up the trail as a young boy. As they crossed the river, Amber looked back in search of his rock high above on the side of the cliff. Seeing it sitting there so open and noticeable caused the young man to remember the day Votan had burned the village.

"Dhin was right." he spoke to himself, "If I had been there when those ruthless men had passed by..." The young man shuddered with the realization of how close King Bolta came to getting his blood.

The three men followed the river for two days, sleeping under the stars at night. They then headed into the woods with their backs to the water arriving at the Temple of Dawn the next day. It was situated the same as the other temple except there were houses instead of huts. Four of them which Gorganis said were the homes of his servants. He himself, like Dhin, had a room in the temple where the main hall was large but void of any furniture. The altar, as Amber had found out the stone slab was called, looked the same. There was a clean white cloth over it and candles were placed carefully on top. Metal lamps hanging from the walls gave off an eerie light. The rest of the temple was bare, cold and unfriendly, causing Amber to shiver.

The young man was glad when Gorganis brought him back out into the sunlight. As they came down the steps Amber saw a statue of the god Apollo. It was standing strong and proud in a clearing on the side of the temple.

"Come," said Gorganis, "I have something else to show you."

They took a path that led behind the temple where there was a large fenced in meadow with about a dozen horses grazing on the green grass. Amber followed his teacher into a large wooden stable. In one of the stalls stood a black pony. Amber could not believe his eyes as he ran his hand over the white star on her back side, for it was his pony.

"She has been here all this time?" he turned and questioned Gorganis.

"Before Yata returned to the village to fetch you, he brought your pony here. We have been taking good care of her." the man answered.

"But why was I not told?" Amber said, a touch of anger in his voice.

"Dhin thought it was best, for you were a frightened young boy when you came to him. He was worried you would run away at the first sign of any trouble from Votan." he replied.

The young man shook his head in agreement. He knew in his heart he would have done just that.

The next morning Yata was waiting for Amber with three of Gorganis' horses and the pony. The young man was curious as to why so many mounts but all Yata would say was that Dhin had ordered him to do so. It was a long time since Amber had been on a horse yet soon he was riding like the wind. Yata had a hard time keeping up with the excited young man while leading the extra steed and pony behind him. By nightfall they were following the river and racing towards the crossing. They reached the Temple of Dusk just as the first rays of a new day were lighting up the sleeping community. In their absence a three sided shed, made from logs with a straw roof, had been quickly put up behind Amber's hut. It was here Yata took the horses and pony while the young man went into his lodging. By the time Yata came in, Amber was fast asleep.

Some hours later Amber woke to find the sun high in the heavens and Yata gone to do his chores. Having nothing better to do he took a goat skin that was hanging by the fire and went out to the rock in the cliff. He set the mixture down so the heat of the sun would keep it warm, then took his place near the edge of the rock and peered into the valley below. Amber was resigned to the fact that the vision would not come again, nevertheless he had to keep trying.

After sitting for some time, Amber was about to leave when suddenly the wind started to pick up. Soon the low hanging clouds were forming around him. With them came the roaring noise in his head. He sat very still, waiting for the clouds to lift and reveal its secrets to him. Instead they stayed close to him like thick smoke.

I am trying too hard, he thought as sweat trickled down his forehead. *I must relax!*

Then, coming out of the thickness, there was a shape. At first it was just a big blob. Then as Amber strained his eyes, it began to take the form of a large horse. She was black like his pony, only without the white star on her back side. This beautiful animal's white star was at the point where the base of the neck meets the top of the shoulder. She stood like a statue in the air. The main part of her body was sleek and well rounded while her long legs were trim and well groomed. Her neck was arched and her alert head tapered to a spherical muzzle with a velvety nose. She was fit for a king to ride.

Suddenly she disappeared leaving the white clouds looking more and more like smoke. Then, as it started taking shape again, it looked like a rubble of rocks. The pounding in Amber's head was getting louder. As his vision started to melt into the air he saw a face in the clouds. It was the face of the 'Old one'.

"Dhin!" the young man called out still groggy.

"Yes, my boy, I am here." Dhin was by his side forcing the warm wine between his lips. It burned his throat and he choked a little. When he had drank all the liquid, Dhin helped him to lay down on the rock. He then placed a fur cover over Amber and let him sleep.

The next day the sun shed its light on the old man sleeping with his back against the cliff. He opened his eyes to see Amber sitting on the edge of the rock looking out into space.

"Well Ambrosius, you have come out of this one much faster." he said as he sat down next to the young man.

"It was not much of a vision." said Amber looking at his old friend, "There was a black horse with a white star, a rubble of rocks like something fell down and you." He stopped short, puzzled over the knowing look in the old man's eyes. "You saw too?" he asked.

"No." Dhin answered, "But come, it is time we got back to the temple."

As they entered the main hall Ronya was busy cleaning the room. Looking up as the two men came in she bowed low to them and hurried from the room. The older man motioned for Amber to sit in one of the chairs in front of the hearth. There was a warm fire blazing and Amber sat looking at the flames as Dhin walked over to the table.

"Ambrosius, we have been friends these past ten years, have we not?" Dhin asked as he poured two goblets of wine. Not giving Amber a chance to answer he continued, "At least I have always felt to be your friend. But now I find there is a lot you have been keeping from me." He sat in the chair next to Amber and handed him one of the goblets.

"Keeping something from you?" he asked, confused by the man's words. "No never, you are my friend. What is it you think I have not told you?"

"You have never talked much of your birth, or who your mother and father are." said Dhin.

"If you have the sight as you claim, you would know I have no answer, for I never knew who they were." Amber said sadly.

"You have never thought about who they might be, no visions?" asked the 'Old one'.

"Once I thought you were my father, but now I know that was foolish of me." Amber caught the gleam in Dhin's eyes but said nothing.

"Nor have you talked about the tower at Larkwood or of the voice that warned you about Votan's intentions." As Amber looked intensely at the old man, Dhin continued, "I do have the sight. True it is not as good as in my youth, but it is still with me."

"The tower is where Lady Viviane said they found me." Amber explained slowly, "I am called 'Ambrosius Myrddhin' because those words were written on the floor beside the pallet."

"So that is the explanation she gave." Dhin mumbled to himself.

Amber looked at him not hearing what he had said, "You spoke sir?" he asked.

Dhin shook his head, "It is no matter." he said waving Amber to continue.

"The voice in the tower could have only been a vision warning me of the danger in Lady Viviane's house." the young man explained.

"You have an answer for everything Ambrosius. How is it you never asked the many questions which must be heavy on your mind? Like where is the book you brought with you from the tower, and the reason I have had you taught so well?" Dhin looked intently at his young friend.

"I felt you would tell me of these things when you thought the time was right." was the young man's answer.

Silence fell over the room as the two pair of ebony eyes locked together searching for the truth. After a few moments Dhin's voice broke the stillness.

"Yes, you are right and also wiser than I thought. I felt you did not want to talk of these things when all the time you were waiting for me to speak. It was an old man's foolishness and he will speak now." He paused for a moment, forming the words in his mind as he gazed into the hearth.

"The day you arrived Yata journeyed here to advise me of your stumbling upon our hidden retreat. He brought with him, your pony carrying the leather bag with the book inside. Taking this treasure in my hands, I felt that what ever was in there was very important and in the wrong hands could be a dangerous weapon against you. My most trusted friend, Gorfan, was getting ready to return to his home after a visit. I gave him the leather bag asking only that he would find a safe place to keep it until the time was right for revealing its secret. I then sent Yata off to retrieve you after bringing Gorganis your pony to care for." Dhin looked thoughtfully at the young man sitting beside him.

"I am an old man Ambrosius." his words interrupted the silence as he turned his eyes once more towards the blazing hearth. "Older than time itself. A year before you came I was gazing into the fire when I saw a boy fleeing for his life. I felt compassion towards this lad as in my youth I too had to escape my enemies. So when you came to me, fear still in your eyes, I vowed to be your friend and help you face all the ordeals of this world." He sat forward reaching out to grasp Amber's hand. "I did not waste my time Ambrosius, for you have turned out to be a fine noble young man." He smiled as he sat back in his chair.

At that moment Amber saw the lines of time that were etched into this good man's face. He felt a kinship towards his benefactor and more, he felt love. A kind of love he had never known before. The kind a son has for his father. When he spoke there was tenderness in his voice.

"We have no kin of our own," he said softly, "so from this day on, you shall be my father and I your son."

Dhin rose from his chair. There were tears in his eyes as he walked over to Amber. He embraced the young man and held him tightly for just a few moments. Then taking hold of his emotions he moved away towards the door.

"I must leave you for a few moments." he said, "I will send Yata in to keep you company while you sit and finish your wine." As Dhin left the room Amber noticed that he walked with a new spring in his step.

Dhin followed the path behind the temple going up the side of the mountain. There, hidden by the large bushes and trees, stood a tower. If Amber had seen it his heart would have stopped beating, for it was the tower from Larkwood. Dhin climbed the stone steps to the top. At the casement he paused looking for a moment at the door to the small room. He then went into his study behind the symbolized oak door. After a while he came out carrying a bundle. When he returned to the temple he entered the kitchen and spoke a few words to Jasper. After handing the servant his bundle Dhin went to join Amber and Yata in the main hall. As the old man took his place in the large chair by the fire a loud rumbling noise shook the temple.

"What was that?" cried Amber as he jumped to his feet. It was a sound he thought he had heard before.

"It is probably just some loose rocks falling down the side of the mountain." answered Dhin, "Finish your wine my son. Tomorrow we must rise early and prepare for our journey."

"We are leaving the temple? But where are we going?" Amber's eyes shone with excitement.

"Like King Lot, Sir Gawain and all the other knights, we are going on a quest, but not for the holy grail. We are going on a quest for knowledge, to the court of King Arthur. On our way we will stop at the village of Amesbury for I wish to pay my respects to an old friend." Dhin then said good night and retired to his room in the back of the temple.

Amber and Yata walked to their hut together. Upon entering they found the servant Jasper there. On the pallet that once was Ronya's the servant had laid out a new tunic. It was the blue color of the heavens just before dusk. There was a good leather belt to use with it and a pair of new sandals. Across the foot of the pallet was a dark blue, almost black, cloak. Placed gently on top of the cloak was a copper brooch with a red dragon embossed on it. Amber picked up the brooch moving his finger over the surface.

"That has been in Lord Dhin's family for generations." said Jasper. "It was given to him by his father to pass down to his son, if he was ever to have one. You are making an old man very happy master Ambrosius. I will be ever in your debt."

"It is as beautiful as is this apparel." said Amber, his face beaming with pleasure while he fondled the expensive folds of the tunic. "The last time I saw anything so fine was on the back of my friend Allon."

As Amber fell asleep dreams of meeting his boyhood friend filled his head. He was dressed in his fine tunic with the brooch pinned to the shoulder of his cloak. All in the court of Arthur were looking with amazement at the handsome man among them. As he slept a smile moved across Amber's face.

Outside the wind blew strong around the temple. Black clouds covered the area for a few moments, then were blown away by the wind. At the end of the path, where Dhin had been earlier, was a pile of tumbled rocks. Could they really be the only remains of a tower that had once stood there?

CHAPTER 6

Dhin was waiting in the main hall when Amber came to the temple the next morning. He smiled as the handsome young man walked into the room. Amber went right to Dhin and embraced him.

"Father, thank you." he said, "I feel like a prince. You are very good to me."

Dhin smiled, "You look very royal. But come now, I have something else for you."

He led Amber out the temple, up the path around to the back. Just behind a rubble of rocks, stood a black horse. As the men approached she turned and Amber saw the white star.

"The horse!" he cried, "It is the same horse. Where did it come from?" he turned to Dhin.

"She was given to me by a very fine man I met in my travels. Her name is Pegasus, and she is now yours. She is too swift a horse for me to ride anymore." answered the old man.

"Pegasus? What a strange name." Amber ran his hand down the horse's smooth neck.

"It is Greek and the story that goes with the name is this; 'Once there was a king of Argos who had a beautiful daughter, Danae. The king, wanting a son, went to the Oracle at Delphi. There the Priestess informed him he would never have a son but his daughter would and that this grandson would be the cause of his death. The king tried to prevent Danae from having any children by hiding her, but Zeus came to her as a shower of gold and she bore him a baby boy called Perseus.

'When the king found out he locked mother and child in a wooden chest and threw it out in to the sea where waves washed it onto the shore of an island. When Perseus had grown to manhood the king of the island wanted to get rid of this young man and marry his mother, so he tricked Perseus into going after the head of Medusa.

'Medusa was a Gorgon, a creature with great wings and a body covered with golden scales. Her hair was a mass of twisting snakes that, when looked upon, turned mortal men to stone.

'With the help of the gods Perseus was able to find the home of the Gorgon. Looking into his mirror-like shield, he aimed a stroke at Medusa's throat. With Athena guiding his hand he cut off the Gorgon's head with one blow. From the blood that poured out of the wound sprang a wild horse.

'This was Pegasus, a white steed with great wings that carried him swiftly through the air. He had great strength and never tired. He was first of all other horses of the gods and was cared for in the stalls of Olympus. When Zeus wished to use his thunderbolts, it was Pegasus who brought the thunder and lightning to him'" Dhin paused. Looking at the beautiful animal standing next to Amber he continued. "I have called her Pegasus for legend has it she was born from the lineage of Zeus's great horse. Her untiring strength has carried me through many adventures. Because she is as swift as the wind, my life has been saved many a time by outrunning my enemy's steeds."

"So this is what my vision meant." said Amber, "This horse, the rubble of rocks, and your face. When I told you about it you knew the meaning but could not tell me without giving away your surprise. I was seeing the gift you were going to give me."

"Yes Ambrosius, I knew." said Dhin, again the gleam was in his eyes.

47

Amber led Pegasus down the path to the stable where Yata and Jasper were busy preparing the other horses for the journey. Amber's pony was packed high with food, clothing and a few books Dhin was bringing. As the small caravan made their way through the forest Amber was concerned that the pony would not withstand the burden she was bearing but she managed to arrive at the village without any mishap.

Lila was pleased to see Amber and could not stop talking. She said that because she could not converse with him before there was now so much to say. She then took charge of showing him the improvements in the village since the fire.

Ronya had ridden back to the village on Yata's horse. She said nothing on the trip and when they reached their destination, she went right to her family's hut. They embraced Ronya fondly, telling her of their happiness in having her back. She was aloof at first because of Amber's rejection of her love. But soon forgot all about this love as the young men of the village were at her heels seeking to be in her favor. Amber was happy with this, now he would no longer feel guilty about the pain he had caused her.

Dhin thought it best to cut their visit short for the river would soon be at its high point and delay their journey. Amber hugged Yata good-bye, thanking him for all his kindness. Dhin told Yata that Gorganis was sending a young man to take charge of the temple and he knew that Yata would serve him well. Even Ronya came to say good-bye, her young admirers following close behind. Jasper stood waiting with four ready horses, the extra horse being used for their food and belongings. The pony would be staying with Yata who promised Amber he would take good care of her.

At the base of the cliffs Amber took one last look at the place he had called home for almost half his life. With tears in his eyes he whispered good-bye to his youth. He could just about see his rock across the valley high on the mountain side. The pain of leaving struck his heart as he quickly turned his back on all and followed Dhin into the river.

Coming out of the cliffs they crossed to the opposite bank from where Amber had entered the water on his arrival. Here was a winding path with hoof prints in it and the faint trace of wheel tracks. The little group followed it into Calleve where they stayed until morning. They hoped to hear rumors about Larkwood but all was quiet and though they learned many things, there was nothing about Amber's birthplace.

Early in the morning they said farewell to the innkeeper and rode down to the river crossing. They proceeded on to the little village Amber had found on the night of his flight. Arriving at noon they were greeted by the sight of a very old man who was trying hard to cut some wood in front of the inn. Amber motioned for Dhin and Jasper to wait by the trees. He dismounted and walked towards the old man who looked up at the sound of approaching footsteps.

"I wonder if there is some work I can do in exchange for a good breakfast?" Amber said, for the old man was Waldon.

He had aged a lot since the young man saw him last. He hobbled around Amber, looking him over from head to foot. Doing a complete circle the innkeeper stopped in front of the young man where he searched the handsome face before him. It was a few minutes before he recognized Amber as his eyesight was failing.

"Ambrosius!" he exclaimed, "Ambrosius Myrddhin. Is it really you? Alicae!" he cried towards the inn, "Come and see who has come back to us looking like a prince."

As he talked he had Amber in his embrace and was moving to where an old woman was shuffling from the inn. Alicae cried out with joy when she saw the young man.

"I have friends with me." Amber said as they were pulling him into the building.

"Anyone who has befriended you is welcome at our table." Waldon said. With that Amber waved for Dhin and Jasper to come in.

Once inside and eating Alicae's good bread and cheese Amber told his old friends all that had happened since he saw them last. However, he did not tell them he had the gift of sight as Dhin had cautioned him not to reveal this secret to anyone.

"What have you heard from Larkwood?" Dhin asked Waldon while they sat before the fire with mugs of wine.

"There was a lot of commotion over the young master's disappearance. For five years Votan scoured the country side looking for him. Then he received word that his brother, Bolta, was laying sick. Without another thought of his quest he rushed back to secure the throne for himself. It was less than three months later when he was proclaimed king upon his brother's death." Waldon got up and put another log on the fire.

"As for the fortress," he continued as he sat back down, "Votan had his engineers move the building site a hundred yards to the west which ended the mishap of cracking walls. Soon all was quiet and Larkwood went back to being a peaceful village once again."

"And what of Lady Viviane or Prince Allon. Has there been any news of them?" Amber asked.

"Lady Viviane died two years ago. They say she was with child again and that her age was too old to live through the birth. The child was born dead, a girl it was. Poor King Lot, he himself almost died too, of a broken heart. Then, on the same day they buried the lady, his fever broke and he recovered. A few months later he returned to his own lands in Orkney." Waldon paused, taking a sip of wine before he continued.

"They say Prince Allon had words with his father about the dividing of Lady Viviane's lands. It seems the prince was told he would have to share the lands as there were some papers the lady had hidden away. They revealed something about the prince having a brother, or something like that. Lot would not show his son the papers but vowed it was true. Anyway it was quite a shock and Allon rode off for the court of Arthur to plead the king's aid in finding this brother. All the village was talking about how Uldin, the household servant, overheard the angry lad proclaim that when he found him, this so called brother would die. He was not going to share the lands that were rightfully his. There was something else." Waldon screwed up his eyebrows trying to recall what it was. "Ah, I cannot remember. This old man's mind fades quite often." He then left with Jasper to get their rooms ready.

Amber looked at Dhin, "What do you make of all this?" he asked, "Prince Allon with a brother. It does not seem possible."

"I think maybe we will have to wait until we visit Larkwood." when Amber looked alarmed, Dhin reassured him, "There is nothing to be afraid of Ambrosius. The Lady Viviane will not be there to hurt you anymore. You can go home now my son, without any fear in your heart." With this the two men retired for the night.

The village of Larkwood was just as Amber remembered it. They stayed at the inn which was run by a young man and his mother. The woman kept to the kitchen while her son took care of the hungry travelers. Dhin introduced themselves as Lord Dhin, of the Isle of Mona, his son Dylon, and their servant Jasper. Dhin felt it better if Amber went under an assumed name. The biggest problem was Amber's looks. The innkeeper kept saying he was sure he had met Dhin's son before. To this Dhin remarked that all young men looked alike.

Now the old man knew he must change Amber's looks as well as his name which would be done just before their leaving for Lady Viviane's estate. Another problem would be getting into the house. However here their host helped them without even knowing. He was a very talkative fellow and it was not long before Dhin found out that Allon was still at the court of Arthur. In his absence, Mored and Uldin were taking care of the house, left with only the cook and a few other servants.

After supper the three men retired to their rooms saying the long journey had tired them. Once behind the closed door, Jasper produced a cloth which contained pieces of black hair, taken from the underside of Amber's horse. Using a sticky substance, he said was from a plant, Dhin took the hairs and carefully formed a beard on Amber's smooth face.

When he was done Dhin said, "There master Dylon, you now look like a Welch lord's son. Now let us see if I can look like a Welch lord."

He then proceeded to cut his long white beard so it hung just below his chin. Then with some dye, made from special roots, he colored it black along with the hair on his head. When he was done he stood by Amber's side.

"Well, Jasper, how do we look?" he said to the servant who was getting things ready for their departure.

Turning around Jasper's mouth dropped open and his eyes stared with astonishment. He stood there gazing in a stupefied fascination for a few moments before he finally spoke.

"My Lord Dhin," he said, "I cannot believe my eyes. If I did not know better I would surely swear that you are truly father and son. Your art of disguise is remarkable."

Dhin smiled, the gleam that Amber had come to know so well was in the old man's eyes.

Leaving some coins to pay for the room and food, they left the inn during the night so the innkeeper could not see their new features. Their trip to the Lady Viviane's house was uneventful and soon they reached the wall that stood around the house. Rumpling their clothing to make it look like they were on the road all night, the three men approached the entrance. After a few minutes the door of the house was opened by a grumpy Uldin who finally answered their continuous knocking.

"Well, what can be so important to bring you here in the dead of night?" he said with rage to Dhin.

"I am Lord Dhin, from the Isle of Mona, cousin to the Lady Viviane. You will please advise her of my arrival. We have traveled the roads all night to get here." stated Dhin in a boisterous manner as he pushed past Uldin and entered the house.

The servant was taken back by this loud, rude man. He stammered then said, "My Lord, I do not know how to inform you of the happenings in this house two yeas ago."

"Happenings?" shouted Dhin, "What could possibly interest me in the happenings of this household? Now will you go and get your mistress or shall I announce myself? I am anxious to see her again as the last time we were but children."

Uldin bowed low to the man and said, "Please my Lord, you must hear me out. It is my unpleasant duty to tell you that your lady cousin has passed on to the heavens above."

With these words, Dhin feigned surprise by teetering on his feet like he was going to faint. Amber, who understood the look in the 'Old one's' eyes, rushed to the man's side to support him.

"Quick man, bring my father some wine." he yelled to the servant, "Your words have caused him much grief." As Uldin ran from the room Amber helped Dhin to a chair. When they were sure the servant was gone, he said to the old man, "What now? We are in but how do we get them to let us stay?"

"Your father is about to have a seizure of the heart. You will demand that they allow you to take me to a room upstairs or I might die. They will do as you ask." Dhin instructed Amber.

Just then the servant rushed back into the room with Mored at his heels. She brought the goblet of wine to Amber who made it look like he was forcing some between the lips of the stricken Lord.

Finishing he turned to Uldin and said, "My Lord father has had a heart seizure and I must get him to a bed." seeing the undecided look on the servants face he added, with a harshness in his voice, "If he is not taken care of fast his death will be on your heads."

With this Mored made a sign used to ward off evil spirits and hastened to show them upstairs. She led them into a large room where Uldin, who had hurried before them, was lighting a fire in the hearth. Jasper had carried Dhin up to the room and now placed the old man carefully on the bed.

"You must all leave me to look after my father." Amber said then added, "Would you please see that our servant is bedded down in comfort." with that he turned to the man on the bed and started to unfasten his tunic.

When they had left and the door closed behind them, Dhin slipped quickly from the bed. Amber watched with amazement as the man walked to the large chest standing against the wall. Without hesitation he reached in, pushed the dresses aside, and drew out a satin covered box.

"While we were sitting by the fire last night, I saw in the flames this box and where it was hidden." Dhin said seeing Amber's questioning look. "How fortunate that we have been placed in Lady Viviane's own room."

He then placed the box down on the table in front of the fire. Sitting in one of the chairs he opened the container and revealed its contents. Amber watched with eagerness as Dhin rummaged through the papers. Picking one up and reading it, he looked deep in thought for a moment.

"Ambrosius," he spoke softly, "do you think you are ready to accept the truth of your birth?" he looked up at the young man standing beside him. "Are you man enough to hold secret what you will find when you read this?"

Amber did not hesitate but answered, "I will do and say anything you tell me I must."

Dhin was pleased to hear this and handed Amber the paper from the box. Looking at the document Amber's eyes went wide with perplexity. "I do not understand. This just says that the Lady Viviane gave birth to twin boys. It says nothing of me."

"I thought you were wise. Can you not put the facts together?" Dhin said, "You know you must have had a mother and father for no one is just born without them, and now you find Prince Allon has a twin brother, a boy born the same night as he......"

"Of course." the light of realization crossed Amber's face. "I was born that same night and there were times I was mistaken for Allon when I journeyed to the village." Amber sat down as the truth hit him. At first he was stunned, then upset. "And Allon is looking to kill me so he can have all the land himself. Ah cruel fate has taken away the only childhood friend I ever had." He went to the window and stood looking out at the black night. His thoughts a jumbled mixture of yesterday, today and tomorrow.

When he finally turned around, he saw Dhin staring into the fire. The old man's eyes were wide and his face was white. It looked to Amber like only the body was still sitting in the chair. Dhin himself seemed not to be there, but off somewhere searching for something. The young man went to the table and poured some wine. He then went to Dhin's bag and took out a bit of a powdered plant. Mixing this in the wine he placed the goblet near the fire to warm. He knew Dhin would need this drink when his spirit came back from its journey. Amber then curled up in a chair next to the enchanted man as there was nothing else for him to do but wait.

CHAPTER 7

Amber was dozing next to the old man when suddenly Dhin moaned. Jumping to his feet the young man hurriedly forced the warm mixture between the 'Old one's lips. Soon Dhin was fully awake. Unlike Amber, he did not need sleep after a vision. Finishing the wine Dhin sat back in his chair.

"Well father, what did the flames tell you?" Amber asked.

Dhin, still looking glassy eyed, answered, "I saw a small hut made from the logs of trees. It was sitting in the middle of a forest. Where, I could not tell, for there was a heavy fog all around it. As my essence drifted into the hut I could smell moldy straw. Suddenly a table in the middle of the room came into focus. As the vision became clearer the drawer opened revealing a book covered in red velvet. For a moment the pages unfolded, disclosing some of its contents; 'I Viviane, Lady of Larkwood and wife to King Lot of Orkney, do here by set down the story of my life…' Then just as quickly as it had appeared the book, table and the hut all disappeared, leaving only a thick fog and the evil sound of a woman laughing."

"But what does it all mean?" Amber asked.

"It means we must go and find that book for in it are the answers you are looking for." With this Dhin went over to the bed and in a few moments was asleep.

Amber curled back in his chair unable to sleep, his mind focused on the red book. When he finally drifted off his slumber was filled with dreams. There was a woman, all dressed in black, laughing as she held a red book in her hands. Amber tried to grab it from her but she only laughed more and floated off in a puff of smoke. From somewhere in the night that hung like an ebony shield around him, came that deep whisper a boy once heard.

"You must go to the court of Arthur. There, if you are patient, you will find your way to the forest of the fairies. Be brave my son, and all will come to you."

Amber woke with a start feeling a cold chill pass over him. The fire in the hearth had died out yet there was the smell of smoke in the room. Getting up he walked over to the window and watched the sky as it lit up with the first rays of dawn. Dhin stirred on his bed but did not wake bringing Amber's attention away from the window and towards the hearth.

"I must get a fire going. It would be thought badly of a son who had let the fire die in his father's sick room," he said to the empty air.

Placing some logs on the dead fire he looked around for the flint to light it. Suddenly he heard the sound of footsteps in the long hall. Panic struck his heart when to his dismay he could find no flint. How was he going to get the fire started before the footsteps reached his room?

"Lay your hands over the logs." came a familiar voice. Amber looked towards the bed but Dhin had not opened his eyes. "Do as I say, quickly!" demanded the voice again. The young man stretched out his hands over the logs. "Now concentrate on the powers of the heavens. Think only of the great bolts of lightning that are hurled to the earth during a great storm. Concentrate, concentrate, concentrate…"

Amber, kneeling in front of the hearth with his hands over the logs, had his eyes closed as he thought of the bolts from the sky. Suddenly Jasper's voice broke into his thoughts.

"Master be careful," he warned, "or you will burn yourself."

Amber opened his eyes to see the flames leaping around his

hands. Quickly he pulled them from the fire and faced Jasper.

"The fire had gone out and left me with quite a chill." he said getting up from the floor. "Have you seen Uldin?" he asked disregarding the servants puzzled look. "I thought he would be with you."

"He is on his way up from the kitchen with breakfast for you and my Lord Dhin." As Jasper spoke more footsteps were heard in the hall.

"I have brought you food." said Uldin as he carried a tray with bread, cheese and mutton to the table. "How is your father?" he asked turning to Amber.

"He had a few bad moments during the night but I think the worst is over." answered the young man.

Just then Dhin stirred. Seeing Uldin as he opened his eyes he played his part well. "Dylon, my son." he said in a whisper.

"Yes father, I am here." Amber walked over to the bed.

"What happened? Was it my heart again?" the father asked.

"Yes but you are going to be fine now." the son answered, "I gave you the herb you carry and they let you sleep well."

Dhin looked at Uldin. "My apologies to you sir, I did not mean to bring you such grief. The knowledge that my beloved cousin was dead…" he paused to feign a sob, "well it was just too much for this old heart to bear."

"Do not worry yourself, my lord," Uldin reassured the old man. "You are welcome to stay as long as you need. I am sure the Lady Viviane would have had it so. I will leave you now as I have my duties to attend to. If you should need anything please call on Mored. She will serve you well." with this he bowed low and left the room.

They stayed just long enough to make Uldin and Mored believe the old man had really been sick. Then, thanking their hosts, they took leave of Lady Viviane's house. As the horses moved out of the courtyard and through the gate Amber turned to look at the debris standing outside the wall. It was hard for him to believe that once a tower had stood there.

Suddenly the young man had a strange feeling come over him. The way the stones were sitting there, one atop the other. He stopped his horse and sat frozen in the saddle.

"What is it my son?" Dhin asked pulling his horse to Amber's side.

Amber was about to say that the rubble of rocks looked just like those at the end of the path behind the temple, when he saw that familiar gleam in Dhin's eyes. "Nothing," he finally said, "I was just remembering a night so long ago."

They turned their horses and headed towards the south bypassing the village of Larkwood. After Amber had told Dhin of his dream it was decided they would go to the court of Arthur, stopping first at the town of Amesbury. Dhin said he had some business to take care of there. As they rode away a dark cloud moved to cover the sun while the wind picked up and whistled through the trees by the rock pile.

A woman's voice seemed to whisper, "You will not get my book so easily, my Lord Dhin, if that is really who you are."

Amber shivered and spurred his horse to a faster gait. He wanted to get away from this place as quickly as possible.

After a few days the three men came to the little village of Amesbury. It was said to be the birthplace of King Uther, Arthur's father. After they had eaten in the inn and Jasper left with the innkeeper to find a room, Dhin took Amber and rode west. Not far from the village was a spot marked by one large stone.

"Many years ago, over a hundred brave British nobles were massacred by the Saxons and buried here in one grave." said Dhin, pointing to the mound of dirt that laid beneath the great stone.

As they rode on Amber asked, "Where are we going?"

"Beyond these woods there is a stone circle some call 'The Dance of The Hanging Stones'. It is said that Merlin, for the love of Uther, brought the largest of the stones from Wales." Dhin answered.

Soon they rode out of the woods. Amber looked about. Mile upon mile the long open plain stretched without hill or valley. There was nothing on it except a few oak trees and clumps of thorn bushes. Soon in the distance could be seen the outline of the hanging stones. As they came near Amber gasped, for the stones were enormous, bigger than any he had ever seen. They had a mighty look about them, as they stood isolated, in a circle, in the center of the vast empty plain.

Dhin rode half way around the circle until they reached a hollow. Here he dismounted and told Amber to secure the horses. When this was done both men walked back towards the circle. The outer diameter was of huge stones standing like a giant's fence across the heavens. Within them were smaller ones, which circled enormous stones that formed a half circle. The largest one stood guard over what seemed to be a grave.

After Dhin had looked around he said, "We will be spending the night in the hollow. We must stay and wait for the dawn before I can fulfill a promise." they walked back to the horses where Dhin took two fur covers from his saddle. "You had better collect some tinder for a fire. You should find all we need at the end of this hollow where there are some trees and bushes. It will be very cold when the sun goes down." he said to Amber.

Doing as he was told, there was soon enough wood to keep a fire going all night. Dhin went to the pile and knelt on the ground. Placing his hands over the wood, he closed his eyes. Soon, as the young man watched in amazement, a spark fell into the pile and caused it to flame up. This was just how the voice had told Amber to light the fire at Lady Viviane's. Could it be that the unknown one who was watching over him was also Dhin's guardian?

The old man then turned to him and said, "Come, wrap this around yourself and try to get some sleep. It will be a long night."

Amber took the fur cover offered to him and sat by the fire. Dhin sat also, not saying anything, just staring into the flames.

Amber must have dozed off for suddenly he was aware of movements around him. As he opened his eyes Dhin said to him, "It is time. We must go and stand at the foot of the large stone."

He followed the old man and as they stood facing the east, the sun came up ever so slowly. Light pierced through the gray air and formed a line from the horizon to the stone at their feet. All around the air was still and filled with a golden brilliance, the brightest ray shining on the grave. It looked like the heavens themselves was paying homage to this person of the past.

Dhin was standing, head held high, his arms out stretched like he was reaching for the very sun itself. His lips were moving but no words came to break the silence. Amber caught the faint trace of tears in his deep black eyes. As the sun moved up into the heavens, the bright light of dawn faded into a gray sky. Dhin lowered his head to look once more upon the grave at his feet.

"He was the greatest man that ever lived." his voice broke the stillness.

"Who was he?" Amber asked in a whisper, still in a state of awe.

Dhin stood tall, his eyes shining with pride. "He was my father." the 'Old one' answered, he then turned and walked towards the horses.

The ride back to the inn was done without any conversation. Amber was still thinking of what he had seen at the hanging stones, wondering what really had happened. It was something that only occurred in a vision yet this time there were no clouds, no voice. No, it was not a vision, what took place was real.

Jasper was waiting for them with hot bread, cheese and wine. He asked no questions as he set about getting the horses ready for their continued journey. Amber followed his example and asked nothing of Dhin knowing the old man would tell him in his own time.

Amber's thoughts drifted towards the days ahead, the court of Arthur and in seeing Allon again. Of course the Prince could not be told Amber's identity. He was wise enough to put the facts together and come up with Amber being the brother that he wanted to find and kill. Time had been put between the two brothers and Dhin was sure the friendship Amber felt towards Allon was not shared by the angry prince.

It wasn't long before the men were looking down into a valley at a town sitting by a winding river. Beyond it on a hill stood a huge gray fortress with towers and turrets shooting up towards the abode of the blessed.

As they rode through the town they passed huts with thatched roofs and small gardens around them. Some stone houses, with no windows were scattered among the huts. The streets were crooked alleys with dogs and children playing in the sun. Following one alley they climbed up the side of the hill and soon reached the breezy height where the huge castle stood. There was an exchange of bugle blasts from the wall as men at arms marched to and fro. As the travelers approached the great gates were flung open and the drawbridge was lowered. Inside Amber could see large flapping banners with the figure of a dragon displayed on them. He looked with confusion at Dhin as his fingers moved to touch the brooch pinned on his shoulder. The old man leaned over and put the fold of the young man's cloak on top of the brooch to hide it.

As they dismounted a young lad took their horses to the stable and they followed an older man who led them to a room on the second floor of the castle.

"You may wash off the dust of your travels while you wait for the king to receive you." he said, then left.

"While you are here in Arthur's court you must be careful and not let anyone see your brooch. I cannot explain now, just have faith in this old man's wisdom," Dhin said as they changed their tunics.

"I understand, father, I will wear it at my waist where the leather belt will hide it." Amber answered as he pinned the brooch to his tunic. With the belt in place it could not be seen.

They had just finished when the servant returned and led them into a great hall. Amber was aghast with the glorious surroundings. Banners were hanging from the lofty arched beams and there were stone railed galleries at each end of the room. Musicians sat playing tunes in one while the other held beautiful ladies, dressed in lavish clothing. The floor was of big black and white square stones. On three walls hung huge tapestries of horses, men in armor and other scenes. Beneath these stood men at arms in breastplates looking every bit like statues. The forth wall was occupied by the largest heath that Amber had ever seen.

In the middle of this massive room, almost as large as the room itself, was an oaken table they called the table round. Sitting around it were a great company of men dressed in such glowing colors that Amber blinked from their brightness. There, in the middle of this, sat King Arthur looking more impressive than all his court combined.

"Ah, your grace. Your welcome to this humble lord is most gracious." Dhin was saying as Amber was trying to stay focused on the conversation before him.

The king smiled at them, then asked, "And who might it be that accepts my hospitality?"

"I am Lord Dhin, from the Isle of Mona. This young lad is my son Dylon, my reason for seeking your illustrious presence. With our servant Jasper, we have traveled here from the Welch border so my son may have the benefit of learning from the greatest teachers of all. Intellectual scholars that could only be found at the court of Arthur, King of all Britain." with this Dhin gave a low graceful bow.

The king looked pleased with the eloquent words of this refine gentleman before him. "My Lord Dhin, your journey has not been in vain. Your son may stay in the company of this court. I will select one of our fine squires, training for knighthood, to be his companion during his learning."

Arthur looked around the room until his eyes stopped on a fine looking young man. Amber's heart jumped as he saw the squire had thick black hair with eyes to match. It was as if Amber was looking into a mirror. Except that he now had a beard while the other was clean faced.

"Allon, Prince of Orkney, you are to be the companion of Dylon." the king said as the squire came over to them. "This is his father Lord Dhin. They are from the Isle of Mona."

"My Lord Dhin." said Allon bowing to the older man. "It will be my pleasure to be guide and companion to your son."

Dhin smiled and said to Amber, "I think if your saintly mother were here to see you taking this big step in your life, she would be as proud as I." only Amber noticed the old gleam in his eyes.

"I am sure your lady wife is just as proud." said the king, "Did she come with you or is she still back on the Isle of Mona?" he asked.

"Neither, your majesty. She passed on to the world beyond two years ago." said Dhin with lowered eyes.

"I am sorry to hear that but now your son will have more in common with Prince Allon as he too lost his lady mother at about the same time." stated the king.

Amber could feel the young man's eyes upon him. He turned sure that Allon had recognized him in spite of his disguise, only to find a look of pity in the others eyes.

"I know how you must feel Dylon." said the prince, "I am sure we will be good medicine for each other. Come I will show you where you will bed down. Have your servant bring your things to my room. It has been a long time since I have had a companion my own age."

Dhin watched as the two young men took their leave of the king. "You would be very surprised, your majesty," Dhin said to himself, "if you knew just how much those two have in common. Even more surprised if it were revealed what you and I have in common." He smiled at Arthur who was holding out his arm to the older man.

"Come, Lord Dhin. Let us walk in the gardens. I would like to know you better even though the feeling gnaws at my brain that I have met you sometime in my youth."

The two men walked out the door with the king telling Dhin how he has been in need of an older man's conversation since he lost his only real friend, Merlin. Arthur was so involved with his talking he failed to notice the gleam in Dhin's eyes. The breeze in the garden seemed to whisper "my sons, my sons." as the two men walked slowly into the sunlight.

Dhin's heart was light as he listened to the king's conversation. But his thoughts were on other matters. All was going as planed. Soon Amber would be on one of the most adventurous quests that anyone had ever been on. Soon too Dhin would be able to share with this young man one of his most hidden secrets.

CHAPTER 8

Amber found being a squire not only hard but at times, quite boring. The information King Arthur's great teachers provided was only repetition of what he had already learned from Dhin and Gorganis. Then there were days when he would spend all his time looking after some knight's armor. He had to keep the helmet, chain mail and sword polished and free from any rust. It was also a squire's job to care for the knight's horse and to follow him into battles and tournaments.

To ready himself for such events Amber had to spend a lot of time working out with a sword and lance. This part of his training brought out mixed emotions. At times he would really enjoy the clash of steel. Then at other times, it sent a shiver down his spine. He tried to talk to Allon of this feeling but his friend just laughed.

"You must have been very sheltered on your Isle of Mona." he said, "If you had been raised like I, you would be quite use to the sounds of battle."

Amber smiled, yet in his heart he felt sad. Not for himself, but for Allon. He knew that his growing up in the temple of Dusk was more beneficial than any court of the king's.

"There are many times when a quick mind can win more battles than all the flashing steel of a knight." said Amber, "Were we not taught that King Pendragon won his battle over Vortigern by his wits?"

"Maybe so." answered Allon, "but it was Uther's sword that put the traitor to his death, thus preventing him from trying to take the crown away from Pendragon again." And so the differences of opinion continued in this manner.

Other than his talks to Allon, Amber never complained. He labored with his sword out in the field the same as all the other squires. In heavy armor he learned to mount a running horse, scale walls and spring over ditches. Long hours were spent wrestling or wielding a battle-axe without so much as raising the visor of his armor to take a breath.

The one thing that really bothered Amber he did not mention to Allon. It was the custom of the court that every untested squire should select a young lady as mistress of his heart, to whom he was taught to refer all his sentiments, words and actions. Amber had no wish to become involved with any lady, at least not yet. They all seemed like giddy little children who reminded him of Ronya and how her presence in his youth had caused him to be very clumsy. A spill down the mountainside would be nothing compared to falling from a horse in full armor. On top of the physical pain he would also become the laughing stock of all his peers. So he avoided making a choice until the king ordered him to do so. At this time Dhin stepped forward and saved him from the scorn of the court. He told Arthur that his son was betrothal of a neighboring Lord's daughter back on the Isle of Mona. This satisfied the monarch and Amber was free to continue his education without any distractions.

After many months of hard work and learning lessons, the time had come for all the young squires to take their vows of knighthood. To ready themselves for this occasion, it was required that they spend the night in the church chapel in prayer and meditation. There were twenty-five squires and as they walked ceremoniously into the church all the court stood outside watching. Amber's eyes moved around the crowd, searching for the familiar face of Dhin. His heart sank as he realized the old man was not one of the spectators.

In the church, twenty-five kneeling blocks had been set up around the altar. Here the young men knelt, paying homage to their god. All around them were placed large, thick candles. The smoke coming from their flame made the chapel appear to be of another world. As Amber took his place on the last block at the end of the line he looked around. The only one allowed to remain in the chapel was the squire's servants who stood against the wall behind a railing. As he turned to face the altar Amber realized that Jasper was not standing with the others.

Time slipped by and the strain of being in this position started to take its toll. Soon, here and there around the church, the young men fell from their kneeling blocks. As they did their servants came to carry them out of the chapel where the crowed mocked and ridiculed them, for it was said if a man could not stand the strain of kneeling all night, he was not fit to become a knight. From Amber's position at the end he could see the others without moving his head. Counting Allon there was only fifteen left.

He will surely last until morn. Thought Amber of his friend, *if I do not, who will carry me off?* He wondered.

Suddenly Amber felt very light headed. The smoke from the candles seemed to close in around him. As he looked at the altar with burning eyes, he became aware of a cold chill coming over him. Immediately a voice, coming from inside his head, spoke.

"Ambrosius." it called. "Ambrosius Myrddhin. You must not take your vows of knighthood."

Amber, looking around, felt as if he were all alone, enclosed in a thick white cloud.

"You cannot be knighted as 'Master Dylon, son of Lord Dhin'." the voice continued, "You must leave this place now before it is too late, to deceive the gods would bring down a great punishment."

"But what shall I do?" Amber whispered to the mist around him. "Dhin is expecting me to fulfill the vows."

"He is waiting for you at the bottom of the hill." reassured the voice, "All is ready for your leaving."

"Where shall I go?" questioned the young man. Panic was starting to grip his heart. "You said I would find the answer to where the forest of the fairies is, here at the court of Arthur."

"Search out the castle of gold." instructed the voice, "There you will meet a fair haired man dressed all in yellow. He will take you in and feed you well. After your meal ask the way to the forest in the glen. When he tells you, leave Dhin and Jasper at the castle. You must fulfill this quest alone. Even I will not be able to help you. Your bravery and wisdom will be your only hope."

With this a great breeze came into the chapel causing the candles to flicker and some to go out.

"*Now, Ambrosius, run as fast as you can.*" the voice cried loudly startling Amber. "You will return some day and become knighted, 'Sir Ambrosius Myrddhin', son of Lady Viviane and.............."

The voice was left behind as Amber lurched from the kneeling board and ran out of the chapel. In the courtyard the first rays of dawn were trying to find their way through the thick layer of clouds. The few spectators that had braved the long night were shocked to see a young squire running from the church. They stood like statues, unable to prevent his flight down the hill.

As he came to the bottom of the hill, Jasper's voice reached his ears, "Over here, Master Ambrosius."

Amber turned to see the servant standing by their four horses. Dhin was sitting in the saddle of his horse with eyes that glowed brightly in the dawn's light. He didn't speak but as the young man mounted his horse there was a smile upon his face.

They spurred their mounts and quickly rode through the sleeping village, across the river and into the woods. When they finally slowed, Amber could not tell where they were. The forest was thick around them yet Dhin led the group as if he knew just where they were going. Suddenly before them could be seen a large and lustrous castle. As they approached a fair-haired man dressed in a long robe of yellow satin came to greet them. Smiling, he welcomed them into his castle as a servant led their horses towards the stables.

When they entered the main hall, which was larger that the one at King Arthur's court, Amber's eyes fell on the beautiful daughters of their host. There were six in all, dressed like their father in long yellow satin robes. As the men reached the hall the women put aside their sewing and came to greet them. Their father offered his visitors food and drink from golden vessels.

No one spoke until the meal was done, then their host asked, "What service can I do for you?"

"If it pleases you to tell me," Amber answered, "I would like to know the way to the forest in the glen."

The fair haired man sat silently at first, then spoke in a soft voice, "I will tell you what you wish to know," he said, "but first be it said that I have warned you of the dangers that await anyone traveling to the glen."

He then told Amber that he was to take the road behind the castle and follow it up the mountain until he came to level ground. There, on the right, would be a path leading to the glen.

"But now come, you must not go until the morning. You will need all your strength for the adventure before you." He then led his guest to their rooms.

When Amber woke to the bright sun of morning his eyes fell on Jasper getting his things ready. There was a new tunic of red satin with a cloak of the same material and color.

"Well my son, I see you are awake." said Dhin as he came into the room. "Come, we must ready you for your departure."

Helping Amber to dress, Dhin placed a lightweight golden breastplate next to his skin before helping him with his tunic.

"Our host was kind enough to give you this for protection against the lance and sword of your enemies." the old man explained, "His daughters fashioned it from threads of gold and it will resist any weapon."

"It feels as soft as silk." said Amber smiling. "I must remember to thank our kind host and his lovely daughters."

When Amber was through dressing, Jasper put his cloak around him while Dhin fastened the dragon brooch onto it. There was no longer any need to hide it. Amber noticed that on the breast of his tunic, as well as the cloak, there was the exact same emblem that was on the brooch, a red dragon on a black background.

"You shall call yourself the '*Red Warrior*', using your own name only when you think it is necessary." Dhin said as they walked to where Amber's horse was waiting.

Pegasus, all saddled and ready for the journey, had red satin trappings that hung down all around her nearly reaching the ground. Here, again, was the emblem of the red dragon on a black background, in the front, the back and on both sides. Just as Amber was about to mount, the fair-haired owner of the castle and his six daughters came to say good-bye.

"My children have some gifts for you," said his host. "They may be of some help, for where you are going is very dangerous. Though their powers may be used only once, I know you will find them useful."

As each lady gave Amber her gift, she explained its use.

"These, my Lord, are winged sandals." said the first, "Just slip them on over your own and they will fly you through the air. Once you set down upon the earth again they will disappear."

"Here, my Lord, is the cloak of invisibility." stated the second, "All you need do is wrap it round your body and you will cease to be in the eyes of those around you."

"A gold ring crown to place upon your head, my Lord." declared the third, "It will give you the power to defeat your mightiest foe, while protecting you lest he scores a blow upon your body, for with its power comes invincibility."

"This star shaped ring I place on your finger, my Lord, has two pills in it." announced the fourth, "The white one, when swallowed, will make the truth come from the lips. The other, red, will bring deep sleep."

"And this moon shape ring which I place on your other hand, my Lord, has but one pill." spoke the fifth, "When taken it will prevent even the devil himself from placing an enchantment on you."

"Here, my Lord, is an ever burning torch." proclaimed the sixth, "When afire it will light the darkest path. Once its flames are put out it will never light again."

"And last, young Master," said the ladies father, "here is a spool of gold thread. It will mark your path so you will be able to find your way out of even the hardest maze."

Amber took the gifts and placed them carefully in the pouch hanging from his saddle. "My heart is warm with thanks to you all for the kindness you have bestowed upon me. I only ask that you give my father leave to stay with you until that day when I shall return." he said.

"Your father is surely welcome to stay as long as needs be." answered the man.

After embracing Dhin, Amber mounted Pegasus and hurried down the road behind the castle. Following this up the mountain it wasn't long before he came to the clearing with the path on the right leading into the woods. The trees were thick making it necessary for him to bend over the neck of his horse to dodge the low hanging branches. At the end of the path was another clearing with a small wooden house sitting in the middle of it. As Amber approached, a short bearded man came out the door.

"Ho, fair sir, might you tell me if this is the forest in the glen?' Amber inquired as he dismounted.

"That it be." answered the man in a gruff voice.

"It has been a long journey and my throat has the taste of straw from being so dry. Could I trouble you for some liquid to quench my thirst?" asked the young man.

The woodcutter looked at Amber for a moment then with an impatient gesture, led him into the house. As he sat at the table, the man poured two mugs of ale.

"It is very cold in here and your fire is burning low." said Amber, taking a sip from the mug.

The man grunted and left to bring in more wood. Quickly, before he could come back in, Amber opened the star ring. Taking the white pill out, he closed the ring and dropped the pill into the other's mug. Just then his host returned with an arm full of wood. After placing it on the dying fire, he sat and took a drink of his ale. Sitting back in his chair the woodcutter closed his eyes for a moment. When he opened them again, they were glassy.

"I would like to know the way to the forest of the fairies." said Amber taking advantage of his host's hypnotic state.

"Go back to the clearing and take the path by the large rock." said the man, forced to tell the truth. "This will lead you to a cave in the side of a mountain. If you find your way through, you will come out in the forest of the fairies."

Amber finished his ale, thanked his host who had come out of the trance without remembering anything, and left the house. Mounting Pegasus he rode back down the path to the clearing. There stood the large rock just as the man had said.

"This is strange." Amber said to himself, "I did not see this rock before."

Even stranger was the fact that besides the path he had just used and the one by the rock, there was no other. The path he had rode on when he came up the mountain from the castle had disappeared. It puzzled him but did not stop him from continuing his adventure.

Following the path, he soon came to the side of another mountain. It was straight up, towering high over the forest. There at its base was the cave entrance. After tying Pegasus to a tree and making sure there was enough grass for her to nibble on, Amber folded his cloak carefully and placed it on her saddle. Then taking the spool of golden thread, he fastened one end of the fiber to a bush near the entrance. He put the spool in the pocket of his tunic, making sure the thread would pull freely without falling out, and then walked cautiously to the mouth of the cave. Carrying the pouch with all the gifts tucked inside, he stopped to light the torch by striking it against the side of the great tunnel. It burst into a bright golden flame, illuminating the darkness before him.

Cautiously the young warrior stepped into the shaft and followed it to a large open area. Its vastness made him feel like a monster was swallowing him. Looking up he could see no roof, only the blackness where the light of the torch ended. Ahead of him was a long wall of stone with five tunnels leading out of the chamber. Amber studied the ground in front of each opening carefully and found that the stone path in front of the middle entrance showed more wear than the other four. He chose to enter this one, knowing that it was the one most used therefore had to be the one leading out of the mountain. As he walked slowly down the passageway he thought he smelled smoke. It could not be coming from the torch, for this just gave off brightness without any evidence of smoke.

Soon the tunnel ended as he entered another chamber. This one was not as big as the first for when Amber looked up, he could see the roof. It had strange rock formations hanging from it that glistened like they were wet with moisture when the light flashed over them. Here and there, around the floor under these rocks, were others that seemed to be growing like trees reaching toward the ones above.

Caught in the marvel of the sights around him, Amber jumped as the sound of laughter reached his ears. Looking in the direction it came from he saw an old woman sitting on a rock. She was dressed all in black and had stringy white hair that hung in a disheveled manner over her shoulders. Her laughter now sounded more like a cackling as she motioned for the young man to come nearer.

"Well...well...well," she said slowly, "what do we have here?"

Her crackling voice sent a chill through this *'Red Warrior'*. "Come my fancy friend, you are not afraid of old Maude, are you now." she cackled again as Amber sat on the rock across from her.

"I am called the Red Warrior." he said without any show of fear. "I have come in search of the forest of the fairies. The old man in the glen told me of the cave entrance."

"So, the old woodcutter has told you of this cave." the old woman laughed so hard she threw back her head and displayed a mouth that was quite toothless. "You must have strong magic to get such information from one as tight lipped as he." she turned a glaring eye on Amber as she continued. "And what magic have you for me? I am Maude, the witch of Fairy Mountain and I challenge any boy who thinks his sorcery stronger than mine."

The torch in Amber's hand shook at these words. He had planned to slip her the red pill from the star ring. Could he really fool a witch? If this old hag was really the enchantress she claimed to be, what gift could he cleverly use to get away from her?

CHAPTER 9

The loud crack of a fire caused Amber to turn his head. He saw a hearth built into the side of the cave wall with a table and a few chairs sitting in front of it.

"Come, my Red Warrior," Maude gave out a vulgar laugh, "Let us celebrate our meeting." The old woman hobbled over to the fire and sat down.

Amber placed the torch in a holder on the side of the chamber wall and followed her. As he made himself comfortable in the other chair, Maude poured wine into two goblets.

Handing him one of the vessels she said, "Now, let us see this great magic of yours." her eyes squinted at Amber as she drank some wine.

Looking into the fire, the light of an idea settled on his face. "If you will put out those burning logs, I will relight them without the use of any flint." he said going to the hearth.

"Will you now?" she said as her laughter turned to a screech. Taking some water from a bucket nearby, she doused the fire.

The young man knelt in front of the hearth and stretched his hands over the wet logs. Closing his eyes, he thought of nothing except the great bolts of lightning that came from the sky during a storm. When he opened his eyes, he saw the look of amazement on the face of the witch as the wet logs burst into flames. The Warrior sat back down, leaving the old hag staring at the fire with open mouth.

"Do you think your magic could do that?" he asked confidently.

Maude gave him no answer as she once again poured water on the fire. Kneeling in front of the hearth she placed her hands over the logs. When she closed her eyes, Amber took the opportunity to open his star ring and drop the red pill into her goblet of wine.

"Bah!" Maude exclaimed as she rose to her feet. "I have an easier way of getting fire," With this she took something from the pouch hanging at her waist and threw it into the hearth. There was a bright flash as the logs burst into flames.

Amber pretended to be amazed as he sipped his wine. "Well, I guess that you are the better fire maker." he said with a smile.

Maude laughed again as she sat down and drank the rest of her wine in one gulp. Before she knew what was happening, her gray head fell onto the table with a great thud. The young man smiled as he bent over and found she was fast asleep. Taking his torch he left the chamber by its only exit.

Amber had only gone a few paces when in the distance could be heard the sound of music. As he proceeded down the tunnel a sweet aroma filled the air. When he came upon a third chamber he paused before entering, peering inside to see what was waiting for him. The sight before him was the same as the chamber he had just left, except instead of an old hag, there was the most beautiful woman he had ever seen. She was sitting on a satin pillow singing a woeful song. All around her, big red roses seemed to sway with the music. The young man marveled that they could grow in such a place without sunlight. Then he noticed there was light that came down in a shaft embracing the lady and the flowers. Looking up, he could not see where it was coming from.

"This sight before me cannot be so without some magic." he thought to himself. "I must take the pill to prevent my becoming enchanted." He opened the moon ring and swallowed its contents then walked out into the cave, letting the lady see him.

"Welcome Red Warrior." she said putting down the lute she had been playing.

"You know who I am?" asked Amber coming near.

"Verna knows everything." When the young man looked towards the tunnel he had just come through, she smiled and said, "Old Maude was never very smart. Mind you, it will not be so easy to fool me!"

Suddenly, as Amber gazed into this lady's eyes, there was a vision of another lady. Standing before her was a little boy.

"It is not easy to fool me Ambrosius." the lady was saying, "I know my dear little Allon would not be so cruel as to put the lizard into Mored's bed, so it must have been you. Come now and take your punishment."

Amber shook the vision from his head as Verna said, "Come now and sit by me while I play you a song." she picked up her lute and started playing again.

The young man stood his ground as she sang a song in the old tongue. Amber knew the language but the words had no meaning, so he just looked blankly at her. When she saw that her magic had no effect on him, Verna threw down the lute and started screeching in the voice of the old hag.

"It will do you no good Ambrosius, you will never get the red book." with this Verna lost her beauty as she turned into the old witch Maude. The warrior stood amazed as Maude then disappeared in a puff of smoke. Without too much hesitation he left the chamber through yet another tunnel.

"I wonder what will be waiting for me in the next cave." he said as he held the torch before him.

But there were no more chambers, for at the end of the darkness, Amber could see light coming from the outside world. His heart pounded with happiness for he felt the end of his trials in the mountain was near at hand.

Stopping short he saw that he was wrong, for in front of him the ground was split wide open. The sides of the tunnel were as smooth as glass and the gaping hole came right to them so there was no way around it. Amber stood at the edge and looked in. Holding the light over the emptiness he could see no bottom.

"Well, there is nothing to do but use the winged sandals." he said as he sat on the ground and put them on his feet. He then stood up and wondering how he was supposed to fly when he found he was floating in the air. Putting one foot in front of the other, he managed to walk on the air across the pit below him. Once over, he floated back to earth where the sandals disappeared when they touched the ground.

As Amber came into the sunlight, he wondered what to do with the torch. Deciding it would be needed on his return he struck the end into the ground at the mouth of the cave. Looking into the woods before him, he started to walk away from the mountain.

Just then there came a loud growl. "Who comes from the mountain of the fairies into the domain of Garth?"

Amber stopped short for coming out of the trees was the biggest man he had ever seen. With one fast move the warrior took the gold ring crown from the pouch and placed it on his head. Then, picking up a large tree branch that lay near his feet, he prepared to defend himself.

Garth stalked Amber like an animal of the forest as the young man advanced with an air of bravery. His enemy charged suddenly, striking Amber on the chest with his gleaming sword. It cut through the breast of his tunic, exposing the gold vest beneath.

"So you carry a great treasure which shall be mine after I have slain you." snarled Garth.

"You will have to slay me first." said Amber. Catching the large man off guard he landed a blow to the top of Garth's head, dazing him for a moment.

Indignation filled the giant as he started to slash at the dwarfish man before him. It was all wasted energy for there was no way he could even draw the others blood. When the weapon struck Amber across the cheek with no results, the angry Goliath stood unbelieving the lack of a wound. Seeing that the gold ring crown was really protecting him, Amber became arrogant and started taunting Garth. He let the large man hit at him, then laughed and jeered as he landed blows on the giant's head with his shaft.

Then, the young warrior's foolish game backfired as he tripped on a tree root and fell to the ground with a thud. Panic struck his heart as he felt the gold ring tumble from his head. Before he could retrieve it, Garth came running full force with the point of his sword aimed at the toppled man. As the fates would have it the enormous man's foot caught the same root. He tried to catch his balance but nothing would stop his sizable body as it fell to the ground. Amber suddenly found the man on top of him, pinning him to the earth. He closed his eyes waiting to feel the cold steel pierce his warm body. Lying like this for some time he suddenly realized Garth was not moving. Using all the strength he had, the warrior pushed the jumbo man off. He looked at his own chest expecting to see Garth's sword sticking out of it. There was no sword but the front of his tunic was wet and as he touched it a red solution was on his hand.

"Blood!" his voice caught as he spoke. "But I felt no pain." then he saw the giant laying face up with Amber's weapon protruding out of his chest. Having held the shaft in an upright position when Garth fell on him, the warrior had killed his enemy.

Getting slowly to his feet, Amber saw the gold crown turn to copper and rust as it lay in the grass where it had fallen. Looking around he sighted his pouch next to a pool of water. Here he washed most of the blood off his body, thankful that it was not his. Yet, as he walked into the forest, he felt a sharp pain in his left shoulder. Before he could see what it was, he heard a loud roaring and smelled smoke. Cautiously he crept towards the noise, using the trees for cover. There in the clearing at the center of the forest was the hut he had been looking for. Standing guard over the entrance, tied by a large chain, was the cause of all the noise and smoke. It was a monstrous dragon with fire shooting from his gigantic mouth.

Amber opened the pouch to find his last gift, the cloak. Quickly he wrapped it around so it would cover his whole body from head to toe. With the folds parted enough for him to see, he walked slowly out of the trees, stopping only to test his invisibility. Sure enough, the dragon looked right at him without even knowing anyone was there. Still slowly, Amber walked past the beast and into the door of the hut. Safely inside he let the cloak fall to the floor where it promptly disappeared.

"Well," he said with a sigh. "I will have to worry about getting out of here when the time comes, but for now I must find the book."

As he turned slowly looking around the room, he spied a table near the hearth. The young man quickly walked over and opened the drawer. There in all its glory sat the book. Amber picked it up, and then went to sit before the fire.

The first page of the book read just as Dhin had said it would. "I

Viviane, Lady of Larkwood and wife to King Lot of Orkney, do here by set down the story of my life." Amber read the words aloud. They struck the walls of the hut and seemed to echo around him. He continued reading.

"In truth, the village called Larkwood was formulated by me many, many years ago. Using the magic taught to me by my grandmother, I transported the villagers from another town and enchanted them into thinking they were born and raised in Larkwood. Today, their offsprings still believe this. My reason for doing this was just the beginning of a well-planned plot to become the Queen of Orkney.

"I chose Orkney because my grandmother and mother both suffered an injustice at the hands of the king and his son. The king had made love to my grandmother with the lie that he would do away with his wife and make her his queen. After he had taken his pleasures with her, he had her thrown into the dungeon where his soldiers were allowed to misuse her. When she became heavy with child, they took her to the forest of the fairies and left her to die. But she lived, by her own determination, and learned the magic of the elf-like people who resided in the woodland.

"There she bore a daughter, my mother, who when she had grown, tried to fulfill her mother's revenge. But the king's son was just as corrupt as his father and history repeated itself. I was born in the forest of the fairies, cared for by my mothers loving hand and taught the magic of the elf-like people by my grandmother. As I grew in years and wisdom, I vowed to become Queen of Orkney and complete an old lady's revenge.

"To avenge my family's humiliation, I needed the help of Merlin the Enchanter. Not only to learn more about the black arts, but also as an accomplice. I could not reveal my plans to him for I knew he would surely refuse to comply and so a plan of deception had to be fabricated. As the fates would have it my chance to meet him arose when Merlin decided to travel across country. I made sure I was in the right place at the right time and when we met I kissed him with a potion of love upon my lips. Instantly he became my slave in romance. Infatuated and very much in love, he revealed the secrets of his art. Having completed the first phase of my scheme, I hurried on to the second stage.

"During a walk in the forest, we sat beneath a tree to embrace and dream as lovers do. I sang to him the song of the wood nymph and soon, under its enchantment, he fell asleep. Using the *incantation of imprisonment*, taught to me by the old wizard himself, I confined him in a tower and whisked him away, tower and all, to the grounds outside my house in Larkwood. The trap for King Lot, now heir of Orkney, was set. I let word out that the wicked Merlin had me captive in the tower and it would take the bravest knight in all the land to save me. Others came but I cast spells upon them, for they were not the knight I was waiting for. All believed it was the magician who kept them from the tower.

"Then one night as I lay asleep, I had a dream that Merlin came into my room and stayed in my bed until morning. I could not stop his advances as I was in a trance. At dawn I awoke suddenly and felt a cold wind pass by me out the window. Merlin, knowing the art of transporting his soul from one place to another while his body was in sleeping form, had come to me in the night and when he left I was heavy with child. It had not been a dream. The old sorcerer would have suffered a terrible death had it not been that King Lot chose this time to come to my rescue. All thought of the enchanter left with the knowledge that my long wait for revenge would soon come to an end.

"When Lot came to the tower I charmed him into believing he had driven Merlin away. It was near the truth, for after his soul returned to his body the old wizard disappeared, never to be seen or heard from again. As a reward for the brave knight who saved me, I gave Lot a kiss. He fell madly in love with me for once again I had the magic potion upon my lips. We were married that same day and after a month I told my husband I was carrying his child. There was no reason for him to suspect he was not the father.

"As the time for my birthing drew near, Lot decided to visit his lands in Orkney. His first wife had been in such pain that he could not stand being around a screaming woman who was giving birth. I was glad of his going for by the movement in my belly, I knew there was more than one baby. I was right, there were two boys born with hair and eyes as black as the night, given to them by their father as a reminder of his treachery. The first born, whose face was that of his father's, had skin like a bronze god and I cursed him to live the life of a child of no birth. While the second babe with lily-white skin and features after my own face. I chose to call him, my son Allon.

"With my magic, I enchanted the entire household into believing they had found a baby in the tower. His name is the reverse of the man who sired him. Myrddhin Ambrosius. Through this son of Merlin I planned to have complete revenge on the man who caused me to bear his children. Allon shall have everything, my lands in Larkwood and Lot's castle in Orkney, while Ambrosius shall have nothing but a black birth. Even though he has escaped from the hands of King Bolta, Ambrosius will never be allowed the lands or titles that come to those of noble birth.

"Now that I am with child again, this time Lot's, I can feel the black heart of Merlin hovering over me. For now my age is too great for any chance of living through a birth. I know I am at deaths door, yet my only fear is that someday Ambrosius will find out the truth and cause my dear Allon to lose all that I have meant for him to have. Now, before I draw my last breath, I am planning evil preparations for Ambrosius. If he should ever find his way through the mountain and past my two guards, Garth and the dragon, my spirit will somehow prevent him from ever hurting my precious Allon."

A cold chill passed over Amber as he finished reading the book. The realization of what was written hit him full force. "Ambrosius Myrddhin is twin brother to Allon. He is the son of Viviane and of Merlin. Merlin the Enchanter..." he said the words aloud.

"Now you know the truth Ambrosius." came a woman's voice, "What do you think you can do with this new found knowledge?"

Amber jumped to his feet looking around the room for the owner of the voice. As he watched, a puff of smoke appeared and took form. It was the woman who called herself Verna.

"You are the Lady Viviane, my mother. Are you not?" said the young man to the specter before him.

"I am the woman who bore you through the curse of the Enchanter, but I could never be your mother. I have hated you since the day you let out your first cry of life. You think you will be the downfall of my fair Allon, but you will not be able to support your claim. At this moment my book lies burning in the fire." spoke the apparition.

Amber turned to find she had said the truth. In his haste to find the owner of the voice, he had let the book drop into the fire. The last of the red cover was now turning to ashes as the flames burned bright.

The lady's laughter filled the room and she began to turn to smoke, "Good-bye Ambrosius Myrddhin. I, like my book, am no longer able to exist. But at least I go with the knowledge that Merlin's son has found his identity to no avail. You are back to where you started before you found my book. If you reveal your true character to Allon, he will slay you for the lands that are rightfully his."

Her laughter lingered a few moments then with a flash of lightning not only did Viviane disappear, but the hut also vanished. Amber found he was quite alone, standing in a clearing with the forest all around. Still bewildered by all that happened, the young man stumbled through the forest towards the mountain.

Suddenly he stopped short, more confused than ever. Before him was the burning torch still stuck in the dirt where he had left it. But there was no mountain behind it. The gigantic mound was now gone, along with the dead body of Garth. Looking past the torch Amber saw Pegasus where he had tied her. The area between horse and torch was flat, barren land with nothing on it except the gold thread running back and forth across the open space. The spool itself was lying on the ground where it had fallen from his pocket during the fight with the giant.

As he staggered towards his horse Amber felt the stabbing pain in his shoulder again. Opening his tunic he found a deep gash with blood running from it. Tearing a piece of his cloak he pressed the cloth hard against the wound, almost fainting from the pain.

"It must have happened when Garth fell on me." his utterance was heard only by the air around him.

Desperately he attempted to mount Pegasus as the ground swayed beneath his feet. Putting his foot into the stirrup and holding the reins with his good hand, Amber tried to climb into the saddle. The pain was more than he could bear. From the sleeve of his tunic the blood was dripping, forming a red pool at his feet.

Unexpectedly the world went black as the young man fell to the ground. Half conscious, laying in a pool of blood, he mumbled, "Twin Brother… Lady Viviane… Merlin my father, my father… my father…"

Then his eyes closed as he fell into an unwanted sleep. He was still and silent, alone, bleeding from his wound in the forest of the fairies.

CHAPTER 10

The moon glimmered through the puffy clouds giving light to the forest below. Its illumination revealed a young man laying in a pool of blood. A horse was next to him, giving protection from the night chill. Unexpectedly a soft moaning echoed through the trees as the man's body was lifted and carried off deep into the woods. A pair of small hands took the bridle of his horse and led her behind the slow moving procession. The forest around them became thicker, preventing the moon's glow from lighting their way. Still they pushed on, almost as if they were floating on a cloud, until they stood before a huge mountain. Slower now, not wanting to bounce the injured man, they carried their burden up a path, coming at last to the mouth of a cave. Once inside they laid the unconscious man on a pile of straw.

When Amber opened his eyes, his vision was fuzzy. His sight became clearer as he tried to sit up. Someone gently forced him back down and he looked to see who it was. Shaking with fright he saw the hand holding him down belonged to an old lady with white stringy hair. She wore a black robe and was tending to the wound on his shoulder.

"Do not be afraid, my boy, I will not hurt you." her voice was soft and gentle. "Lie still and give your wound time to heal." she finished washing his shoulder with a liquid that smelled peculiar.

"Your Maude." Amber said in a weak voice.

"Maude! What ever gave you that idea?" the woman asked as she gave him a puzzled look.

"You are not Maude, witch of fairy mountain?" the young man inquired.

The old woman laughed. Not a cackle like Amber had heard coming from Maude, but a pleasant soft laugh. "I assure you I am not a witch," she said, "though I may look like one. My name is Reena and I live here alone."

Amber looked around the cave which was very plain. There was a hearth in the wall with a table and some chairs, crudely made from logs, sitting in front of it. The floor was dirt but had been swept clean. Amber was lying on the bed that was set in one corner. In the other corner, looking very much out of place, sat a large wooden cabinet with different kinds of containers on its shelves.

"How did I get here?" he asked, "Surely you do not have the strength to carry me."

"No, I do not have that kind of strength." said Reena as she covered his wound with a clean piece of cloth. "The animals of the forest are my friends. When they come to me being sick or injured by the hunters arrow, I cure their ills, and heal their lacerations with my many kinds of roots and herbs. Two weeks ago I went to the forest over the hill, where grows a special kind of flower needed to ease pain. There I came upon a young man lying in his own blood. I could not leave you there to die so my friends helped me bring you here knowing I could care for your wounds as I do theirs."

"Two weeks!" Amber repeated with surprise. "I have been here for two weeks?"

"Yes, and there was a time when I thought I was going to lose you to death. But now I see you will make it after all." She reached for a gold goblet and held Amber's head up while he drank the liquid inside. It was sweet and warm, soothing his dry throat.

He started to ask her more questions when she stopped him saying "There will be enough time for talking later when you are stronger. For now lie back and sleep with an easy mind for you are safe here with me." she smoothed the young man's hair away from his forehead and soon he was fast asleep.

"Ah yes, sleep my dear Ambrosius." she whispered, "When you wake the pain will be lessened." she smiled and if Amber had not been sleeping he would have seen a warm loving look in her eyes.

When Amber awoke the cave was dimly lit by a fire in the hearth. Reena was sitting in front of it staring into the flames. As the young man moved and turned on his straw bed, she looked towards him. Her face was wet with tears and her eyes reflected the appearance of a vision passed.

"You are sad Reena. What is it that makes you cry?" Amber asked, concerned that this gentle woman should be upset.

She quickly wiped away the tears with the back of her hand and came over to his bed. "It is nothing Ambrosius." she said, using his given name. Suddenly she stopped short realizing what she had just said.

"You know my name?" the young man said very puzzled over this new turn of events.

"Yes, I know your name." she answered softly.

"But how did I tell you in my unconscious state?" he questioned.

"You did not tell me." was all Reena would say as she went back to the fire and returned with a bowl of meal. "Eat this, you need to build your strength." she said handing him the container.

Amber took the bowl from the small hands that offered it. "Will you talk to me as I eat and tell me how you know my name?" he asked.

Reena smiled, "Yes Ambrosius, there is much I must tell you for you have a right to know." She pulled a chair over to the straw bed and sat down. "While you were overcome with the fever of pain, you spoke about the forest of the fairies, rambling on, calling out the names of Maude, Verna, Garth and Lady Viviane. You also mentioned one name over and over again. That of Merlin the Enchanter. You kept calling out, 'my father, my father'. I then realized you were Ambrosius Myrddhin, son of Viviane and Merlin, and..." she hesitated as her tender black eyes searched the young man's face. "And grandson to Reena, mother of Merlin."

Amber stopped eating, his wooden spoon held in mid-air. "You are my grandmother?" he said softly, tasting the words as he spoke.

"Yes, I am your grandmother. Now finish eating and I shall tell you the story of all that is." she settled back in her chair and stared into the fire as she talked. "I was the daughter of the King of South Wales. My father took the side of Vortigern when the latter caused the death of his sovereign King Moines and drove the two brothers of the late king into banishment. The names of these two brothers were Uther and Pendragon. A few years after the exile, I was riding in the hills near my father's lands when I came across a young man who had been injured in a fight with some robbers. He was left for dead yet as I bent over I could see that life was still in him and with my help he managed to mount my horse. Taking him to a cave in the hills, I tended his wounds and fell very much in love with him. He then told me he was Uther and I feared for his life. When he was well enough to leave he wanted to take me with him, but my fear and love of my father caused me to refuse." she stopped speaking to wipe the tears that were running down her face, and then continued.

"He stayed with me for a while loving me, not wanting to leave. Finally his love for his home and the desire to win back his fathers crown compelled him to return to his lands." A sigh escaped her lips as she tried to stop the tears caused by the memory of a love lost.

"After Uther left I found I was carrying his child in my belly." her voice was stronger now as she regained her composure. "I knew I could not reveal who the true father was as my brothers would have sought him out to kill him. So the story I gave to my father was that the Incubus, one of a class of beings not absolutely wicked but far from good, had come to me in the night leaving me heavy with child. When the many beatings would not change my story, my father chose to believe me rather than have me lose his grandchild. When the child was born I baptized him myself calling him Myrddhin Ambrosius for Uther was sometimes called Ambrosius. The name Merlin is what I told my father and his court the child had been named. The only other person to know his given name was Viviane." Reena took the empty bowl from the young man. He watched as the old woman washed it in a bucket of water that sat near the hearth. All he had learned since leaving the castle of gold was buzzing around in his head.

"I cannot believe it." he marveled, "First I find that Merlin is my father. That in itself was a shock to my brain. Now you tell me that Uther was my grandfather." he paused to gaze into the fire across from his bed. "Why that makes King Arthur my uncle and half brother to Merlin. Viviane was wrong. I was born of noble blood. Does Arthur know of his kinship to Merlin?" he asked.

"I told no one except my son when he returned to me a grown man, and now you." Checking his shoulder she added, "I think you had better rest now. In a few days I will be able to remove the bandages."

Amber did not argue with the old woman, she was right for he was very tired. Soon he was asleep with the dreams of his parentage in his head.

In the morning he felt stronger and his grandmother said a sit in the sun would do him a world of good. Going down the path he used his good arm to brace himself against the mountain. Reena helped him on the other side, carefully so she would not break open his healing wound. Once down the path joy came to his heart as he saw a horse tethered to a tree.

"Pegasus!" Amber cried, "You have kept her for me." he ran his hand down her sleek black neck.

"Of course." Reena answered, "A good knight must have his horse. Come now, sit and let the warmth of the sun do its work."

Amber left his horse's side and went to sit at the old woman's feet. "What shall I do now grandmother?" he asked, "If I return to the court of Arthur and reveal my true name, Allon will surely want to kill me."

Reena sat with knitted brow seeking an answer from within. Finally she spoke, "As I see it, Allon is looking for a brother. He was not told that this brother was a twin and I am sure the document that tells this is now destroyed. So there is no reason not to show yourself at the court of Arthur as Ambrosius Myrddhin, 'son of no birth'. You have had all the training of a squire therefore should find it easy to gain your knighthood even if you seem to be of no noble birth."

"But grandmother, I left the chapel before sunrise. How can I become a knight now?" Amber asked sadly.

"I am not wise in the ways of the court but I am sure there is some way for you to be knighted. Lord Dhin will help you find a way." she answered.

"Dhin!" Amber exclaimed, "I had almost forgotten about my friend. He will think I am dead."

"He knows you are safe for he has been watching you in the fire at the golden castle." said Reena, "As I have always watched him in my fires."

The young man saw a warm loving look in the old woman's eyes. "You have watched Dhin?" He looked confused as he tried to sort out her words in his mind. Then he realized something his heart must have known all along. "Dhin," he spoke the name again with love and respect. "is Merlin, my father."

"Yes Ambrosius, Dhin is my son Merlin. After the Lady Viviane's treachery, he thought it best if he never used the name Merlin again. He could not use his given name either for that would reveal his royalty. So he chose the last four letters of Myrddhin, thus the name Dhin. The night you were at your worst and sure to die, I felt a cold breeze and knew his spirit was there in the cave. When it left, the color came back to your face and I knew you would live."

She looked at her grandson and, smoothing the hair away from his forehead, continued. "In a day or two you will be strong enough to travel. Then you must go back to your father. Stay with him always Ambrosius, as his love for you is the greatest you shall ever know."

"And you grandmother, what shall you do when I have gone?" he asked.

"I will keep on doing what I have done all these years, take care of my animal friends and watch my son and grandson in the flames of the fire." But Amber noticed a tear in the old woman's eyes and the sad tone in her voice. In his heart he knew she was trying to spare him the grief of parting.

The next few days Amber helped his grandmother gather herbs and roots in the forest around her mountain. When it came time for him to return to the golden castle, he was dressed once again in the red tunic and cloak. Reena had mended his clothing so it appeared as if they were newly made.

The young warrior kissed the old woman as he said with sadness, "Will I ever see you again?"

"Yes Ambrosius, you shall see me again. Whenever you are in need of me, I will be there. All you need do is keep me always in your heart." Reena embraced her grandson then hurried up the path to the cave where she stood watching until he was out of sight.

Amber rode through the forest in the direction that Reena had told him to go. It was not long before he came to the path leading down the mountainside, behind the golden castle. As he rode nearer he could make out the form of a man sitting on the outside wall.

As the rider approached the man on the wall, who was Dhin, got to his feet. "Jasper come quickly, my prayers have been answered. My son has come back to me." He was at the young man's side before this Red Warrior had a chance to dismount. Jasper held Pegasus as Amber scrambled down out of the saddle.

"Father!" he said embracing Dhin, "It has been a long time. I am happy to find you in the best of health."

"And I am so very pleased to say the same to you." the old man answered.

The three men walked off towards the castle as a stable boy took Pegasus. There was food waiting for Amber in the main hall. Their host stayed just long enough to welcome him back then left with the story of work to do. After Amber had his fill of the bread, cheese and mutton, Jasper filled the golden goblets with red wine and then settled in the chair next to Dhin listening as the young man told of all that had happened.

When he finished Dhin sat thoughtfully before he spoke. His voice showed great emotion as he then said, "Reena is a very fine woman. She has always been in my heart." He sat quietly as he sipped his wine. When he spoke again he had his feelings in control. "Well Ambrosius, now that you know the truth there is no reason why we cannot speak of the past without playing any games."

"Then it is all true? What was written in Lady Viviane's book and what Reena told me?" Amber asked.

"Yes, it is all true," Dhin answered, "Reena is my wonderful mother and I am Merlin. I had been very busy at the court of Arthur when I told the king it was time for me to get away for a while. As I was touring the country I met Viviane. She thought the potion upon her lips caused me to fall in love with her, but in truth, I needed no potion for she was a very beautiful woman and I found it easy to love her. It was not long before this love caused me to trust her and reveal my most secret magic to her."

"This is why in my youth you told me to be careful of any woman I might fall in love with." said Amber remembering Dhin's words of so long ago.

"Yes, I did not want you to make the same mistake your foolish father did," Dhin smiled, then continued, "Anyway she used this knowledge against me and one day I woke to find she had enclosed me in the strongest tower in the land. Peering out the window I saw that it stood outside the walls of a large manor house. My books and clothes were in the room she kept me in, but all the magic in my head could not free me.

"Then Viviane came in and said I was to stay her prisoner for reasons she would not disclose. When her use for me was over, she would snuff out my life as one does the light of a candle. She had forgotten my gift of the sight and after she left I searched the flames in the hearth to find the truth. There in the fire it was revealed to me the lady's reason for my imprisonment.

"I turned to my books and it was not long before I found the answer, not only to freeing myself, but also how to bring down my revenge upon the wicked lady. I learned the secret of transporting my soul from one place to another while my body lay in sleeping form. In this way I visited the lady in her bedchamber and planted the seed of my child in her body. Once my retaliation was completed I used the incantation I had found and freed my self from the evil lady's spell.

"I left the tower and took refuge in the temple of Dusk, living there until my son could find his way to my retreat. I could not go to him for fear that no matter how I disguised myself, Viviane would know and somehow end my life."

"Grandmother said Uther was your father. That would make you first born and successor to the throne at the time of his death. How is it you did not bring this fact to court and claim that right?" Amber asked.

"When Reena told me of my father, she asked that I tell no one. I was compelled to keep that promise as the gods spoke to me and said that my help was needed in bringing about the birth of a great king," the old man explained. "It was I who helped Uther by changing his appearance into the likeness of Gorlois Duke of Tintadiel. In this manner he was able to enter the bedchamber of the duke's wife, thus Arthur was conceived. After the Duke's death Uther married the Dutches. I think you know the rest of the story." Dhin settled back in his chair sipping his wine.

"Yes, but I am still confused as to why you helped. Did you not know this child of Uther's would steal your rightful inheritance?" Amber looked at his father baffled by his words.

"Ambrosius!" the old man said sternly, "As you will find out, a man such as I, born with the sight, has only one road in life to take. I have lived my life by following the gods and doing as they ask. It was not in the stars for me to be king as it was the gods who told me of the coming king. I did as they asked for Arthur was that king." he paused looking at the young man. When he continued his voice was composed once again. "You see my son one does not go against the direct orders of the gods for fear of their wrath." They sat quietly for a moment both being deep in thought.

Then Dhin's voice broke the silence. "I have been happy in my roll as King's wizard." he said, "And upon his death bed Uther gladdened my heart by acknowledging me as his own. We were alone and as he closed his eyes for the last time he said my name and called me son. It was the happiest moment of my life." There was the slight glint of tears in his eyes as he continued. "I made the promise that if ever I should have a son, I would bring him to the foot of the hanging stones for his grandfather to see."

They sat drinking their wine and gazing into the fire. After a while Amber spoke, "What shall we do now father?" he asked, "Grandmother said you would know a way for me to become a knight. Is this so?"

"Yes, there is one way," answered Dhin, "You must return to the court of Arthur. You will go as the Red Warrior, wearing the red cloak over your armor. Your shield will be the red dragon on the black background."

"Will this not cause talk at court, as the red dragon is also the king's shield?" the young man inquired.

"If you are asked it will be told that you fight in the king's name. You will challenge the strongest young knight. Winning this, you will redeem yourself in the eyes of the court and the king will have no choice but to knight you." his father answered.

"That would be Allon!" Amber said in horror.

"Yes, Allon," Dhin replied, "and you will have to beat him in the games."

"But he is my brother." stated the young warrior, "What if I should kill him by mistake?"

"You will not, but if it happens, well you know he would not hesitate to kill you." Dhin spoke with no emotion looking soberly at his son.

Amber stood up shocked at his father's words. "Father, I have never seen you so cold. He is your son also. I thought you had a kinder heart than Lady Viviane. How can you hate one son, yet love the other?"

Dhin sat quietly staring into the hearth. It was Jasper's voice that broke the silence, "You must tell him my lord." he said.

"Yes, I must." the 'Old one' answered as Amber looked on puzzled.

"Tell me what?" The young man was more confused now than he had ever been.

"That......" Dhin faltered, "That Prince Allon is not my son."

His words echoed around the room and hit Amber like the blow of a club. He sat back down spilling the wine he had been holding.

"How can that be? You say Allon and I are twins, that you are my father. How can you say now that Allon is not your son?" The young man's head began to hurt as the pounding noise entered his brain. Suddenly the fire in the hearth seemed to leap higher and brighter.

"Look, watch the flames." the voice in Amber's head spoke as smoke encircled him, closing out the presence of the other two men.

Dhin settled in his chair, "It will be a while before my son comes back to us. We must wait and see what the fire is telling him," he said to Jasper. The servant nodded his head yes and waited with the old man.

CHAPTER 11

Sounds of a voice trickled through the fog and echoed in Amber's brain. "Here, Master Ambrosius, drink this." it said. He opened his eyes to see Jasper holding a goblet of wine. He drank the warm liquid, then settled back trying to clear his head. Jasper woke Dhin telling him of his son's return to this world. The old man drew his chair closer to Amber.

"What did the fire tell you?" he asked, his voice almost a whisper.

"I am not sure I know what it meant." answered his son as he shook his head still trying to free it from the clouds of vision. "I saw Lady Viviane laying on her bed. A shapeless form hovered over her, then seemed to lower into her body. When it left, I could see the seed of a child had been planted in her belly. Then smoke filled the scene. When it cleared Lady Viviane was again upon her bed. This time it was her husband, King Lot, who was laying in her embrace. When he left her I could see that a second seed was left in her." he paused to drink more of the wine Jasper was offering him, "What did it all mean father?" he questioned.

"It means that as I was in spirit form when I planted the seed of your life, it was possible for Lady Viviane to receive the seed from a mortal man also." explained the old man. "Therefore, in truth, King Lot is Allon's father."

"How do you know that it is not the other way around." Amber asked, "I could be King Lot's son while you are the father of Allon." The pain that this might be true etched the young man's face.

"You are the one who has the sight, you are a child of magic!" stated Dhin adamantly. "Viviane saw that of the two babies you were more like me and so gave you my name. Allon never went to the tower for the gods kept him from it, because he was the child of a mortal man."

Amber nodded in agreement remembering that every time the two boys had planned an adventure in the tower, something always happened to keep Allon from completing the experience.

Dhin stood up and held his hand out to his son, "Come now, it is time we got some sleep." he said, "We will leave tomorrow for the court of Arthur."

In the morning they again thanked their host and said good-bye to his six beautiful daughters. Amber was still trying to sort the pieces of what he had learned and remained quiet during their ride. Dhin chose to let him be, knowing he needed time to think about all this new found information.

It wasn't long before they were once more looking down into the valley at the town by the river. Below the fortress the flat land was now set up for the tournaments. Bright colored banners flew from high wooden poles that marked off a rectangular fighting field. At the head of this area sat two wood thrones with benches around them where the king would sit with his court. Seats were also set along one long end of the field for spectators. On the other side, directly across from this, small tents were set up for the comfort of the knights who were in the games. Beside one of the tents flew a banner with a white cross on a green background. A gold half moon was positioned in the center of the cross. Amber knew this to be the coat of arms of Allon, showing him as the second son to King Lot.

"I see Allon has chosen to remain at court rather than to go crusading with his father." said Dhin as he watched Amber's face. "It is the will of the gods."

His son showed no emotion at the mention of his half brother's name. He sat on his horse watching a red and black tent being set up away from the others. Jasper had gone on ahead to get every thing ready for their arrival.

"We will wait here under the protection of the trees until dark." Dhin said, getting down from his horse. "It will be better if no one sees you until you are ready to challenge the king's knight."

Amber followed his father and tied Pegasus to a nearby tree. Sitting down on the ground they watched the games as mounted knights moved back and forth across the field, their lances held out in front of them for the joust. Once one was knocked off his horse the fighting continued with swords until one knight would yield. Bits of golden flecks danced in the sun as its rays bounced off the jeweled hilts of the weapons. Amber sat almost hypnotized by the flashing steel. His father's voice brought him back to reality.

"After you have beaten the king's knight you will go before Arthur." he was saying, "Kneeling down in front of him you will declare yourself by your given name, explaining to the court why you left the chapel." As Dhin talked, Amber marveled at his father's optimism. "When you have finished, the king will have no choice but to knight you." exclaimed the old man excitedly.

"You have no doubt at all that I shall win?" Amber asked.

"You cannot lose." his father answered, "It is in the stars. Just do not get over eager if you find you are getting the best of your foe." there was a bit of mockery in his voice.

"Like with Garth?" the young man smiled.

"Yes, like with Garth." the old man then settled down to watch the games along with his son.

As the moon rose above the forest two men on horse back slowly made their way down the hill from the woods. As they dismounted and tied their mounts behind the red and black tent, Amber looked around the area. The only people he saw were a few squires cleaning their lord's armor from the dust of the day's games. The winning knights were at the castle celebrating their victory. The losers nursed their wounds in their tents where could be heard the groans of men in pain.

Dhin and Amber entered their tent to see Jasper grinning up at them. he was kneeling on the ground with a pile of shining armor in front of him. A small fire was set away from the canvas sides in the middle of the tent. It not only kept the dampness out of the air but also provided the light by which the servant was cleaning the equipment.

"You have done a good job." Dhin said to Jasper as he inspected the pieces of metal. "They look newly bought. How do you like your fighting attire?" he said turning to Amber, "It belonged to your grandfather, the one thing I managed to keep for myself."

"It will be an honor to wear Uther's armor when I compete in tomorrow's games." the young man answered with pride.

"Just keep in mind there is no longer a gold ring crown to protect you." his father reminded him, "It will take wisdom and skill to win. The gods have said you will be the victor but you must not let them do all the work." Dhin then helped Jasper put the armor to one side of the tent, giving them room to bed down.

The night seemed long to the young warrior who turned restlessly on his fur pallet. He was not able to fall asleep as quickly as his father and Jasper for his head was filled with too many thoughts. Then as a white mist seemed to settle on the anxious young man, he closed his eyes and was soon drifting among the clouds of sleep.

The sun was shining bright the next morning when the bugles blared to start the day's competition. As was the custom the older knights would joust first. Amber stayed in the tent watching from behind its flap as the magnificent collage of armor rode by. The bravest of these knights would challenge all others. The young man recognized some of them from his days as a squire. Sir Kay, foster brother to the king; Sir Launcelot, the queen's champion; Sir Bedver and Sir Hector de Marys. Amber could not help but get excited over this display of the best fighting men in the land. As the games began the hills echoed with the sound of clashing steel and the moans of the defeated.

Soon it was time to stop for the noon meal. Behind the field servants had set up tables with enough food to feed the whole of Britain. Fresh roasted boars with large red apples sticking out of their mouths. Huge platters of venison and mutton with all kinds of cheese set out around the meat. And the bread, newly baked, was as long as the table itself. Wine and ale flowed like water from the nearby river. The delicious smell made Amber's mouth water and when Jasper appeared in the entrance of his tent carrying a large platter of food, the young man rushed forward with open arms.

"Master Ambrosius," the servant laughed taking the goatskin of wine from his shoulder. "It looks like you have never eaten a meal in your life."

"You must be careful not to over stuff yourself." cautioned Dhin who had come in behind the servant. "The games of the young knights will be held after the meal. You cannot afford to be weighed down, the armor will be heavy enough."

"I will only eat until the growling in my stomach is satisfied." said Amber as he took a sip of wine. "There will be plenty of time to celebrate after I have won my match." Dhin smiled, pleased with his son's confidence.

After the meal Dhin and Jasper went out to watch the young knights telling Amber they would return when it was time to get him ready. As the young man waited he fell into a light sleep from the food and wine.

"Come Ambrosius, it is time to prepare yourself." Dhin was saying as he bent over the sleeping man.

Jasper helped him into his armor, while Dhin instructed him on what was to follow. The old man then left to mingle in the crowd and watch. When Jasper finished he wrapped the red cloak with the dragon emblem around Amber's shoulders, handed the young man his helmet, and then led the Red Warrior to the side of the field. The servant helped him onto a waiting Pegasus then stood holding the horse's bridle.

Amber sat not really aware of what was going on around him. His head was starting to pound in the same wild beat of his heart. Suddenly he heard a familiar voice coming out of the air.

"Do not worry my boy." it whispered, "As I promised you so long ago, I am with you. Just be brave and remember all you have learned."

Amber now felt his heart slow down to a normal beat and the pain in his head vanished. He sat up tall in his saddle as a keen awakening shot through his youthful body.

Then he heard the bugle blast and saw a young knight sitting on a white charger. The herald standing next to him was saying, "Hear ye, and hear ye, men of Britain. If there be so bold a knight amongst you who will challenge our strongest knight, let him come forward now."

Jasper wished the young man luck as Amber went forward to meet his destiny. The crowd of onlookers let out a murmur of surprise as the dashing young knight rode onto the field, his black horse with the white star moving almost silently towards their king. Their amazement grew as they noticed by the lack of a plumage in his helmet, that he was not a knight after all.

"Your majesty, even though your court may feel I am not worthy of the honor, it would give me great pleasure to challenge the king's knight." Amber gave a bow from his saddle.

The king, looking at the sight before him, sensed something familiar about this knight who was not a knight. "So be it." he finally answered. Then as the young man rode away, he turned to Queen Guenevere and said, "Why do I get the feeling I have met that young challenger before?" His queen gave no answer as the sound on the field told them the contest was about to begin.

Amber had ridden back to Jasper who handed him a lance. He then turned towards his opponent and waited for the signal. It came in a shout from the king, "Let this contest begin!" The young warrior had no need to spur Pegasus, for at the sound of the king's command, she lifted her head and sprinted across the field.

There was little time to even think; before he knew it Amber felt the thud of his lance as it hit the charging knight's shield. Veering to one side he managed to evade the on coming pointed implement as the white horse accelerated past him. Pulling on the reins, Amber turned Pegasus to face his oncoming foe once again. This time his piercing lance hit the other knight on the chest, causing him to topple to the ground. Faster than the blink of an eye, Amber was off his horse with drawn sword, rushing towards the fallen man. The challenged knight was not to be caught off guard and was on his feet with sword in hand when his opponent reached him. Soon the clash of steel resounded over the field as the two young men slashed back and forth trying to unarm the other.

From where Dhin was sitting he could see his son still full of fire and energy, while the other knight appeared to be tiring. Then almost faster than the eye could see, the king's knight stumbled. Amber took full advantage of this windfall and kicked the sword out of the man's hand.

"Do you yield?" he asked, holding his pointed sword to the throat of the defeated man.

"Yes, I yield to a better knight than I." he said pulling off his helmet to reveal Prince Allon. "Now sir, will you give me the honor to see who it is that has beaten me?" the young man asked as he rose from the ground.

Amber obliged by removing his helmet and as the winning knight turned to face the king and his court, a baffled prince looked on.

"Your gracious majesty." he said bowing low. "I am Ambrosius Myrddhin, bastard son of Lord Dhin, know to many as the '*son of no birth*'. I have also been known as Dylon, squire in the court of Arthur." he paused as the sound of a falling helmet came from behind him.

"You are the friend of my youthful days?" Allon spoke in a whisper.

Amber continued without either answering or turning to his friend. "The reason I did not remain in the king's presence to take the vows of knighthood is because of the rumors of my birth. I knew I would have to prove myself worthy of being a knight. That is why I have come now and challenged your strongest knight. My future is in your hands, mighty ruler." the young man honored his king by kneeling down before him.

Arthur sat quietly for a moment while the court around him whispered to each other. When he spoke his voice filled the field with words of wisdom.

"Ambrosius, you have indeed proven yourself strong, but to be accepted into this court and receive the title of 'Sir', you must show that you are also brave and wise." Not a word was spoken as all awaited the king's decree. "It has come to my knowledge that in a cave on a mountain called Saint Michael's Mount, there lives a giant who for some time has been carrying off the people from a near by village. They have sent up a cry, pleading for me to free them from this disaster. To prove that you are worthy, you will ride on a pilgrimage to this mountain and slay the giant. When you have done this, come back to my court with his head upon your lance and I will not hesitate to bestow upon you the title of 'Sir Ambrosius Myrddhin', the king's own knight." This mighty ruler of Briton then motioned the young man to leave.

Amber rose to his feet, bowed low and with his head held high, left the field. Dhin was waiting for him at Jasper's side and while the servant led Pegasus, the old man walked with his arm around his son.

"I am so very proud of you." said Dhin as they entered their tent.

"You will do as the king wishes and in no time at all, receive your title. Being the king's own knight is the greatest honor a man can acquire." He embraced his son then helped Jasper remove the young man's armor.

"I must find Allon." Amber told his father as Jasper moved about the tent preparing for their departure. "There are things that must be said."

"Use caution." Dhin recommended.

"Do not worry." the young man responded. "I was taught by a master." He smiled at his father and teacher then turning to leave, came face to face with Allon who had just arrived at the tent's entrance.

"Amber!" said the prince seizing his friend's arm. "I find it hard to believe it is really you. My mother sent word that you had been killed when lightning hit Merlin's tower. How is it you are alive?" he asked.

"I was not in the tower at the time it crumbled." Amber answered, "After you left with Uldin to meet the royal visitor, I walked to the village. There I met a traveler telling the story of an old man who was the keeper of the temple of Dusk. He said this man knew who the parents of the 'child of no birth' were. Not knowing I was that child, he led me to the temple, which was hidden away in a mountain retreat.

"There the keeper told me of my father on the Isle of Mona, Lord Dhin, as he was called. He had taken up with one of the village wenches and left her not knowing I had been conceived. She left the village full of shame at her condition and found refuge in the temple of Dusk. When she was ready to give birth, she ran away again from fear. The keeper, following her, found the woman at the base of Merlin's tower. There beside her dead form was the child she had just given birth to. Not knowing what else to do he placed me in the tower then took the young lass back to the mountains to be buried."

Amber paused to give his childhood friend a goblet of wine. As he pored the drink, he caught the smile on his father's lips and the look of approval in the old man's eyes.

Turning back to an astonished Allon, he continued. "After finding out who my father was, I started my quest to the Isle of Mona. Once I met Lord Dhin and revealed my identity, he accepted me with open arms."

The prince sat absorbing all his friend had said, "But why did you come to court as 'Dylon'?" he asked, "What was the purpose of this deception?"

"My father had found that Votan used trickery with your mother. His real reason for being in Larkwood was my blood. I had to travel as Dylon until I was sure Ambrosius was safe." Amber saw that Jasper had finished packing. "It is time for us to leave." he said as he walked the prince out of the tent.

"I am sorry we do not have more time for conversation, but I want you to know that I wish you a speedy and safe return." Allon said as he embraced his friend. Amber thought he caught the gleam of a tear on his half brothers cheek.

"I wonder if I will ever be able to tell him the truth?" the young man asked himself as he stood in the tent entrance and watched Allon. As the prince walked past the scattered tents he stopped for a word with his servant then disappeared from view. "At least I go with a happy heart knowing that my friend and half brother does not wish me dead." He then went to join his father and servant who were now ready to leave.

Amber had no idea that at this very moment the thoughts in Allon's head were not very pleasant. As he reached the castle's wall, Allon stopped and watched the three men mount their steeds and ride slowly towards the mountains in the far distance.

"So Ambrosius Myrddhin, offspring of a wench. You have come out of my past like a ghost to haunt me." Allon whispered, "You will be sorry you have shamed the king's knight by toppling me in the games. If you return, I will show you what happens to a serf when he belittles a noble born prince. You will not take my title away so easily." he sneered through his teeth as the men became one with the landscape and were soon out of sight.

CHAPTER 12

The clearing at the foot of Saint Michael's Mount was scattered with wood houses spread out along the flat land. The inn that sat by the little used road looked as if it had been pounded with a great mallet. The mountain itself loomed high above, casting a foreboding shadow over the land. From the inn Amber stared at the sinister cloud that clung to the top of the mount.

"I am Ambrosius Myrddhin called the Red Warrior." he said to the innkeeper, "Bring food and drink for three weary travelers." After the man had set bread and cheese on the table with mugs of ale, Amber said to him, "I have come in the king's name to free your village from the giant of the mount."

"The lord be praised!" said the innkeeper, "Our great king has heard the cry of his poor people." He bowed to Amber and continued, "But you must hurry for not more than a few hours ago the giant came and took the good Duchess of Brittany as she rode with her attendants. We fought to retain her but his strength was greater than ours and he carried her away to his fortress. He left many of us dead or wounded. I was one of the lucky ones." With this he raised the sleeve of his crudely made shirt to reveal a bloody wound that had been left to dry without salve or bandage.

Dhin motioned to Jasper to bring his pouch with the special medicine and while his son continued questioning the man, he tended the ugly wound.

"I will do all in my power to free the Duchess but first you must tell me where I can find the abode of this giant." said Amber.

"If you follow the road out front, you will come to a path leading into the mountain. Keep to this until you see two great fires. There you will find your quest along with more treasure than I think is in the whole of Britain. All travelers passing the foot of the mountain have fallen into the evil hands of this monster who, after disposing of his captives, has hoarded their valuables." the innkeeper shook his head sadly.

The three men finished their meal then sat before the great hearth planning their venture. They would go into the mountains at nightfall as it would be easier to conceal themselves in the dark. At dusk the three men left the inn. As they came to the foot of the mountain, Amber told his father and Jasper to wait for he would go up the hill alone. He left Pegasus in their care and walked the path until he saw the light of a large fire. Cautiously he peered out from behind the trees that concealed his presence. The scene before him was not a pretty sight. There sat a woman by a newly made grave, crying and praying while her body rocked to and fro. Coming out of the darkness he approached the woman.

"Madam," Amber interrupted her, "I have come from the king of all Britain to talk of the law's of Arthur with this tyrant."

"There is no way you can talk with such as him," she replied, "for he believes in no king's law. Only in the laws of his own strength."

"If talk will not stop his useless killings then I shall have to halt him in another way." Amber left the woman to her sobbing and went to the crest of the hill. There he saw the giant, sitting before another great fire, gnawing on the limb of a man. Three fair maidens were lying bound by heavy ropes on the ground, set aside to be devoured in their turn. When the young warrior saw this, his heart bled as great compassion filled him.

"By the gods who have given you life, your shameful death is closer than you know." Amber said with anger, "You have murdered innocent attendants of the Duchess, therefore you shall die by the hand of the Red Warrior."

The giant was not one to wait for the first blow to be hurled at him. In an instant he was up on his feet swinging a large club over his head. With a mighty thrust he caught the young man, grazing his shoulder and knocked him to the ground. Scrambling quickly to his feet Amber plunged his sword toward the hulk towering over him. The sound of steel cutting through skin and bone as his weapon entered the giant's belly, sent a shiver of nausea to the young man's stomach. When he withdrew the blade, red blood poured profusely from the deep wound, infuriating the giant all the more. He threw away his club and caught Amber in his arms, squeezing him with the strength of a great snake.

The battle that followed caused the earth to rumble and the trees to quiver for as the young man squirmed and wrenched both he and his adversary fell to the ground. Wallowing about still caught in the giant's grasp, Amber managed to pull his dagger from his belt. Slashing at the enormous body that held him, the warrior tried to free himself. His mighty foe only tightened those large arms as they rolled down the hill like a massive landslide.

As the fates would have it, the two fighting men landed at the feet of Dhin and Jasper. Seeing Amber covered in blood, held tightly to the giant's breast, the servant came to his young master's aid by plunging his sword deep into the gigantic man's back. In death the giant retained his incredible strength so that it took both of Amber's companions, tugging and pulling, to free him from the grips of the dead man. When he was finally on his feet again, the young man took his bloody sword and with one swing, cut off the giant's head.

Whirling around on his heels, Amber ran back up the hill towards the great fires. "Jasper!" he yelled over his shoulder, "I will need your help."

The servant ran after the young man with sword drawn, expecting more trouble. As he came into the clearing, he saw Amber bent over three maidens, cutting the ropes that held them captive. "There is a coach over by the other fire." Amber told Jasper. "We can use it to take them back to the village. The woman sitting at the grave of her attendant is the Duchess and will have to be persuaded to come also. I will leave her to you as I have another matter to tend to." With this he left the clearing.

Jasper's struggle with the Duchess finally ended when he picked her up and carried her to the coach. The servant had just finished setting down the woman when Amber reappeared leading five horses with four large sacks tied securely on each back. "The fortune of Saint Michael's Mount." he said smiling at his friend's bewilderment.

Dhin stood at the foot of the mountain scratching his white head in astonishment as he watched the strange procession coming down the path. When Amber reached his father's side he explained the situation then climbed up on Pegasus's back. With the Red Warrior in the lead and holding the head of the giant high in the air, this indescribable parade moved slowly down the road to the inn. The villagers, who had been watching from a safe distance, now came out and danced along behind singing praises to the hero who had freed them.

When they reached the inn Amber ordered the sacks of treasure to be brought into the building. Once inside the people pushed through the door to get a look at more wealth then they had ever dreamed could exist. When all the sacks were emptied out onto the tables, their contents were separated. Not a word was spoken as the onlookers stood in the glare of the gold and silver.

Amber took one of the sacks and filled it to the top with some of the golden coins. "This is enough payment for me." he said, "The rest of this great treasure I leave to be divided among all the population of this settlement. Your innkeeper is a fair man, so I give him the task of seeing that my wishes are carried out." He turned and climbed the stairs to the bedchambers on the second floor, with Dhin and Jasper following behind.

"I think we better look after your wounds now my son." said Dhin when they reached their room. "We have waited too long already."

The young man did not argue with his father for he was beginning to feel weak from the loss of blood. Jasper cleaned the gash on his young master's shoulder where the giant's club had hit him. When Dhin was done putting salve on the injury, he placed a clean cloth over the area.

"Well it is nothing that will not heal in a day or two. Come now, sit by the fire and drink some of this wine." He led his son to the chair in front of the hearth.

The yellow red glow of the fire seemed to draw the tired young man's attention. As he stared into the flames, he knew that a vision was about to come to him. He waited patiently as the smoke closed in around him. When it cleared he saw the face of his half brother, Allon.

The prince was talking to a man Amber recognized to be Maugantius, minister to King Arthur, who had once been King Vortigern's wizard. After Pendragon took back the throne, he had remained in court and by clever schemes, managed to acquire his post. Now, as Amber watched the minister and Allon, he knew they were plotting against someone.

"There must by someway we can cause his downfall." The prince's voice came like a hollow sound in his half brother's head, "You, above all, should be able to come up with a plan."

"What makes you think I will help you in this awful intrigue of yours?" asked Maugantius, but his voice only strengthened Amber's belief in his evilness.

Allon, too, was aware of the minister's reputation, for he said, "You may be able to fool the king and his court, but I know you for the schemer you are. You have no choice but to help me for I fear the king would not be happy to know that the man who was once Vortigern's wizard had almost caused the death of Merlin, Arthur's friend."

Maugantius smiled, "Your wish is my command, oh mighty Prince." he said, giving Allon a mocking bow.

"Now that we understand each other, let us make our plans before he returns to court. Messengers from Saint Michael's Mount have brought the news to the king of his victory. They say the giant's head is being kept by the people of the village as a reminder of their great hero. When he arrives he must not become aware of our intentions. If there could be…oh maybe an accident…or something." As he spoke, Allon led the minister down the hall of the castle and the smoke once again closed in around the Red Warrior.

"Some more wine my son?" Amber looked up to see Dhin standing over him with a goblet. "It was something unpleasant. Was it not?"

The young man took the liquid and after sipping some answered, "Yes. Very unpleasant." he said, "It seems my half brother would like to be rid of me. Whether it is because he has discovered our relationship or because I am about to take his title, I do not know." He sat for a moment, staring into the fire. When no answer came from the flames, he spoke again, his voice cold and solemn. "I am not to know his reason. So be it, but I will not be caught unaware."

It was near dawn when the innkeeper and all the people of the village gathered to see their benefactor on his way. The singing and celebrating that had started the night before, continued as the three men rode off into the rising sun. At the crest of the hill Amber turned to look back at the Mount. The sinister cloud that had been there on their arrival was gone and the trees seemed to dance to the voices of the singing peasants.

As the music faded in the distance, Amber turned to Dhin. "I have always wanted to see Wales. Is there any place we could go and be accepted?" he asked.

"You will remember that my grandfather was King of South Wales. His lands that lie on the outskirts of Meridunum, were confiscated when Vortigern was killed. Then when Uther lie dying he declared that they be returned to my mother. The estate with its large manor house was left deserted as she chose to stay in her mountain cave." Dhin's eyes grew cloudy as memories of his past life crept into his thoughts.

"Then that is where we shall go. With this money we can restore the house and lands." said Amber as he patted the money belt Dhin had carefully made to hide their gold. Each of them had one tied tightly like a belt under his tunic. The rest of the gold coins were safely tucked inside their packed clothes. "We will travel to the mountain by the golden castle," Amber continued, "and persuade a gracious lady to come with us."

Dhin smiled at his son; proud that the young man should give such concern to a grandmother he had not known long.

Reaching the golden castle they were greeted with great respect for the news of Amber's encounter with the giant of the Mount had reached the fair-haired man. As it was near dark when they arrived, Dhin thought it best if they waited until the next morning before riding up the mountain to the cave of his mother. The six beautiful daughters brought a fine meal of cheese, mutton and mugs of wine into the great hall where the weary travelers talked with their father. After eating, the men retired to the large room they had shared once before. As the sun rose they again thanked their host and departed up the path behind the castle. By mid-day they reached the forest at the foot of the mountain where Reena lived.

As they dismounted and tied their horses a strange sensation came over Amber. Not waiting for the other two men he ran stumbling, up the path to the cave entrance. Inside was dimly lit as the fire in the hearth was nearly out. Quickly he threw some wood from the pile on the floor into the dying embers. In a flash the interior of the cave became bright, revealing Reena lying white and still upon her bed. The sound of death was rattling in her throat.

"Grandmother!" the young man cried as he raised the frail old body in his arms.

"Ambrosius, is it really you?" her voice was barely a whisper. "Or is it just an old woman's heart playing a cruel trick on her dying body?"

From behind him, Amber heard the rustling of his father's cloak as the old man hurried into the cave. He stood, frozen to the ground, as he saw his son with the dying woman in his arms. Tears of grief stained the grandson's face as he held the small body close to his chest.

"Mother!" Dhin spoke the word with great sorrow in his heart. He knelt next to Amber so the woman could look easily upon the face of her son.

"It is not a trick." she said weakly, "My son and his son are really here. This old woman is not cursed to die alone, without her loved ones near." She reached out her bony white hand and touched her son's cheek, wiping away the tear that rested there. "Do not weep because my soul is finally going to rest." she said, "I will be with my love once again, in a land far better than this one. My only wish is that you take my lifeless shell and lie it to rest beside that of his."

"It will be done." said Dhin, trying not to let her see how deep his grief was.

Turning her eyes to her grandson, she smiled as she said, "You must not be sad either Ambrosius, for you have given a woman great happiness. I have had the pleasure of watching my grandson growing from youth to manhood. My eyes were always peering into the fire to follow all your years. The fates even allowed me to care for you when your need for care was great." The rattle in her throat grew louder as Black Death closed in around them.

The horses that carried the litter of the dead woman between them moved slowly across the barren plain leading to the hanging stones. The men that rode beside them were silent, each in his own thoughts of the great woman, gone now to join a love that had lived for many years in her heart.

At the circle of stones that was to be the final resting place of Reena, Dhin broke the silence by saying to his son, "When Uther was buried here I had surmised my mother's wishes upon her death. My father was put deep into his sleeping bed so that there would be room to lay the woman of his heart in the same spot. This way there would be no questions asked by the people of Britain as to why there was a new grave at the hanging stones."

As the days sun set in the western sky, the dim light fell on two men with heads bowed. They were standing at the foot of the largest stone, the dirt on the grave below it showed little signs of being newly dug. As the last glimmer of daylight faded, Dhin and Amber joined Jasper who was waiting with the horses in the hollow.

"On to Wales?" Amber asked as they rode slowly away from the stones.

"Yes." said Dhin as his hand touched the paper in the pocket of his tunic. It was the deed to the lands of his mother, given to him as she drew her last breath. "If our appearance must be explained, it will be said that after leaving her lands upon her father's death, Lady Reena married the Lord of the Isle of Mona. As the son of her marriage, I, Lord Dhin, am rightful master of Logan Manor."

They rode on in silence for a while until Amber spoke, choosing his words carefully. "Father, you know it is not from fear that I do not wish to return to the court of Arthur. It is the knowledge that an encounter with my half brother would result in his death. I am not ready to have this sort of thing on my conscious."

Dhin smiled at his son. "I knew it was not fear." he said, "We will turn our backs on Britain. Maybe Wales will be kinder to us."

"Wales, a new start." thought Amber. Then a puzzled look came over his face. "Father!" He said aloud, "What of your trusted servant Gorfan and the book I brought with me from the tower at Larkwood? So much has happened since we left the temple of Dusk that I completely forgot about them. Where are they now?"

"Waiting for us at the end of our journey." said Dhin. By the gleam in the old man's eyes, Amber knew that questioning him any further would do no good. So he filled his mind with thoughts of the adventures that lay ahead, wondering what perils the fates had waiting for them.

CHAPTER 13

Amber stood in awe anticipating their journey across the vast waters that appeared before them. The ship that was going to carry them to the coast of South Wales was sitting in the harbor at Hercules point. Its tall mast swaying to and fro as the large frame bounced lightly in the water's tide. Jasper left Amber and Dhin to board the ship with the horses. He led them up the great wooden planks, through the cargo entrance and disappeared into the belly of the frigate. He would stay below to keep them calm during the voyage. Father and son climbed the wooden planks that led to the upper level of the ship. As they stepped onto the deck, Amber took hold of the railing to keep from losing his footing on the water soaked boards. Already the sway of the ship was getting to his stomach. Dhin led the young man to the cabin they had been assigned.

"I see you have your father's taste for the sea." he said trying not to let his son see the smile on his face. He knew only too well that being seasick was not a laughing matter.

Amber never answered his father for the sickness was too great for him to suppress. The whole two days and nights at sea were spent with his head hanging off the side of his bed so any retching could be done into a bucket sitting on the floor. The third day's light found the ship anchored at the mouth of the Tywy river. Two long boats were waiting for the passengers to disembark while one flat boat, looking like a large raft, was waiting to receive the animals and cargo.

Dhin managed to shuffle his son out of his sick bed, onto the deck of the ship and over the side. Then, climbing down a rope ladder, they stepped into the waiting boat. Once on shore the old man propped his son against a tree and waited for the flat boat with Jasper and the horses.

"Father, could I have a sip of wine?" Amber spoke his first words since entering the ship at Hercules point. As Dhin held the goatskin of wine to his son's lips, a soft cool breeze blew in from the open sea. "Ah!" said Amber sucking in a long breath. "I never thought I would be so thankful to the winds for such refreshing air."

Now that the sickness had passed, Dhin could no longer hold in his amusement of the situation. When his son looked puzzled he said, "I do not laugh at you Ambrosius. I laugh at the young lad who, upon taking a similar voyage, was also kept to his sick bed." As he laughed, the young man joined in. Softly at first then, as his head cleared and the wine eased his hurting stomach, just as loudly as his father.

By the time Jasper had reached the two men with the horses and their belongings, Amber was ready to mount and ride to their new home not far away. As they followed the river inland he could see barges, loaded with cargo, on their way down to the waiting ship. Large sturdy ropes were attached to the two huge workhorses who trotted along on both sides of the river. These horses kept the barge from getting out of control as they drifted down to the open sea. On the way back to the town of Meridunum, the horses would be used to pull the barge through the water against the current. It was a quicker route than using horse and cart, and kept the cargo safe from would be robbers.

The road leading from the sea brought the three men into the bustling water front area. Men of the town were busy loading and unloading the barges of their freight. Then the road turned away from the water and curled its way towards the village, which was set on a hill high above the river. Across from the dock there were wood stairs that had been built into the dirt hill. They also led to the town and made the work easier for the men carrying cargo. In the middle of the busy village sat a large stone building, which was the inn.

Dhin led the way through the town towards the deserted estate of his grandfather. Villagers peered out their doors as the horses plodded their way down the road. Strangers were very rare in Meridunum and the town's people were curious to see who these might be. The young man's head pounded with excitement for he knew that they were entering a new and adventurous point in their lives.

As they rode, Amber looked over the countryside. South Wales was a beautiful place, with green rolling hills, flat meadows holding yellow flowers and cattle grazing lazily in the sun. Not far from the village a path broke away from the main road and followed an old stonewall. Here Dhin turned and rode the trail as it climbed further up the hill. On the other side of the wall stood stone buildings that were situated in such a fashion that Amber knew they must have been the military barracks of the old king's soldiers. Soon they came to an opening in the wall with a wider path that led to a large and magnificent looking structure.

"Welcome to Logan Manor." Dhin said as they dismounted in front of the house. "If I remember correctly there are some stables around back." he said to Jasper. "See if there is anything for the horses to eat while we evaluate the house and see what repairs are needed." Turning to Amber he said, "Come, my son, let us see what is left of this fine old house."

The two men walked carefully up the loose stone steps, through the large doors and into an entryway. This area also served as a waiting room and held some small chairs and stools. There were two doors set into the wall on the right, one in the center, and the other at the far end. Straight ahead on the back wall were two more doors set together and on the left near this same wall was a staircase.

Using the closest door on the right wall they entered the hall. It was large with a great hearth on the wall to the left. The room itself was void of any furniture except for a huge wooden table and some oak chairs around it. The tapestries on the wall were in dire need of mending and the whole room was covered in dust.

In the corner, on the same wall with the hearth, was a door leading into a small sitting room. The door in the same corner only on the next wall led back out into the waiting area. As they came out this door, Amber saw the staircase situated across from them. Before climbing the stairs, Dhin opened the two doors on the back wall.

"The kitchen area." he said to Amber as he closed them.

At the top of the stairs, the landing went to left and right following the length of the house. There were nine rooms in all, the largest being set at the end of the landing and overlooked the front courtyard. At the opposite end there was another staircase, closed in against the back wall. This led down into a small alcove coming out into the kitchen. Like most of the others, this room was very large. Small food storage chambers were scattered around the area. Two great cooking hearths stood on one wall and serving tables were in the middle of the room.

Off to one side there was a long stone-enclosed corridor, which led to the servant's quarters. At the doorway to one of the rooms, Dhin stopped. Placing his hand on the wood portal he stood looking as if he were in a different time and world. After a few moments he turned to his son.

"This is where most of the days of my youth were spent." he said with tears in his eyes. "Being the bastard grandson of a king, my presence in the main house was frowned upon. Some times in the dark of night, my mother would sneak me up to her apartments by the back stairs. There she would talk to me of far off lands and sing softly until I was fast asleep. Then her kindly servant woman would carry me back to the room we shared."

"Were you never at all allowed into the main hall?" Amber asked.

"Only once," the old man answered, "when a Baron came asking for the hand of my mother. My grandfather had tried talking her into marrying to hide the shame of my birth. I was called to the main hall so the Baron could get a look at his prospective son. But my mother refused his offer and that was the last time I saw my grandfather on his bidding."

"Father, if I may be so bold to ask, why did you leave your mother's side?" his son spoke softly, trying not to break his father's reminiscent mood.

"Ah, my son," Dhin replied, "that is a long story. But I will tell you this much. Upon my grandfather's death, my mother's brother became king of these lands. He was in with the Saxon leaders and because my mother was the elder child of the dead king, I was a threat to him and his crown. I was sitting before the fire in the kitchen when the flames told me of an accident he had planned for me. Knowing he would not harm my mother, I slipped away that night and became a man of the world at the tender age of eleven." Dhin turned and walked back through the corridor into the kitchen. His eyes were steady and clear again as he said, "Come, it is time we met Jasper in the courtyard."

As they came outside, Amber noticed the gardens to one side. What once had been filled with beautiful flowers and shrubs was now over run with weeds.

"Men will be needed to care for the grounds also." said Dhin, "Those trees over there on the far side of the yard bear different kinds of exotic fruit. My grandfather brought them out of the Orient when he returned from the first crusades. It is a wonder they have thrived so well without any care." Walking over to the trees he picked one of the fruits for his son.

"I have never tasted anything like this before," said Amber smacking his lips, "so sweet and juicy."

"Well, you will be able to eat all you want now." said his father smiling. "Let us go and contract the help we will need." he then said to Jasper who had come from the stables with the horses. "We will have to stay at the inn until all the work is done."

On the way back to the village Amber's thoughts wandered to the people who had watched their arrival. He wondered if they would accept them or maybe they would discover who his father really was. Looking at the old man, he realized that there was no way he would be known as Merlin. He had been much younger when he disappeared. Now, with the black washed out of his hair and beard, he looked older than time itself.

At the inn the young man found that his thoughts were right. When Dhin told their story, they were welcomed as masters of Logan Manor. Jasper, who would be head servant of the entire household, was given the task of hiring all the help he would need. Their stay at the inn was very pleasant. Amber got to know the people of the village and discovered they were far friendlier than those of Larkwood.

Jasper contracted only the best tradesmen and it was not long before they were able to move into the manor house. Dhin had said he wanted to be settled before the winter came and it was a good month after their move when the first snow fell on the countryside.

They soon adjusted to the everyday life of the widowed Lord and his son. While winter winds howled around them they made plans for the spring planting. Dhin decided it would be best for them to work the land and cultivate the orchards, selling their corps to the village for a living. He was wise enough to know the money from the giant's treasure would not last very long. The thought of living out the rest of his life as a land Baron made him happy and content. Jasper too, was satisfied with running the house and supervising the other servants. Only Amber became restless as the long winter nights passed slowly by.

One night as he sat with his father in the sitting room, the young man revealed what was eating at his heart. "I know you are happy in this life, father, but you are old and have had enough adventures to carry you to your death bed, while I am still a young man not yet twenty and five. There must be more purpose to my life than just freeing a village from a giant." The young man sat with a long face, brooding into the fire.

"So, my son, you are bored with the life of a land Baron already?" said Dhin smiling, "Well, I guess it is time to fill your days with some excitement."

Amber looked up at his father trying to read the old man's thoughts and the meaning behind the gleam in his eyes.

Dhin continued, "During our stay at the inn, while you were meeting people, I was searching for some news of Gorfan."

"Gorfan!" cried Amber sitting on the end of his chair, his interest aroused. "Did you find out where he is? Does he still have the book? Where is he? Can we go there?" he rattled the questions so fast that he had to stop to catch his breath.

"Hold on, one question at a time, I cannot follow you." Dhin laughed at his son's eagerness. "If you will listen I will tell you what I have learned."

Amber sat back feigning calmness as he waited for his father to continue.

Dhin took a sip of his wine, sat comfortable in his chair, then said; "About seven years ago a traveling man of medicine came to

114

Meridunum and rested at the inn. As he refreshed himself with food and drink, he told the innkeeper that he was from the town of Galava and was on his way to the court of Arthur. He said that he had barely escaped with his life as the Saxon's had broken the fortifications around his town and had taken over rule of the village. Arthur's fighting men tried to push them back but were unsuccessful. All of Sir Ector's lands were now in the hands of Caw who proclaimed himself king." As the old man paused to take another drink of wine, his son spoke.

"But what does that all have to do with Gorfan or the book?" he asked, not quite sure what his father was leading to.

"When my servant left the temple of Dusk, his destination was the quiet village of Deva which is just south of Galava. If anyone has seen him, I am sure this man has."

"But it was seven years ago that he came through Meridunum, on his way to the court of Arthur. Surely we are not going to go there in search of him?" Amber did not relish the thought of facing his half brother.

"You have not let me finish." Dhin said sharply, "Our traveler from Galava is here. A sturdy wench, the miller's daughter, changed his mind about continuing his journey. He married her and stayed on as the town's physician. His name is Toran and he lives, quite happy, in the mill he took over after his wife's father died."

"I still do not understand." said Amber getting inpatient with his father.

"One of the things that Gorfan knew best was the making of herbs, for I taught him myself. If Toran stopped in Deva, there is a chance he could have met my friend." The old man rose from his chair and moved slowly to the window. Looking out into the moonlit night he said, "Today's sun has melted much of the snow. By tomorrow we will be able to ride safely into the village and maybe have a talk with Toran." Dhin ended the conversation by retiring for the night.

The next morning Dhin and Amber rose with the sun and quickly made their way into the village. The one place in Meridunum where everyone gathered on the first day after a harsh winter was the large warm room of the inn. When the two men arrived, it was quite crowded and the noise of voices exchanging news met them at the door. They found a place to sit in a corner and as they made themselves comfortable, the innkeeper brought them warm mugs of wine.

"Is he here?" asked Amber when the man had left to take care of some new arrivals.

"Yes, he is that thin gray haired man, sitting with those dock workers." Dhin answered nodding his head towards the table nearest the fire.

Amber saw that Toran was indeed a very thin man. He held his mug of ale in long bony almost blue white hands. His hair was white and scarce, leaving a bald spot on the top of his head. Unlike most men of his age, whose beards were long, Toran's face was without any hair at all. The physician from Galava looked quite out of place talking to the hard, broad men who worked the river barges. He was sitting with hunched back at the long table and Amber noticed that his body stayed in that same bent position while he shuffled over to the keg of ale for a refill.

"Shall we go and talk with him?" asked Amber rising from his seat.

Dhin placed his hand on his son's arm to bring him back onto the bench. "There will be no need for that. Toran's curiosity about us will bring him over soon."

The old man was right, for as soon as his mug was filled, Toran hobbled towards them. "Ah, my Lord Dhin, is it not?" he said as he slid into the place across from Dhin.

"You are correct, my good man." said Dhin, "And who have I the pleasure of meeting?"

"I, my lord, am called Toran, physician and miller of this village." he responded.

"So you are the miller. Well sir, you are just the man I need to talk with." Dhin replied.

"You have a need to talk with me, my lord? What service could I be in a position to offer you?" the man asked.

"As you must know, I have taken over Logan Manor. Unlike the last owner, I am not a king and therefore must work the lands for a living. I will need a market to bring my wheat to at harvest time." Dhin explained.

"Ah, I see. And I being the only miller in this village, you will have to do your business with me. Well, my lord, I am sure we can come to a favorable agreement. Is this your head man?" Toran looked towards Amber.

"This is my son Ambrosius. My man, Jasper, did not come with us. You will have to pick a day that he can meet with you." Dhin smiled politely.

"There is plenty of time for that." Toran said, wiping the ale foam off his lips with the back of his sleeve. "So, you come from the Isle of Mona? And how do you like the warmer climate of South Wales?' he asked.

"It is not really very different from my birth place, except maybe the wind that comes off the open sea is more severe on the island. So severe that when I was a young lad, my father would send us to Deva before the winter set in." Amber saw the gleam in his father's eyes and marveled at how the old man had maneuvered the conversation to his chosen topic.

"Deva." the miller said with feeling in his voice. "I have not heard that town mentioned in a long time."

"Was that your home?" Amber asked.

"So the young master has a voice after all." Toran laughed as he answered the young man's question. "My birth place was the town of Galava, north of Deva. But when I left my village and came south, I stopped there for a spell. Had a close call too. You see," he leaned over the table as if he wanted to be sure no one overheard. "the Saxons had crossed over the boundary and when I reached Deva the king's men were already there. Under orders from Arthur it was told that no one was to enter or leave the village until the invaders were routed. But I had a friend who was able to sneak me in after dark.

"When the Saxons were stopped from advancing any further than Galava, a border patrol was set up at Alana. But that did not stop the murdering dogs for they slipped past the soldiers and raided the countryside. They came into Diva on the day I was preparing to leave and set themselves to drinking our good ale. The drunker they got the louder they became and we began to fear for our lives. They boasted that they were on a scouting mission, looking for British slaves. Then just as one of them came towards me saying I seemed like servant material, this man jumps up from a stool by the fire and distracts them, saying that good King Arthur would make short work of them very soon. Well I recognized him to be the one people called the herb maker. I had bought some roots from him just the day before. A good mixture they were too." He paused to call for more ale.

Amber looked at his father who seemed to be calm, as if he were listening to the story about some complete stranger rather than his servant and friend.

Dhin saw his son's anxious glance and said to the miller, "How lucky you were that this herb maker took their attention away from you. Did they leave then?" he asked.

"Leave? Not them dogs, oh no. They latched onto this brave man and decided to make him their slave instead of skinny me. He could carry their belongings, they said. The last I saw of the poor devil, they were dragging him out of town over the north road. A chain was around his neck and bundles were piled high on his back." Toran took a long drink that emptied his mug and called to the innkeeper to fill it up again. He never finished this one for all the drinking and the warm closeness of the inn got to him. Soon he was laying face down on the table snoring away like a sleeping babe.

Dhin rose from his seat and motioned to the innkeeper. When the man came over to them, the 'Old one' said, "I feel our friend the miller has celebrated the coming of spring way beyond his capacity." He pressed some gold coins into the man's burly hand and continued, "I think this is enough to cover all he has drank, with enough left over to provide him with a soft bed to sleep off the effects of your fine ale."

The innkeeper's eyes lit up as he saw the amount in his hand. Smiling at Dhin, he picked Toran up, threw him over his shoulder and carried him off to a room in the sleeping quarters.

Once out in the cold air, Amber pulled his fur cloak around him and asked, "When do we leave for Deva?"

"As soon as we can get the house in order and plans for the spring planting settled with Jasper." his father answered, "I am afraid our friend is going to be disappointed, for he will not be able to go with us this time."

"Are we going in disguise again?" the young man asked.

Dhin laughed at his son's apparent excitement, happy to see the color back in his cheeks and the spirited look in his eyes. "I think this time I will be a man of medicine and you shall be my herb finder. Your time spent with the master of the temple of Dawn can now be put to work. What names do you think we should use?" he asked, getting caught up in his son's enthusiasm.

"How about if you are the physician Gorganis and I am your man Yata?" said Amber, delighted to be once more planning an adventure. "No one would know those names so far away from the mountain and yet Gorfan will recognize them."

"Gorganis and Yata, ah yes, that will do nicely." Dhin's voice showed all the merriment of his son's. Yet in his thoughts were all the dangers they would have to face if they were going into a Saxon camp to steal one of their slaves. If anyone recognized them for who they were, their lives would be snuffed out in a second. The excitement now surged through his old body and it made him feel young again, as if he were still at the side of King Arthur. He turned and looked at his son as they rode the path pack to the manor.

How like your father you are, craving for adventure. he thought while aloud he said, "No matter what happens to us in the land of our enemies, I will never regret having a son as you."

"It is my pleasure being your son, but do not despair, for nothing is going to happen to us." Even as he spoke, Amber felt a cold prickling sensation crawling up his spine to the back of his neck.

CHAPTER 14

The town of Deva was unlike any town Amber had ever seen. The houses were left unattended and the streets were littered with scraps of bones and broken wine bottles. The hour of their arrival was early, the sun having just peeked over the nearby mountains. Yet the streets were heavy with people, young and old, sitting around the buildings with tattered clothes, many were shoeless. Young girls danced around in a vulgar fashion, while men in strange uniforms ran after them with lust in their eyes.

"They are what is know as 'war wenches'." said Dhin seeing his son's eyes following this spectacle. "Every village has its share of wanton women. When there is war and soldiers, they seem to flock all the more. Do not be alarmed for this is a way of life for them."

They had left their horses hidden in the forest on the outskirts of town in the care of Edgar, the servant they had taken with them. Jasper was upset when he found out he was to stay home, but he did make sure to lecture the man to do what he was told without any question and to maintain strict loyalty to 'Master Dhin and Master Ambrosius'. Dhin had no doubts that Edgar would prove himself to be a very faithful servant and friend.

At the inn, which was at the far end of the street, Dhin gave the innkeeper some coins in exchange for food and lodgings. The man then led them through the kitchen to a room with two pallets its only furnishings. They needed no more because the only things they had brought with them were a few books on healing and the tools of a physician. All this was carried in a leather bag Jasper had made for Dhin. The only clothing they had were the ones they were wearing for the life of a man of medicine was a poor one.

As Amber looked around, Dhin noticed his unpleasant look. "Do not turn your nose up at our living quarters, for they may save our lives." he said in a low voice, not wanting to be overheard.

Amber smiled; "It is not the lack of finery but rather the strange odor. It smells like they have soaked the house with wine and ale." he said.

Dhin laughed as he led his son out through the kitchen and back into the eating room of the inn. It was filled with men in uniforms and the lusty women bustling around them. The innkeeper showed them to a table near the hearth where cheese and mutton with a loaf of fresh bread was waiting for them. After pouring the ale into thick mugs, he left them to enjoy their meal.

"The innkeeper tells me you are a man of medicine." the words came from a large, bushy haired man. His clothes were dirty with a tear in his sleeve just above the elbow. A wound with dried blood could be seen beneath the ragged material. "You are to fix this gash in my arm." he ordered in a thick Saxon accent as he grabbed Dhin by the arm.

Amber rose from his chair and by the look on his face his father feared he was about to do something foolish. "Yata!" he said in a loud voice, "Go get my bag of medicines from our room." He gave Amber a little push, to remind him what they were there for. "It is very hard for a poor man as myself to get a good servant." Dhin said to the Saxon soldier. "This one was given to me as payment for curing a sick lord. He is not too bright but he has learned the art of herb finding very well. Now let me see your arm."

Taking his dagger from his belt, Dhin cut away the dirty torn garment. The wound had been made a few days before and the lack of care had left it festered and oozing with infection. When Amber returned with the bag, the old man cleaned the sore area with medicine and bandaged the Saxon's arm. As he finished the soldier threw a gold coin at him and grunted his thanks.

Amber's face grew red as he tried to suppress his anger at the brash Saxon. "When we have found Gorfan and freed him, I will personally see that the war-monger regrets his treatment of you, my father." he said when the soldier was far enough away not to hear him.

"Do not be revengeful my son." Dhin answered, "You cannot expect compassion from invaders. Our main purpose is finding Gorfan and nothing else. If we must bear some ill treatment during this time, then so be it. You must remember that our very lives depend on being able to deceive the enemy." He saw his son's eyes had cooled some but they were still on the Saxon they had just tended.

"What do you watch so intensely?" Dhin asked.

"The man that was just here is talking to the others. I cannot hear them too well, but did catch the words, 'he could be used at camp'. Do you think they mean to make you their slave?" Amber's voice shook with fear. If that was the case, he was ready with his hand on the dagger stuck in his belt. There was no way he would let them harm his father.

"I do not know too much of the Saxon ways, but this I do know. They do not harm men of the church or men of medicine. Both kinds of men they hold in high regard. I think we will be asked to take the position of camp physician." As Dhin set his mug down and turned to call the innkeeper for more ale, he saw the familiar Saxon coming towards his table. Behind him were three others, just as dirty and massive as he.

"You will come with us?" the husky man asked. "If you choose to, there will be more gold coins than you can get here." he said, "We are going to leave for Galava at mid-day. If you do not join us by then we will know your wish is to remain here. Keep in mind, Caw rewards them that serve him well." He then turned and left with his friends close behind.

Amber looked at Dhin, smiled, and then rose to tell the innkeeper of their change of plans. He knew, when Caw's name and the town of Galava were mentioned, what his father would do. When he came back to the table and sat down the smile was still upon his face.

"How are we going to get word to Edgar?" he asked.

"We will have to take someone into our confidence." Dhin answered as he looked around.

The room was filled with the fair-haired men of Saxon blood and a few native Britons. Already, after only seven years of conquest, there were young children with yellow hair and blue eyes running in and out of the inn, doing errands for the warlords. Suddenly the old man's eyes fell on a black haired boy of about twelve years, sitting on a stool by the fire. His black eyes showed all the hate his heart held for the invaders of his land.

"There is our helper." he said to Amber, "Go and fetch him by asking if he would like to be of service to a good man of Briton and Arthur."

When the young man did as his father asked, the boy's eyes lit up and he nodded his head yes. Hurrying over to the table, the lad sat next to Dhin with eagerness written on his face.

"My boy, would you do a great service for me and in doing this, also serve your good King Arthur?" the old man asked in a whisper.

"Oh yes, sir, there is nothing I would not do for our King." he answered.

"You realize there is great danger in being a king's man in this town, do you not?" When the boy nodded yes, Dhin continued. "Then what I tell you must be kept in secret. No one can be told of your mission or my life and that of my servant's will be ended." He paused again trying to read the boy's eager look. "How do you feel about your Saxon neighbors?" he asked.

"If I were older and had the strength, I would cut them down like the dogs they are. They killed my father and older brother because they wanted our farm. And when their filthy hands ravaged my sister, she took her own life. My mother died shortly after of heartbreak leaving me all alone in this Saxon world and those pigs are to blame!" He said this with so much feeling; Dhin feared the others in the room would know what they were talking about. But a quick look around showed that they were more interested in cavorting with the women and drinking ale to worry about what a young boy and old man were saying.

"Well, I see you are the right one to trust." Dhin said with a laugh. "Here is what I want you to do. Do you know the glen just off the main road?" As the boy nodded, the old man continued. "If one should follow the path just behind the thick trees, he would find an old deserted stone fort. Half the walls are tumbled down from the first war."

"Yes, I know it well." the boy's eyes danced as he answered, "I use it to hide in when things here get too much for me to bear."

"Well there you will come upon a man who is camped taking care of three beautiful steeds. You will tell him you come from the 'Old one' and give him this note." To the boy's wonder, Dhin pulled out a piece of parchment and proceeded to write on it with a piece of burnt stick. When he saw the fear in the boy's eyes, he said, "There is nothing to fear. My friend Merlin showed me how to write without the help of a stylus. Burning a stick slowly turns it into chard wood that can make marks on the parchment. Now hurry and make sure you are not seen. Tell the man that he must carry out my wishes and no more." He handed the folded note to the boy. "Return and let me know you have done as I asked."

"Will you have Edgar stay hidden in the ruins?" Amber asked as the lad slid out of his seat. Slowly walking to the kitchen, the boy left by the back door.

"Edgar is to follow us at a safe distance." Dhin answered his son's question. "He was chosen to accompany us for his ability to track anything that walks. He will find a safe place to hide when we reach our destination and make sure we know of it." He then called the innkeeper to fill their mugs once more, for they still had a while before the Saxons left town.

Leaving Amber at the inn, Dhin went in search of the Saxon leader to tell him of their plans to join the camp of Caw. When the leader told the rest of the men in their own tongue the news, they mumbled among themselves. Dhin pretended not to understand and the leader said they were very happy of his decision. Dhin smiled and moved back towards the inn.

"Well, that was a short walk." said Amber as Dhin sat down on the bench next to him.

"I wanted to be sure the boy's leaving was not seen." his father replied. "I spoke to the Saxons and let them know of our plans. The leader says they were very happy. What they really said, not knowing I knew the language, was that Caw would be glad to have a physician instead of just an herb maker. But to them we were just more mouths to feed."

"Ah!" Amber's eyes lit up. "Then it is possible that Gorfan is still in the camp of the Saxons."

Before Dhin could answer, the curtain by the kitchen was moved aside as the young lad came back into the inn. Without looking around he went and sat by the fire. After warming his hands near the flames he turned his head slightly and nodded at the old man.

"Well, Yata." Dhin said loudly, "I think it is about time for us to leave. We would not want our new friends departing without us."

Outside the Saxon leader was waiting with the reins of two nags in his hand. They looked more like plow horses than anything anyone would ride. "I was told you came into town on foot." the man said, "You would not be able to keep up with us walking, so I found you and your man something to ride. They are not much but it is better than wearing out your sandals."

Dhin bowed saying, "You are most kind."

Mounting the horses they took their place at the end of the column and rode out over the north road. This was not the main road but led into the mountains and bypassed Alauna. Taking this route would eliminate the chance of running into King Arthur's patrol, who still had control of that town.

At night when they stopped and made camp, Dhin sent Amber out to search for herbs. He came back with a bag full of roots and information for Dhin on the lay of the land. Such knowledge was important for their escape from the Saxon held town when the time was right.

On their second night of travel, as Amber went in search of the special roots, Dhin set up a spot on a flat rock to prepare the ones from the day before. The Saxons were content to sit and eat their meal of dried mutton and bread. The wine from goatskin containers flowed like water as they drank themselves into a drunken stupor. Only the leader drank sparingly as his squinting eyes watched the physician.

Coming over to Dhin the man muttered, "My arm has stopped hurting. Should the binding be taken off?"

"Let me have a look at it." Dhin unwrapped the bandage carefully so the healing skin would not be disturbed. The area was still red and raw. "I think some more of the salve should be put on and it will have to be covered for at least another day or two." When the man nodded his approval, Dhin took the medicine from his bag and tended the wound.

"Your servant has been gone a long time. These woods are a bad place for anyone to get lost." said the man as his eyes searched the old man's face.

"There is no need to worry about Yata, he will find his way back. The herbs he is looking for grow abundantly in these hills and they will be of great help in caring for the sick at your camp." When he finished putting the cloth on the man's arm, Dhin went back to mixing his medicines.

Seeming to be satisfied with Dhin's answer, the Saxon went to bed down near the fire, unaware of the gleam in the old man's eyes. It was not long before the old man found a place near the fire and also bedded down.

"Father!" Amber shook the old man awake. He motioned to Dhin as he crawled away from the sleeping men. "I have made a discovery." he said in a whisper. "Over the next hill I came across a glen where yellow flowers were growing wild. Happy at my find, I set to picking them when my eyes caught something moving beyond the trees. Going to investigate, I came upon a very ragged and dirty boy with his foot trapped in the tangled roots of an over turned tree. When he saw that I was going to help him, he stopped struggling and let me free his foot. He thanked me in the old tongue and as we talked I realized he was from a tribe of hills men that lived nearby. He told me how they hated the Saxons for raiding their forest homes and taking their women. He also said that his people would be willing to help us for they knew our true identity. The boy is going to watch for Edgar and lead him to an old deserted temple not far from the camp of Caw. We are to meet him there when our mission is done."

As Dhin listened to his son his eyes started to glisten, "I remember these people." he said excitedly, "I took care of their chief once. They are what is left of the people that the Roman's pushed into the mountains. Soon, if Arthur is unable to stop the invaders, all the people left of Briton descent will have to join them in their hiding." He stopped talking for one of the men stirred in his sleep. "We better get back for there will be questions if we are found talking in secret. We will speak of this at another time."

They then crawled back to the fire and settled down for the night.

In the morning as they rode on toward their destination, Dhin noticed small figures darting between the trees following them. Slowing his horse so Amber could catch up with him, he said softly,

"Your young friend is true to his word. They watch us from behind the trees. It is good to know we shall have help."

By mid-day they were on a hill overlooking a valley. Below them was a small lake with farms doting the landscape around it. At the head of the lake sat the town of Galava. As they rode down the hill and past the farms, Dhin noticed the figures that had been following them were staying under the trees. They would camp there and be ready for Dhin when he needed them.

Caw had his camp set up in the high walled fortress once owned by Sir Ector. Dhin had been acquainted with Sir Ector who was once lord of all the land around Galava. As they rode toward the stronghold, he noticed there were no familiar faces among the slaves and surmised that the servants of the original owner were either killed in the battle or had fled for their lives. Here, as in Deva, the streets were not kept clean and again there were war wenches, dresses torn from rough hands, running playfully from the yellow haired soldiers.

The main building in the fortress, which had been the home of Sir Ector's family for generations, was now the quarters of the Saxon who professed to be king. Dhin and Amber were brought into the main hall where Caw was waiting to receive them. He was a tall man of around forty years, with the golden hair and blue eyes of the Saxon blood. Across his right cheek was a thick scar, left from some battle. It made his features look strange as the hair on his face that formed a large bushy beard, did not grow near this scar. It looked like someone had taken a dagger and shaved one stroke of the beard from his cheek.

"So you are a physician." Caw said in the Saxon language. When Dhin just stood there pretending not to understand, the warlord spoke in a whisper to the man who had brought them there.

"It is the Briton tongue he speaks." the man answered.

Turning back to the old man, Caw said, "I do not like using the alien words unless it is necessary. Most of my slaves have taken the time to learn their captor's language."

"Am I to understand that my servant and I are your prisoners?" Dhin asked as black sparks shot from his eyes. "Your man asked me to follow him to this camp as my services were needed."

"Do not get yourself upset." Caw answered, "You are free to come and go as you wish. If you choose to stay there will be plenty of work."

"My work is taking care of the wounded and sick. If I am needed here, I will stay." was Dhin's reply.

"There is so much sickness that my slaves are dropping like flies. As for wounds, your work will begin here." Caw removed the cloak that was over his left hand, hiding it from view until now. Amber winced at the sight of the Saxons badly mangled hand. Part of his thumb and the top of his first two fingers were missing. Yellow infection oozed from the sore ends. "I received this in battle about two weeks ago. There was no one of knowledge to care for it, now you will."

"You have no other man of medicine, no herb maker who could have cleaned and dressed it for you?" Dhin asked.

"There is one who calls himself that, but I do not believe him. He looks like a common servant, I do not trust him." There was something in his voice that made Dhin wonder if anything was wrong with Gorfan. But for now he would have to concentrate on the Saxon's injury.

After cleaning the hand with special medicine that formed on the decaying skin, Dhin inspected the wound thoroughly, and then said, "It has been left too long. Poison has set in and done its worst. One could die from such an infection."

"Then take my sword and lop off the hand. I am of strong will. I can take the pain." Caw pulled his sword from its sheath and handed it to Dhin.

"There will be no need of that." the old man said handing the sword back to Caw. "I will just cut off the poisoned skin. We must go into your sleeping area and I will need a few things."

The 'would be king' nodded towards the soldier Dhin had tended and said, "Just tell Walter what you need and he will see that you get it."

In Caw's bedchamber, Dhin had him lay down. Moving the man's arm out to the side, he placed a piece of wood that had been covered with a clean cloth, under the injured hand. From his bag he took a small bottle of liquid and poured it onto the fingers and thumb, then over the hand.

"This will cause the hand to lose its feeling until I have done my work." the old man said as he drew out his dagger.

Going to the fire in the hearth, he placed the blade over the flames until it turned red-hot. He then poured some wine over the steel to cool it. Under his instructions Amber put some of the hot coals from the fire into a metal dish and placed it on the table near the bed. Taking his son's dagger, Dhin put it into the hot coals in the dish then turned to Caw.

"I am now ready my lord." the physician said as he bent over the Saxon's hand.

Without waiting to see if the man was ready, Dhin proceeded to cut away the infected flesh with his dagger. He did one finger at a time, sealing the cut area with Amber's hot blade. The smell of burning flesh filled the air, causing Walter to leave the room. Amber was so interested in what his father was doing that he was not aware of the odor. When all the poison flesh was removed, Dhin took some leaves that had been soaking in a thick black medicine and placed them over the wound. He then covered the hand with a clean white cloth making sure the leaves were pressed tightly against the area he had just cut.

"When the feeling comes back into your hand it will bring great pain." Dhin said, cleaning his implements as he put them away. Taking a small vial from his bag, he poured some of its contents into a goblet of wine and handed it to the warlord. "This mixture will ease the pain and help you to sleep. Drink it now before the pain starts."

Caw took some then settled back and said; "My servant will show you to your sleeping quarters. You will be lodged in the room across the hall in case you are needed in the night. Your man can bed down in the servants quarters in the court yard."

"It is the Briton ways to have their servants sleep in the same room. If it is all right with my lord, I would have Yata stay with me." Dhin said as he bowed to the Saxon.

"Strange customs you people have but so be it." He then gave his servant orders in the Saxon language and turned again to Dhin, "What is your name physician?" he asked.

"I am called Gorganis, my lord." he answered, then followed the man out of the room.

While Dhin was getting settled, Amber took a walk around the compound. Out in the spring air, he pulled his cloak around him against the chill that came with the setting sun. he walked passed the small buildings that were used to house the soldiers. To one side were the stables and more buildings that served as the servant's quarters.

"We are lucky to be lodged in the main house." he thought as the odor from this area reached his nose.

The slaves of the Saxons were kept so busy by day that when nightfall came they would lie exhausted on their straw beds, not able to clean up their own living area. The male children had been taught by the invaders only of fighting and were gone following the soldiers from sun up to sun down. The Saxons knew that the boys of the Britons would be of help in their quest to conquer all of Britain. Young females that were old enough to walk were put to work doing odd jobs.

Amber was about to return to his quarters when he heard a weak voice coming from one of the shacks. "Yata, Yata!," it called. Turning around he saw a man dressed in rags clinging to the doorpost. He had been beaten and his face was covered with blood. The back of his tunic was torn to shreds and showed the swollen and bleeding marks of a whip on the skin. Amber hurried and caught him just as his strength gave out.

The man gave a slight smile as he was carried into the building. Amber was placing him on one of the straw beds when the man cried out, "You are not Yata!," then passed out.

As the young man took care of the wounds, a shadow crept out the back door and hurried towards the main house. There would be gold coins for the information that was just overheard. The stranger who had arrived with the physician was not who he said he was.

Amber placed a cloth with cold water on the back of the unconscious man, unaware of the treachery about to be brought down upon him and his father by one of their own countrymen.

CHAPTER 15

Amber made the man as comfortable as he could then turned to leave. He stopped short for there in the door stood Dhin with a Saxon soldier behind him.

"Master," he said catching the look in Dhin's eyes. "I was about to call you. The herb maker has been beaten. He is so bad, there was doubt in his mind that I was 'Yata'. You must hurry and tend to him for I fear he is dying."

"Do not worry Yata; I would not let my old friend die." Dhin said as he went over to the bed.

The Saxon started to follow, but when he saw the bleeding man lying on the straw bed and smelled the stench the house held, he changed his mind and waited by the door.

Gorfan opened his eyes to see the face of Dhin bending over him and felt the cold cloth the old man had placed on his head.

"Do not try to talk, herb maker, you have been badly hurt and must let your wounds heal." Dhin said trying to let his friend know they were not alone.

Gorfan looked towards the door and saw the soldier standing

there. He closed his eyes again as the Saxon looked at them. Amber covered the wounded man with another cover as their guard stepped out into the clean air.

"It seems one of our own people is in with the invaders." Dhin said to Amber in a low whisper. "He was in back of the room when you brought Gorfan in. Hearing him deny your identity, he ran to the main house with his story. Caw was still sleeping from the drug so he told his tale to Walter. He in turn sent this man, who speaks our language, to see what was going on. I was allowed to come also for if we were not who we said, Walter wanted to be sure he had the both of us." Turning to Gorfan, Dhin quickly explained why he and his son, Ambrosius, were using other names.

All the time Dhin talked, the injured man kept his eyes closed like he was sleeping. When the story was finished, Gorfan moaned loudly to attract the Saxon's attention. Their guard came over to the bed just as the herb maker opened his eyes.

Seeing Amber at the foot of his bed, he said in a weak voice, "Yata, what are you doing here in Galava?" Before receiving an answer he turned his head towards Dhin. "And Gorganis, it has been a long time since my eyes have had the pleasure of seeing you. What are you both doing here?" As weak as he was Gorfan managed to help his friends.

"We have been asked by the Saxon King to care for the sick and wounded of his camp. You were out of your mind with pain when Yata came upon you, even to the point of not knowing him." Dhin stopped talking as the Saxon pushed him aside and stood over Gorfan.

"You are sure you know these two men as the ones named 'Yata' and 'Gorganis'? There is no mistake?" he grunted at the battered man.

"How could I not know my own brother, Yata? Or the man who is his master and had taught me to be an herb maker." Gorfan stated then shut his eyes in pain.

The soldier, satisfied with what he had heard, left to report back to Walter.

Dhin made sure there was no one else in the house then said to his friend, "That was a close call."

"Are you really the brother of Yata?" Amber asked.

"Yes, through the years my people had no one coming from the outside world so there was much intermarrying. When a man did stumble across our village he would decide to stay and you could almost bet he would father a large brood of children. In my family alone there were seven sisters and nine brothers." Gorfan gave out a weak smile as he saw the amazement on the young man's face, and then added, "My father had three wives."

"Enough of this small talk." Dhin said, "Tell me now, why were you beaten?"

"About two months ago, the Saxon soldiers went out on a raid looking for more slaves." he said slowly, "They do not take good care of the people they capture, as you can see. This ill treatment brings many deaths and so these war mongrels have to replenish their supply. Caw is very demanding and says a king must prove his royalty with a large number of servants. But like most conquering rulers, he tends to abuse them." He paused to drink some of the wine Dhin was offering him.

"This time," he continued, "they came back with a young girl bound at the wrists." tears started to fill his eyes. "It was strange to see this as most of the young women coming into camp did so willingly. Only the old ones, used for household chores, were brought in by force. As I drew nearer, to get a better look, I felt there was something familiar about her face. The laughing soldiers took her into their quarters where there was much screaming and I knew what they were doing to her. Then her voice came no more. It was not long before these Saxon dogs came out, still laughing and made their way towards the main gate on their nightly journey to the village inn." Gorfan's hands started to tremble as the tears ran down his face.

"You must rest now my friend." said Dhin fearing for Gorfan's life. "You can finish your story tomorrow when you are stronger."

"No, no my lord," he said desperately, "I must finish now for tomorrow might be too late."

"Very well, but if you feel the strain is too much you must stop." Dhin said as he gave him more wine.

"I waited until they were out of sight" Gorfan continued, "and I was sure they would not return, before I went into the building. She was lying, without clothing, on the floor where they had molested her, sobbing and retching at the same time. As I went to wrap my cloak around her she thought I too had come to lay hands on her. She tried to scream but there was no voice left in her. I gently covered her bruised body and talked softly to her. She did not understand me, so I spoke the words of the old tongue. Her eyes softened and she stopped crying. I asked her name and when she answered I sat, unable to move or speak. I could not believe my ears." he started to sob helplessly.

Dhin placed his arms around the despairing man, trying to comfort him. "Who was it?" he gently asked.

"My Lord Dhin," he said as fire flashed in his eyes, "first I must tell you that the men who desecrated her young body, are now dead. The day before your arrival the last one met his fate, the same as the others, in a very brutal manner by my hands." Gorfan's face now showed the hate that was in his heart for all Saxons. "They found out it was I when the traitor, the same one who ran to them this night, saw me completing my act of revenge. You will not have to soil your hands on that task. They are all dead... Dead...like her."

"Who was she?" Dhin's voice was more demanding and his body shook as if he already knew the answer.

"She was my brother's child, a girl that had never been touched by a man. Her name was Morlan, a child of only sixteen years. A beautiful babe she was." Gorfan lost control of his emotions once more. The sobbing caused him to cough and spit up the blood that was seeping into his stomach from the beating.

Dhin was trembling as he held the man in his arms and forced wine down his throat. Amber stood at the foot of the bed. He neither moved nor spoke as he became consumed with all he had heard.

After giving the man some of the medicine made from the pollen of the yellow flowers Amber had picked, Dhin placed him gently back down on the straw. Tears were in his eyes as he said, "Poor little Morlan. She was a pretty child. How did she die?"

Gorfan's voice was very soft now as the medicine started to take effect. "As I sat holding her, trying to soothe her with words of comfort, she saw my dagger in its place beneath my belt. Before I knew what she was doing, or could even stop her, she plunged the blade deep into her heart. She was dead without another breath." his voice trailed off as he drifted into a drugged sleep.

Amber was now at his father's side and placed his hands on the old man's shoulders, trying to console him. "I remember her well, father," he said with great emotion. "On the rare occasions she came to visit the temple, Morlan would sit at your feet and listen to the stories of the far off places you had seen."

"Ah yes," Dhin joined Amber in remembering the child of Yata's younger brother. "She would sit with eyes always opened wide as if she were about to lose them. It added to her beauty."

Amber's grip on his father tightened as he tried to contain himself. He could see the child, sitting on her sister Ronya's lap as he taught the older girl his language. Everyone had agreed, she was the prettiest child in the valley. Now she was dead, her life taken by her own hand because these foreign monsters had molested her. Tears flowed freely and anger gripped his heart as the memories formed in his mind.

The rest of that night Dhin and Amber spent at the bed side of Gorfan. All through the dark hours, the dying man moaned and called out the name of his brother's child. Every once in a while, Dhin would force wine between the man's dry lips, knowing there was no hope in saving this pitiful life. In his mind he blamed himself for Gorfan's suffering. If he had not asked him to take the book to a safe place, this man would now be sitting at his brother's side. *Yet, how was it that Morlan was captured?* He wondered. Then, seeing his friend sleeping once again closed his eyes to rest.

Soon the golden rays of dawn began to climb through the only window. As Dhin opened his eyes, he saw Amber bent over Gorfan, talking.

Coming fully awake he heard his servant saying, "You do your father justice Master Ambrosius." his voice was trembling and there was a rattle in his throat. "Ah, my lord, you must not grieve." he said seeing Dhin's sadness. "As you know, whether we live or die is written in the stars."

"That may be true, but I should have foreseen this in the fire and kept you safe at the temple." said the old man.

"I do not know how they got their claws into my brother's child. But it does not take a scholar to realize that they must have found the valley of our home. If I had been there I would have died defending the people of my village. You must believe this, for you cannot go on blaming yourself." Gorfan said trying to give comfort even though he himself was dying.

Dhin knew the man spoke the truth, yet it did not ease the pain of watching his long time friend's life flow out before his eyes, while he stood by helpless.

As Gorfan started to talk again, Amber leaned over to hear for the dying man's voice was very low. When the young man moved away, Dhin could see that his friend was gone.

After a few moments, Amber spoke; "He said we can find the book hidden in the altar of an old temple that lays deep in the forest on the hill." There was much sadness in the young man's voice.

Dhin left Amber with the body of Gorfan while he went to see Caw. His permission was needed before they could bury their friend. The Saxon King was sitting up in his bed having a light meal of broth and bread. There was good color in his cheeks as he greeted the physician.

"Ah, Gorganis. Have you come to see the wonder of your work?" he said in a happy tone.

"Yes my lord, and I see I have done it well. Does the hand pain you very much?" Dhin asked.

"Somewhat, but nothing I cannot take. You are truly a man of medicine. I doubt if even this Merlin I have heard about, could have done better." Caw let out a loud laugh and motioned for his servant to bring a seat over to the side of his bed. "What is the payment you ask for your fine work? A bag of gold coins maybe?" there was a twinkle in his eyes as he motioned for the old man to sit down.

"I have only one wish and that is not gold." Dhin answered as he sat down and looked the Saxon dead in the eyes.

"A physician who asks for no gold? What could be better than gold?" Caw questioned.

"Permission to bury the body of a friend." came Dhin's reply.

"That is all? Well, my good man, you have it." said the Saxon.

"You have not heard who that man is. Maybe you will change your mind. He was beaten to death by your own soldiers for killing some of your men." Dhin watched Caw's face as the Saxon answered.

"The old herb maker. Yes I knew." there was no change on the proclaimed king's face. "My man told me you and your servant watched over him through the night, until he drew his last breath this morning. I also know he killed because of an injustice done upon his family. His brother's daughter, was it not?" Now it was Caw who watched the other's face.

"Yes my lord, a young lass just sixteen years, who had never been touched by a man." Dhin kept the emotion he was feeling out of his voice.

"Gorganis, I hope you will believe me when I tell you I knew nothing of all this until after the herb maker was beaten. I am a warrior. If I kill, it is because it is my destiny to become king of all Britain. I do not condone the bloody actions of my men. Yet until there is peace and the lords and barons of this land sit by my side for the good of the country, I need these men. You can understand my position, can you not?" he watched his physician closely, waiting for an answer.

Dhin sat silently for a moment before speaking, "If I may be so bold to speak freely without you taking it as an insult, I will say that, even though I can understand your not being able to control all your men, I cannot see why you want to take all the lands of Britain. My people cried out for the Saxons to free them from the Pics and Scots. In return for your help we gave you the island of Thenet for your home. Now you want to drive us from our lands. This, to me is an injustice hard to swallow." Dhin tried to keep his anger under control but this confrontation with his country's enemy seemed to fuel the fire.

"I admire you for your honesty." said Caw, trying just as hard to stay calm. "Another man I would have thrown to the mercy of my men, no matter what his age. But you I will answer even though it will never solve the differences between us." he paused to gather his thoughts. "It is true we made a bargain for the island, but through the years my people out grew the land. In need of living space, we tried to live in peace with the people of Britain, but they refused. So it was our duty to take the land we needed. This is the way of war." His eyes flashed as his anger grew.

Dhin knew he was playing a dangerous game, yet he continued his accusations. "It was not enough for you to push your way into the southeast corner of our land. Now you feel the whole country must become Saxon. You said so yourself when stating it was your destiny'. Do you take the Britons to be children? That they can be sweet talked into surrendering their lands to an invader and then, bowing down to him, call him their king. You will not be able to conquer them that easy."

Without realizing it, Dhin's eyes acquired the look that comes with a vision. "I see much death and the country engulfed in flames." he said, obviously in a trance. "It will be more than a hundred years before peace will come again to this land. But you will not stay the victors for very long. Soon others will come from across the waters. Again war will rage over field and farm and you will know how my people felt through their suffering. You will no longer be the might and the power for you shall become downtrodden, the slaves." Suddenly Dhin slumped forward in his chair as the vision ceased.

Caw sat in his bed with the look of terror on his face. Then getting a grip on his emotions, he spoke in a harsh voice, "You have permission to bury your friend, but you will be accompanied by four of my soldiers. I want you at my side, for I now feel there is more to you than just a physician's mind. You will remain here at camp, a prisoner if you wish to call it so, but you will be treated with all the respect due you. My men will not be allowed to harass you or your servant. I shall warn you, do not repeat what you have just told me or you will no longer be under the protection of Caw, Saxon King of Britain." his angry face turned away as he continued, "Leave me now but return after your task is completed." With this Caw went back to his meal without giving Dhin another look.

As the old man left, Walter rushed into the room, having heard his leader's angry voice. Going over to the bed he bowed and said, "You are troubled your Majesty. Can I be of some service to you?"

"It seems there is more to my physician than meets the eye." said Caw. "I want you to do a little spying. Find out who he really is and what he is up to." his brow wrinkled as he became deep in thought. Suddenly he said, "Perhaps Arlo will be of some help in this matter. When the opportunity arises, I want you to put him in the position of meeting our dear man of medicine. He should be back sometime today."

"But sir, you know Arlo is for the cause of the Britons." Walter replied, "How can he be of any use to you? He will not tell you anything the physician would admit to him."

"No, he would not," Caw agreed, "willingly that is. But if one of your spies should overhear them in conversation, then we might have some answers." his eyes glowed with all the evilness that was in his heart.

CHAPTER 16

There were tears in Dhin's eyes as Amber placed the last of the dirt over the grave. They had found that Gorfan had buried Morlan on a hill overlooking the valley. Finding the spot marked with a cross made from tree branches they laid their friend next to her. As the two men stood with bowed head saying good-bye, Caw's four soldiers sat off to the side playing a game of 'stones'.

This was done with two pieces of square wood the size of a coin, with markings on each side. They would be thrown on the ground and gold was bet on what mark would come up on top. Dhin had never played this game, but had watched many times while the soldiers of Pendragon rolled out the 'stones'. Now he was thankful that the Saxons were kept busy so he could speak to his son.

After Dhin finished telling him what had happened in Caw's bedchamber, Amber stood deep in thought.

"There is only one thing for us to do." he finally said, "You are the one who will have the Saxon eyes upon him while I am but a slave and not worth their attention. When I think there is no chance to fail, I will escape. With the help of the hills tribe I will contrive a plan to free you from Caw's hands. This must be done soon before he finds out who you really are."

"I am sorry I put us into this spot." Dhin said looking at his son, "But you will find out as you get older that sometimes you cannot control a vision. That is what happened this morning."

"It is true then? The Saxons will succeed in conquering our land?" Amber asked.

"Yes, and very soon now," his father replied, "I saw it would take a hundred years. It has already been over eighty years that we have been fighting them."

"And who is it that will come across the sea and defeat the Saxons?" Amber questioned.

"For the next five hundred years they will fight among themselves." his father answered revealing what the vision had shown him. "There will be more than one king of '*Angle-Land*' as they will call our land. Warriors will come with brutal force, burning, raping and killing as they bleed this land of its riches. They will seize the throne only to lose it again to the Saxons. Again the country will be divided and many kings will rule until sometime in the ninth century when one king will unite the people. But in the eleventh century, an invader from the lands of Normandy will claim the throne after a battle in which many will lose their lives. From that time on the Saxons will become the lesser people, while the Normans will gain lands and position." Dhin turned to see the guards were still playing their game. "We must go back now. They will tire soon and come to see what takes us so long."

"Shall I carry out my plan then?" the young man asked.

"Let us wait a few days before we decide upon our course of action. There may be some other way to foil Caw's plans." his father answered.

When they returned to the fortress, Amber went to mingle with the other servants in the hopes of finding some information on what the Saxon king planned to do with them. Dhin headed towards Caw's bed chamber only to find that he had dressed and was holding court in the main hall.

"My lord." Dhin said as he approached Caw's side. "I do not think it is wise that you should be up and about. The seriousness of your wound calls for at least another day of rest."

"It will not be necessary physician; Saxons are stronger than you think. That is why we shall be the masters of this land." he turned a sly look towards Dhin to see what feelings his words had aroused, only to be disappointed at finding the man's face quite calm. "Just look at my hand and do not advise me." he said, angry at the old man's lack of emotion.

Dhin unwrapped the bandages carefully. As he did, he found the Saxon king was not as strong as he would pretend. Pain clearly showed on his face, turning it to a chalky white. The area that Dhin had cut seemed to be healing nicely. The rest of the hand was swollen but showed no signs of infection. Dhin placed some salve on the raw area at the end of the cut digits and put on a clean cloth. When he was done, Caw slumped back in his chair, exhausted from holding in the cry of anguish that was on his lips. Dhin called for some wine and held the goblet as the Saxon drank.

"It is healing very well." Dhin said seeing Caw's questioning look. "Tomorrow I will have you start bathing it in warm water, three times a day. It will not be long before all the soreness is gone."

"No matter what else I may think of you, I do have to admit that you are a good physician." Caw said as he took the goblet of wine from Dhin.

"Then perhaps you will listen when I say you must rest today." the 'Old one' persisted.

Caw laughed at Dhin's assertiveness. "All right Gorganis, you shall win this battle. I will return to my bed chamber." he rose from his chair and with the help of his servant started toward the stairs. Suddenly he stopped and turned back to Dhin, "I think it would be a good idea if the camp Physician would take the time to look at all my servants. I would rest easier if I knew what was killing off my slaves."

"And would you take the word of a medicine man, and do the things he advises when the cause is found?" Dhin asked.

"If it is within my power." Caw said as he took the steps to his bed chamber. "Walter will see to your needs." he threw over his shoulder without looking back.

Walter could see the face of his king as he was coming down the stairs. Understanding the order in Caw's eyes, he walked towards Dhin saying, "I am sure Arlo will be only too happy to help you."

Dhin thought there was mockery in his voice and wondered just what kind of person this Arlo was. "Thank you Walter, have him meet me at the servants quarters." he said as he turned towards the door.

Walking around the camp, Dhin found that most of the sickness came from the dirt and garbage that was all around the area. Two small children were fighting over some scraps of meat that had been thrown out for the dogs. It was hard to tell the sex of the children as they were all covered with dirt and wore ragged clothes. Dhin supposed they were girls seeing how the Saxons only took care of the male children of the camp. The living conditions of these people were deplorable. Tears filled the old man's eyes as compassion for his country men touched his heart.

"It is a very sad way to live." A voice broke into the grieving man's thoughts. Dhin turned to see a young golden haired soldier. His blue eyes did not show the strong determined meanness that most of his breed had. Instead there was friendliness about him. Even his clothes showed a marked difference as they were neat and clean, patched here and there where a rip had occurred, maybe even in battle. But Dhin doubted if this gentle youth was capable of killing.

"Here is the reason for all the sickness and dying of your king's servants." Dhin said, "If Caw will allow it, I am going to have this place cleaned up." He walked over to the children who were chewing on the dogs meat and gave them each a gold coin, saying "Go into the village and get something decent to eat." They scurried off before anyone could take their new wealth away from them.

"Surely you cannot afford to do that for all the children of the camp." the young man said smiling. "I know my father will let you have your way if you are sure it will stop the dying."

"Your father?" Dhin looked with new interest at the young Saxon.

"I am called Arlo, son of Caw the Saxon King." he declared. "Walter said I may be of some help to you."

"So you are Arlo and you are the king's son." Dhin looked puzzled, still trying to figure out why Walter had chosen this man to help him. "You come willingly to help a Briton?" he asked.

"Yes, I do." said Arlo, "I also wanted to meet the one man who stood up to the mighty Caw and still lives." he laughed. There was no anger in the young man's voice, only admiration.

"How did you find that out?" the old man questioned.

"My father's body servant is very talkative. I also know that Caw is planning to spy on you and hopes that he will learn who you really are through me. But this you shall know, I will have nothing to do with his plans." there was determination in his voice.

"Are you sure you are a Saxon?" Dhin asked, then seeing Arlo's confusion he explained, "It seems funny enough that the king's son would be happy that I have not let his father rule me. But then, telling me of his plans." Dhin looked into the eyes of the young man before him, "Why are you warning me?"

"I do not like what my people are doing. It is true they were in need of living space when the island they were on became over crowded. But they have more than enough now, yet they keep on pushing. They will not be happy until the people of this land are pushed into the sea." He looked sullen now for this was a subject that bothered him very much. "My father and I fight bitterly about my belief, which is why he tries to keep me hidden." then, changing the subject, he said, "I was sorry to hear about your friend. I was not at camp when it happened, but away on a mission of peace to Arthur. I returned this morning while you were away burying him."

"You were at the court of Arthur? Tell me, how fairs my king? It has been a long time since I have seen him." Dhin looked slyly at Arlo to see if his words had upset him, and was pleased when he saw they did not.

"He is having trouble with Mordred again." Arlo stated, "There is talk that the king's bastard son is getting together an army to take the throne away from him. Your king did not look to be in the best of health. He refused Caw's proposal, which he felt was unfair and I tend to agree with him." Arlo stopped talking and looked to see if there was anyone listening for he was in enough trouble with his father over his refusal to fight the Britons. It would make Caw even madder to find that his son was giving out information about the enemy king. When he was sure that no one was paying them any attention, he continued.

"It seems he is also having problems with his queen. The knight Launcelot was found in the queen's bed chamber. A fight ensued during which the knight managed to escape with Guenevere to his castle. Arthur pursued and surrounded them. he then challenged Launcelot to meet him on the field of battle. The knight refused, some say because he feared Arthur would be injured, but his refusal left the king no choice but to attack. It was not long before the castle fell and the queen was back with Arthur. The king, under pressure from Rome, spared both lives. Instead he banished Launcelot from Britain and ordered his lands confiscated while the queen was shut up in a nunnery." Arlo saw the look of sadness on the old man's face.

"It seems my vision of the future was correct. It will not be long before the greatest man and king will be overthrown." Dhin was very upset to think of Arthur defeated.

"Then it is true, you do possess the sight." Arlo was seeing the old man with a new reverence.

"So you know that too. Have you also learned what your father plans to do with me?" Dhin asked.

"I am not sure." the young Saxon answered, "But no matter what he has in mind, I will find out. You can be sure of that. Right now his only interest seems to be in finding out who you are. He says you are not the physician Gorganis."

"Did he say who he thought I was?" There was a gleam in the old man's eyes.

"If it were not that Merlin is said to be dead, he would think you are him." Arlo's eyes searched Dhin's face trying to read his mind.

"Your father is being silly, I am Gorganis, just a man of medicine and nothing more." Dhin was silent for a moment, and then he said, "I still cannot help but find it strange that you inform me of your father's intentions."

"As I have told you, my friend," Arlo responded, "I do not condone my father's actions and refuse to be the prince of an oppressed people. I have vowed to help them in any way I can. Is it so strange that I, a creature of the gods, cannot stand to see other creatures of another god so misused?"

Dhin put his arm around the young man's shoulder and smiled warmly at him, "no, my son, it is not so strange for such feelings to be in the heart of a good man."

"Master, I was beginning to worry about you." Amber said as he came towards them.

"Arlo, I would like you to meet my servant, Yata." Dhin said to the man at his side. To Amber he said, "Arlo is the Saxon king's son. He is going to help us rid this camp of its infection."

Dhin kept his son wondering about Arlo until that night when they were alone in their room.

Then Amber, not being able to wait any longer said, "Now father, are you going to tell me what happened today or will I have to peer into the fire and find out for myself."

Dhin laughed at his son's eagerness and revealed all that had passed between him and Caw's son. When he was through Amber sat deep in thought.

"Do you think we can trust him? After all it could be that Caw put him up to all this to find out your identity." the young man said.

"I have not forgotten that possibility. We will reveal nothing that could hurt us until we are sure of his true feelings." Dhin answered his son. "But I am certain we will find my first impression of that young Saxon is right."

"I hope so father," said Amber, "for I too liked him as soon as I met him. We may find that he can even be of some help in retrieving our packet of value."

"That may be true. Now my son, I am not as young as you so I think it is time for me to lay this weary body to rest." Dhin walked over to his bed.

As he and Amber stretched out for a good nights sleep, neither one was aware of the shadow moving slowly away from their door and into the one across the hall.

"Well, my faithful Walter, what did you find out?" Caw was sitting by the fire. As his soldier told him what he had just overheard, the Saxon king's eyes danced with merriment.

"So, it seems the young man is not only his son but has the sight also. That is interesting." He ran his hand over his bushy beard as he thought. "I wonder what kind of treasure they have and where it is?" he said softly.

"That they did not say my lord." Walter answered, "But I am sure it is not anywhere in the camp. I had the men search the house where the herb maker died but they found nothing. Tomorrow, while the physician is busy, I will have a look in his room. Maybe I will come across something there.

"You have done well my friend. Now leave me as I wish to think." Caw then turned back to peering into the flames in the hearth.

As the door closed behind Walter, Caw whispered to the room

around him, "I will come up with such a scheme, my dear Gorganis, that you will fall into my trap without even knowing it." he let out an evil laugh that would have made even the wicked Viviane herself turn green with envy.

Amber tossed in his sleep, almost as if his mind could sense the plotting going on in the room across the hall. Suddenly he sat up in bed, heavy sweat forming on his brow.

"Father," he whispered, shaking Dhin awake. "There is evil in this house. I am afraid Caw knows why we are here. He thinks we have a treasure hidden and is planning how to take our parcel away from us."

One look at his son's face told Dhin that the young man had seen a vision in his sleep. He was greatly concerned that Caw might find his book. He knew that the Saxon must be stopped at all cost. After thinking for a moment he said, "Then our only escape is to tell him who we are."

"How is that going to release us from that tyrant?" Amber questioned, "He will just have more cause to keep us here, in the hopes that one of our men will pay a high ransom for our return."

"Ah, but that is where his greed will come in." his father explained, "If he thinks we have a great treasure hidden somewhere around here, he will let us go in the hopes of following us to it. Then he can have it and the ransom too. But we shall fool him for that is when we will escape." Dhin lay back down and said in a low whisper, "Yes that is what we will do. But first things first. We will let him wonder a while longer until the camp is free from its sickness." Before Amber could say anymore, the old man was fast asleep.

CHAPTER 17

The days following, were spent trying to rid the camp of the germs that had been killing off the slaves. Caw gave them permission to do anything necessary to keep his servants alive. Arlo was in charge of getting the houses and grounds cleaned up. He did his chore with no complaints and would not take any from the soldiers he ordered to help. While the Saxon's scoured the area, Dhin and Amber prepared the medicine for everyone to take and prevent the sickness from entering the body.

It was during this time, while working closely together, that Arlo and Amber became bonded in friendship. To the so called 'son of no birth' it was almost like being back in Larkwood with his friend Allon only better, for the prince was not so arrogant as Amber's childhood friend. It made the heart of Dhin glow with contentment to see these two men, from two different worlds, express such brotherly love for one another. It gave the future the glimmer of hope that kept mankind wanting to go on.

When all the cleaning was done and the medicine taken, Dhin said to the Saxon prince, "Our task is almost accomplished. All that is left now is to convince Caw that the clothing, also diseased, will have to be replaced." He had been careful in his conversations with Arlo, for Walter's spies were always near.

When Dhin approached Caw, he saw that the Saxon was in a merry mood. The Saxon had been happy lately for his hand was near healed and the pain was no longer in it.

As his physician came towards him he said aloud, "Here comes my left hand man." The soldiers around him gave out a hardy laugh at their king's sense of humor.

"If I might have a word with you my lord." Dhin said, "There is something we must talk about." After Caw waved the others to leave and they were alone, Dhin continued, "I will need a bag of gold my lord." he said.

The Saxon's eyes went wide, "A bag of gold! What makes you request such a thing?" he asked.

"You have asked that your servants be spared from the death that has struck your camp." Dhin answered. "I have been successful in eliminating the cause, but to keep it from coming back, all the servants' clothing will have to be burned and new ones obtained. If this is not done the germ that caused the sickness will return." Dhin watched the warlord's face as he finished explaining.

Caw sat thoughtful, his good hand stroking his beard, while he pondered over what Dhin had told him.

"I have heard all about your healing among the slaves." he finally said, "They are even doing their work better. So, if you say it is necessary to burn the clothing then that is what you must do."

Calling Walter over, Caw ordered him to bring the physician as many bags of gold as he would need.

Smiling, Dhin bowed to the Saxon king and turned to leave with a very confused Walter. Waiting at the door was Arlo, with a grin on his face from ear to ear. Falling in step with the old man, they walked behind the Saxon soldier, towards the room where the many treasures of Caw were kept.

After giving them the two bags of gold asked for, Walter returned to the main hall to talk with his king.

"My lord, have you been bewitched by the old physician?" he asked, "Why should you really care what happens to the slaves of your camp? When they die we can just go out and capture some more as we have always done."

"You have found nothing to tell me who this man of medicine really is, so I have come up with a plan." Caw answered with the fire of mischief in his eyes. "I want the good physician to think that the Saxon king is mellowing so he will accept the next part of my scheme." He took Walter's arm and headed for the door. "Now here is what I want you to do. The speech I am going to give tonight, you will tell to our soldiers now. Pick ten of my best men and tell them of my plan. They will seem to leave camp in order to follow another Saxon warrior. In reality they will hide in the forest overlooking the village. They must be very careful not to let the hills men see them for then our pigeon could be warned."

The two men walked out the door arm in arm as the plotting for Dhin's downfall thickened.

When Dhin and Arlo returned from the village with their supplies, the servants were told to disrobe and wash thoroughly before putting on the clean clothing. When they were through, the infected garments were gathered together and placed in a pile in the middle of the large courtyard. Even Caw was there, standing beside Dhin with Walter close behind him. All the servants were standing around the yard looking like different people in their clean new clothing. Amber lit a torch and handed it to Arlo who flung it onto the top of the pile. As the flames shot high in the air, it gave an eerie glow to the area, mixing with the semi-darkness that came with the falling dusk. All watching stood in solemn silence, caught up in the effect the dancing fire emitted. Suddenly, like one great voice, the shout of victory resounded through out the valley as the servants began dancing, joyfully around the fire.

"You have made your people happy, my lord." said Dhin turning to Caw. Catching the Saxon king off guard, the old man thought he saw the fire of anger shooting from the other's eyes.

Caw recovered his composure quickly as he said; "It was not I who cleared away the pestilence. You, Gorganis, are the hero today." He sighed deeply, "You have taught me the one thing my son has been trying to make me see for some time now."

"What is that my lord?" questioned Dhin.

"When kindness is handed out, service is given with a happy heart." he looked into the face of the old man standing by his side and proceeded to put on the best lie of his life. "I cannot stop the invasion of the Saxon people. Not because I do not want to but because it is impossible. Yet I can and will stop my own slaughter of your people here in this camp. I will be happy to rule the area around Galava and restore it to its original beauty. We will get back to the matter of living in peace and friendship."

Caw saw the expected doubtful look in Dhin's eyes and turned to Walter. "Have all my soldiers gather in the main hall right after the evening meal. I will speak to them of matters which will be of great importance." the merriment twinkled in the Saxon king's eyes and Walter had all he could do keeping a serious face. Caw then moved around to face Dhin again.

"Will you take your meal with me Gorganis?" he asked.

"It would be an honor my lord," Dhin answered "but I have promised the village innkeeper I would eat with him. I will be back in time to hear what it is you have to tell your soldiers."

"Very well, at that time you will see kindness has really reached my heart." Caw then walked off towards the main house.

Arlo and Amber had arrived at Dhin's side to hear Caw's last words. "What did my father mean by that?" the Saxon prince asked as they headed towards the village.

While they walked, Dhin noticed they were being followed by two of Caw's soldiers. He told the young men what had transpired between him and the Saxon king, making sure his voice was kept low.

"Can this be possible?" Amber asked the other young man. "Do you thing your father has really had a change of heart?"

Arlo shook his head, "It is but a trick." he said in a solemn voice. "I fear he is planning to trap you somehow."

"Do you think it is wise to carry out our plan?" Amber said to his father who was now deep in thought.

By this time they had reached the inn. As they sat at one of the tables, Arlo noticed that the two men sat at the one next to them. Now they would have to wait until their return trip to continue their talk.

To the disappointment of the soldiers, the three men they were sent to spy on ate their meal without any conversation. When they were done Arlo paid the innkeeper and they headed back to the fortress. Once outside, Amber asked his father again about their plan.

"I have thought it over and have come to the conclusion that we will have to hope our plan will work. There is no other choice for one way or the other, Caw will soon find out who we really are." Dhin then told Arlo that he was Lord Dhin and the young man called 'Yata' was his son Ambrosius.

"The only chance for us to escape is to tell Caw our true identity." the old man declared as they walked through the fortress gates.

The Saxon king was waiting for them in the main hall with his soldiers sitting around him. When the three men entered, he motioned for them to sit next to him at the head of the great table. Servants were passing among the men, filling their goblets with wine and there was the din of voices as they conversed with each other.

Caw stood and raised his hands for silence. "I have come to a decision." he stated, "It will affect all of you gathered here tonight. I will no longer need an army of fighting force. I am going to settle here in Galava and be happy to rule the people with kindness and wisdom. Any of my men who wish to feel the sword of war still in his hands will be free to leave my camp and join some other Saxon leader. Those of you, who will remain with their king, shall be the garrison of the castle I intend to build on the hill behind this fortress. You will decide what you will do. If you leave, Walter will see that you are given your payment before your departure." As the Saxon king sat down, finished with his speech, a mumbling arose in the room. Then, ten men that had been sitting together at the end of the table stood and came towards the king.

"My lord," said the spokesman for the group. "We feel our blood still yearns for the cry of battle. Only for that reason do we wish to leave the court of Caw."

"So be it." Caw answered with a smile. "If the day comes when you tire of that life, you will be welcomed back into my presence." he nodded to the men and they left with Walter to receive their payment. "Is there anyone else who wishes to leave?" when there was no answer Caw said, "Very well, you may all return to your duties."

Soon the great hall was empty except for Caw, Arlo, Dhin and Amber.

After calling for more wine from his servant, the Saxon king said, "Gorganis, you have the same choice as my soldiers. You may stay at my court as its physician, or you can be on your way. What ever you wish." Caw's heart was beating so fast anticipating the answer that he was afraid all there could hear it.

"Father, I cannot believe it is really you." Arlo said the words he knew his father would expect to hear. "I have been trying to show you what kindness can do and you always called me a weakling. Now you are going to stop your war against the Britons and rebuild their village. What has come over you?"

"You are not happy with the change, my son?" Caw asked.

"Of course I am but I fear for your sanity." Arlo answered.

"There is nothing to fear," Caw stated, "I have just come to my senses. I am not getting any younger. I want to settle into a place and I also what my son to rule my kingdom after I am gone. You have said you want no part in oppressing the people of this land, so I have stopped oppressing. Will you now claim your title of Prince?" When Arlo gave no answer Caw said, "I see you need time to think things over. Very well, you do not have to give me an answer yet." he turned back to Dhin, "Well, man of medicine, have you made a choice?"

"My work here is at an end." he answered, "Tomorrow you will be able to rid yourself of the bandages that cover your healed hand. As long as you keep the houses and grounds clean and feed your servants and their children the proper food, the disease will not return." Dhin answered.

"Then you will be leaving us?" Caw tried to keep calm, for the next step in his plan was coming near. "Before you go, will you tell me who you really are?" Now he would know if he had been able to fool the old man.

Dhin hesitated for a moment, like he was trying to decide if he should reveal this secret to the Saxon. Only Amber recognized the gleam in his father's eyes.

"I am called Dhin, Lord of Logan Manor in the village of Meridunum, and this is my son Ambrosius." said Dhin proudly.

"You are a nobleman!" Arlo exclaimed, happy that he sounded so surprised.

"A nobleman, passing himself off as a physician?" there was more disappointment in Caw's voice then there was surprise. He had been convinced his physician was the mighty Merlin he had heard so much about.

"Why would you pass yourself off as a man of medicine?" he asked still not sure the old man was telling him the truth. "Surely you were not sent here by Arthur to spy on us."

"If Arthur wanted to spy on you," Dhin answered, "he would have sent a man who is known for that kind of work. We came because we discovered Gorfan, my servant and herb maker, had escaped to this area." Dhin waited for the next question he knew Caw would ask.

"You went to all that trouble just to find a runaway slave?" the Saxon king eyed him with distrust. "Surely Lord Dhin, you must know you can now trust me with the truth. I said you are free to go and nothing you may tell me can change that." Caw sat on the edge of his chair waiting for Dhin's next words.

"When Gorfan left my house, he took something of value with him." was his reply. "We came hoping to reclaim it. But the servant died before he could tell me where it was hidden. We searched his house but found nothing, so our only choice is to return home and hope whoever finds it will benefit from it."

"This is an interesting story." Caw mused, "You must be very rich to be content and return home without it."

"We are not rich but manage to make ends meet by selling our crops in the village." Dhin explained, "Our time is precious as it is near the planting season and we will have a poor crop if we do not get home soon."

"Very well my friend, you are free to leave whenever you wish." Caw rose and feigned a yawn, saying "I fear that the excitement of this day has tired me. I will say good-bye now for I will not see you in the morning."

Once in his room, Caw motioned for Walter to be silent until he was sure the physician and his son were in their bed chamber. He then said, "Well my friend, it seems they have fallen into my trap. Have the men left?"

"Yes my lord," his faithful soldier answered, "and the two you will have following the old man will be ready in the morning. I told them they are to be sure they are seen."

Caw let out a laugh, "Perfect, Lord Dhin will think the men following them are the only spies and not be aware that the soldiers who left tonight are waiting for them in the hills." He laughed again as he raised his goblet of wine to toast the success of their great plan.

In the morning, when Dhin and Amber were ready to leave, Arlo was there to bid them a safe journey. "Be careful, my lord, for you do not know the true depth of my father's treachery. I fear he is out to get your treasure and nothing will stop him." Arlo's face clearly showed all the concern that weighed on his heart.

"We will be on our guard. There are friends waiting in the hills to see us safely away." Dhin said, then looking at Amber he added, "I am also protected by a brave and powerful son who is know as the Red Warrior. He even killed a giant and freed the people of the nearby village. One day, when he returns to the court of Arthur, he will be proclaimed the king's own knight." The pride in his voice could only be that of a father for his son.

"That is one story I would like to hear some day." said the Saxon prince as he took Amber's hand,

"I am proud to have known such a brave man." he said as he held his friend's hand tightly.

"May the gods watch over you as you ride off into this adventure." Arlo said to Dhin, "Before you depart, remember if anything should happen and you once again become the prisoners of Caw, I will be there to help you. Good-by my friends and god speed." Arlo turned and hurried away before his friends could see the tears in his eyes.

Dhin and Amber mounted the two steeds Caw had given them and slowly headed their horses towards the gate, saying good-bye and shaking the hands of the servants as they went by.

Caw stood watching from the window of his bed chamber. "So, my Lord Dhin, you would have me believe that your treasure is lost and you have no interest in finding it."

He turned his attention to the two Saxons below his window. As he signaled to them, they rode out after the departing Britons.

"Soon, your great treasure will be mine. Then we will see just how rich you really are, when your household gets the news of your confinement until a large ransom is paid." the Saxon king laughed loudly as he watched the horses slip past the gate.

"So, it was all a trick." Caw turned on his heels to see his son standing in the door.

"Well I will not let you get away with it. I am going to warn Lord Dhin and his son of your plans." as Arlo started to leave he found his way barred by the massive build of Walter who had come in behind him.

"See that my son is detained." Caw said to the Saxon. "We cannot have him running off our pigeon just when our magnificent trap is about to be sprung."

"You would lock your own son in the dungeon for some gold?" Arlo was shocked that his father could do such a thing.

"You will be kept there until Lord Dhin is in my hands again, for then it will be too late for your warnings." Caw said gleefully.

The laughter from his father's lips followed Arlo down the stairs as Walter dragged him to the dark dungeon below the main house. Even after the soldier's footsteps faded away in the darkness, the young man could still hear that evil laughter. Throwing himself down on the straw bed he cried out in anguish. He was more ashamed of his failure to help his friends, than of the tears he was shedding.

CHAPTER 18

As Dhin and Amber rode away from the fortress, the old man moved his horse to his son's side. "It is just as I thought, Caw is having us followed." he said.

"Well, that is what you expected. What do we do now?" the young man asked.

"It is evident we cannot ride to meet Edgar. We will have to make it seem as if we are going to stay at the village inn until tomorrow." said Dhin. "Then when the night is at its darkest we will leave on foot for the forest at the top of the hill. In this way we will evade our watch dogs."

Amber laughed at the prospect of fooling the Saxons. He also marveled at the fact that his father never ran out of ideas. Then, as he saw the mountain in the distance he remembered the talk they had about the future of Britain.

"Father," he said thought fully, "when the Saxons rule the land what will happen to our lands in Meridunum. It fills my heart with remorse to think that the invaders might be lodging in our manor."

"It will be some time before Wales is conquered by the foreigners and will not happen in your lifetime, nor in your son's lifetime. That is if you should ever have a son." Dhin laughed at his son's embarrassment. "You mean to tell me you have not thought of taking a wife or of having children." Dhin teased the young man.

"You know there has been but one woman in my life and she was just a friend of my youthful days. I have no wish for any other companionship but that of my father and the friends I have around me." Amber's face grew red as he spurred his horse to a running pace, keeping his father from continuing the subject any further.

Once at the inn, as the stable boy took their horses, Dhin looked to see the two Saxons riding into the village. After he and his son were seated and drinking their mugs of ale, the spies came through the door of the inn. Seeing Dhin and Amber near the fire, the men found a table in the corner of the room and ordered mugs of ale from the innkeeper.

"Landlord," Dhin called loudly, "my son and I wish to rent a room. We are returning to our home in the morning and wish to say our farewells to the good people of Galava."

"You are the physician, who has rid the fortress of its sickness, are you not?" the man's eyes were wide with excitement.

"That is who I am, my good man." Dhin answered.

The rest of the day was spent visiting with the people of the village. Some wanted healing medicine; others just wanted to see the man who had helped bring peace to their valley. By dusk they were back at the inn, eating a meal of mutton and cheese. The innkeeper brought out his best wine and all toasted the good physician. The celebrating went on into the night. Dhin and Amber drank sparingly of the wine for it would do their plan no good if they were to fall asleep.

"It is time for us to go." Dhin whispered to his son. Amber looked over to where the two soldiers were and saw that the Saxons were sprawled across the table sleeping off the effects of the wine.

Slipping unseen out of the back door, father and son crept away from the village on foot. When they came to the hill overlooking Galava, Dhin motioned to his son that there was someone following them. Amber took out his dagger as both men stepped behind a tree. Soon the rustling of leaves came to a stop on the other side of their hiding place.

"My lord Dhin?" the words were spoken by a very young voice in the language of the old tongue.

The two men, daggers in hand, stepped out from behind the tree and came face to face with the young boy Amber had helped on their way to the Saxon camp.

"We thought you were one of Caw's men." Amber said, relieved that it was not.

"I was in the village and saw them watching you. Edgar gave me some red liquid to put in their wine." he grinned at them. "It worked well, yes?"

The two men joined the boy in his laughter over the trick he had played on the Saxons.

"My name is Wallin." He said, and then led them into the woods towards the temple.

After a short visit at the grave of Gorfan and Morlan, they continued on their way without stopping. By the first rays of dawn, they were within sight of the stone ruins.

The temple was nothing like the one that had been Amber's home for ten years. It had no stairs as it sat flat on the ground and there were no doors, only openings in the massive stone. The main section of the building was still in one piece, while the back, which had been used for sleeping quarters, lay in a rubble of rocks. It was an eerie sight and Amber felt a shiver run through his body as they walked towards the awesome structure.

As they entered, Edgar came from out of the shadows with open arms. "My lords, how happy I am to see you. After all that has happened, I was afraid I would never look upon your faces again. The hills men had ways of knowing all that went on in the fortress and had kept me well informed."

"Now Edgar, there was nothing to worry about for the gods were always with us. Although I must admit that there were times, I myself was worried." Dhin said as the servant stood grinning at them.

"Father, there is the altar." Amber cried out with excitement.

Behind Edgar stood the remains of an altar. All that was left was half of the large slab, making it look like someone had chopped it in two with a giant sword. As they searched around the stone, Dhin told Edgar about Gorfan hiding the book somewhere in the stone slab.

"It's here, it's here!" Amber's voice came from out of the shadows.

160

He was laying at the back of the stone with his arm part way into a large crack on the side of the altar.

As Dhin hurried over to him, the young man pulled his hand out and produced the leather bag. Inside was the book they had been looking for. The old man helped his son to his feet and smiled with happiness as Amber handed him the book.

Suddenly Dhin's smile turned to bewilderment as the sound of shouting from the woods reached his ears. Wallin came running, all excited, into the building.

"My lords, you must flee. The Saxon soldiers are coming up the hill towards this place. The woods are full of them there may be twenty. Run, run for your lives." he yelled as he scampered out the back opening.

"It is a trap." Amber shouted, "Caw knew all along that we would see the two men following and once we were rid of them we would feel safe enough to find the treasure."

Dhin placed the book back into its leather bag and shoved it into his son's hands. "Edgar, take master Ambrosius and hurry from this danger. I shall run off into the woods to attract their attention." Dhin said to his servant.

"Father, no!" cried Amber, "If anyone should lead them off it must be me. I am younger and can run faster."

"My son, I did not tell you that on the night we left our home, I saw in the flames the death of someone near to me." Dhin said trying to convince his son to leave. "It was not myself as I saw my own form standing over the body. You must obey me and leave now. I know that harm will not come to me. Go now, before it is too late."

Amber wanted to refuse but the look on his father's face and the sound of his voice made him do as he was told. Edgar brought Pegasus to the back of the structure while Amber placed the book beneath his belt. Then, mounting his horse, he followed the servant away from the temple.

As they left they heard the shouts of the Saxons, "Do not harm them, Caw wants them alive. Both of them."

Then Amber heard one of the men call to the others, "Here, this way men. There goes the old man off into the woods." With a clatter of hoofs, the Saxons rode out after Dhin.

Amber reared up Pegasus and before Edgar could stop him he was following his father's pursuers. Just as the soldiers caught up with Dhin, Amber came charging at them from out of the trees. Taken by surprise, two of the Saxons fell mortally wounded from the angry young man's sword.

"No, no my son, go back!" yelled Dhin, "There are too many!"

By now there was a full force confrontation of soldiers on one side and Amber with a few of the hills men on the other. Dhin's warnings came too late for as Edgar came upon the clearing, the sight before him was that of a young man lying in a pool of blood. The Saxons were at full gallop with the old man in their grasps, leaving his son for dead.

Edgar jumped from his horse and looked at the men lying on the ground. The two Saxons were dead, as were the hills men that had tried to help free Lord Dhin. The servant ran over to Amber's side.

"Young master," he cried out, "how could you have been so foolish."

As he held what he thought was a dead body, Edgar suddenly realized there was a heart still beating. With the leader of the hills men helping, the servant managed to get Amber onto Pegasus' back.

Soon they were riding deeper into the mountainous forest, where no man dared to roam. When Amber finally opened his eyes, he was laying on some straw in a fire lit cave. Edgar had just finished tying a bandage around his middle to keep the wound in the young man's side from losing any more blood.

"Where are we?" Amber asked. For a moment he thought he was at another place in time and looked around for Reena.

"We are in the caves of the men of the hills tribe." Edgar replied. "The Saxons will not find you here." As the servant gave Amber a sip of wine the young man's mind came back to the present.

Slowly as he came back to the world of reality, Amber's thoughts turned to his father's capture. He started sobbing so hard he caused the wound to bleed again.

"Your father will be all right. His sight is never wrong." said Edgar, trying to comfort the young man and therefore stop the bleeding. "He has told me his son has the sight also. Why do you not try and see what is happening in the Saxon camp."

Amber stopped sobbing and stared at the servant, "You are right. I was so put out at the loss of my father I had forgotten the power that is in me."

He rose to his feet and, like already in a trance, staggered to the cave entrance.

"Master Ambrosius, you must not move until the wound heals." Edgar called after him.

"I will be all right." Amber answered from the opening in the cave. "I must find a lofty place where I will be able to communicate with the gods."

In the warm sunlight, Amber stood for a moment to get a look at the land around him. High above the mouth of the cave, the mountain rose straight up, leading to a flat ledge at the very top.

Amber wrapped his cloak tightly around his body and started to climb up the rocks. Sharp fragments dug into his hands as he scaled the steep bank. Blood came from the cuts they caused, but he went on as if they were not there. Soon he reached the ledge at the top and as he sat on the protruding rock trying to catch his breath, he saw in the far off distance, little dots that were the houses of Galava.

Concentrating on this, he let himself be drawn into the vastness of space that separated him from his father.

Suddenly the pounding came to his head as he felt the clouds closing in around him. Without realizing what he was doing, Amber stood up on the ledge and stretched his arms out as if he were embracing the heavens themselves, oblivious to his wounded body. The clouds grew thicker and the wind picked up, blowing the cloak he was wearing. He stood like this for some time, communing with the gods, looking like a god himself.

Then as quickly as it started, the wind stopped. Amber's body dropped down on the rock as he tried to clear the vision from his head. Slowly he raised himself to his feet and climbed back down to where Edgar was waiting.

As he reached the flat ground again, all the men of the hills tribe kneeled and stretched their hands out towards him.

"What are they doing?" he asked Edgar.

"They saw you standing on the ledge above." the servant explained, "They say you are one of the gods, like your father and they are pledging their life to you as they did to him. I must say, the sight of you with your cloak blowing like there was a wind, impressed even me."

After leading Amber back into the cave, Edgar got the goatskin of wine and poured some into a wooden bowl which he handed to the young man. Then he tended to the cut hands and wounded side of his young master.

"Is your father all right?" the servant asked.

"They have taken him back to the fortress," Amber answered, "where the Saxon king is questioning him. They have not harmed him yet as Caw hopes to get the item of value that my father foolishly said he lost."

"Your father is a wise man." Edgar said with anger, then seeing that the young man had not meant any disrespect, he added, "He will keep the Saxon dangling until we can rescue him."

"At least he has one friend among the enemy." Amber said, "Arlo will see to it that he has food and wine. I must some how get a message to the prince so he can let my father know I am alive."

"This prince could have been in on his father's trap. How can you be so sure he is a friend and will help you?" Edgar voiced his concern.

"Because I saw that my father was placed in a cell where they had locked Arlo so he would not be able to warn us of his father's treachery." Amber answered. "I also heard as Caw ordered his son to stay away from the prisoner. There was anger in the eyes of the Saxon king and the threat of a tyrant in his voice. But I know Arlo will risk all to make sure my father is treated well."

Amber stood on shaking legs and started to leave the cave once again. "We must go back to Galava and wait for Arlo. He will try contacting me so plans for my father's rescue can be made." he said.

"You must rest first," the servant insisted. "As the traces of your vision are still on your face. You will do your father no good if you should fall from the back of your horse. We will leave when the sun sets, for there will be less chance of being seen." Edgar helped the young man to lie back down.

"You are right my friend. The pounding is still in my head." he said and was soon drifting among the clouds again.

As the servant laid down for some rest, the hills men sat among the cliffs keeping a watch on the woods around the cave.

Suddenly Amber let out a cry of anguish as he jumped to his feet. Edgar, not knowing what had happened, ran to his side with his dagger drawn.

"Master Ambrosius, what is it?" the servant asked as he looked around the cave.

Amber sat back down on the straw and with his arms wrapped around himself, began rocking back and forth. The servant brought the bowl of wine and tried to force some between the lips of the sobbing man. Finally he managed to make Amber drink and then helped him to lay back down on the straw. Soon he was fast asleep with the servant watching over him, wondering what had caused his young master such grief.

For the next few hours Edgar tended Amber as the young man tossed around on the straw. He wrapped him in a fur cover and kept a wet cloth on his head trying to keep him still so the wound in his side would not start to bleed again.

All the while Amber murmured "Oh father, my father!" over and over again.

Finally, after what seemed like a lifetime to Edgar, Amber opened his eyes. This made the servant even more frightened as there was a glassy look in the two black pools. The expression on the young man's face sent chills through Edgar's body.

"Master Ambrosius. It is I, your servant Edgar. Do you not know me?" he said as he bent over the stricken man, "Please Ambrosius, answer me."

Amber turned to face the servant, "Oh Edgar," he said in a weak voice, "I saw who is to die, and by his father's sword." he put his hands over his face, trying to blot out the memory of his vision.

"No, no!" cried Edgar shaking Amber so his hands fell back down on the straw. "Your father would rather die himself than ever do you any harm. You must have been mistaken."

The young man's face was white with horror. "No, not my father." he said with a hollow sound in his voice.

"Who then?" Edgar shook the young man again, trying to bring him back to his own world. "Ambrosius, you must tell me, who is going to die?"

"Arlo," came the young man's words, "by the sword of Caw." he then slipped back into the sea of clouds.

CHAPTER 19

When Amber opened his eyes again, he saw Edgar sleeping propped up against the wall of the cave. The fire in the middle of the floor was nearly out. For a moment he could not remember where he was or what had happened. Then as the memories drifted back into his head, he let out a moan. The servant jumped to his feet and rushed to Amber's side.

"Master Ambrosius, are you all right?" he said as he placed his hand on the young man's forehead.

"Poor Edgar, I must have filled your heart with great fear." Amber said, "I am sorry my friend, but as my father has often stated, there are times when you cannot control a vision." He sat up slowly, his head throbbing with pain.

"My only fear was for your life." said Edgar, "It seemed as if the sight had made you lose your mind."

"The ranting I did was from the deep grief of finding out that Arlo was going to die." the young man explained.

"There is no mistake then? Caw is going to kill his own son?" the servant said looking sadly at Amber.

"I saw the Saxon king standing over the body of Arlo with the blood of his son still fresh upon the sword in his hand." Amber spoke with great emotion.

"You must push it from your mind." said Edgar, getting ready for their journey into Galava. "Perhaps there is some way to foil the fates." he added.

"Of course!" said Amber, his face lighting up. "I should have remembered. Long ago, when I had my first vision, the village of Yata was going to be invaded by Votan. Preventive measures were taken and instead of dying like in my vision, the people hid in the hills and the only damage was done to the houses. If we can warn Arlo, we may be able to save his life." The knowledge that his vision could be changed took a great burden off the young man's shoulders and in no time at all he was ready to leave.

The moon was high in the heavens when the two men left the cave to journey to Galava. It was by this lunar light that Amber was able to see the beauty of the land around them as they rode towards the temple. The caves were high in the mountains and they had to watch their step going down. The forest was thick with trees and underbrush and there was no path to follow. Yet the men of the hills tribe led the way as if they could see through the tangled limbs, missing any ruts or rocks that might cause the horses to stumble.

When they reached the temple, they were not surprised to see that the remaining half of the altar was now laying in shambles. The Saxons had torn the stones apart looking for Dhin's treasure.

"What are you going to do with the book, Master Ambrosius?" Edgar asked as they sat to rest. "Do you think it will be safe to take it with you? If you are captured it will fall into Caw's hands."

"Edgar, when this book was first and last in my hands, I was but eleven years of age. Now that I have it again, I am not going to let it out of my sight. But you are right; I will have to think of a good place to hide it." Amber sat peering into the sky, looking for an answer. Suddenly the sound of Pegasus pawing the ground made him jump to his feet.

Edgar looked startled. Ever since Amber's vision the servant was very jumpy. "Are you all right?" he asked in almost a whisper.

Amber laughed and said, "Just fine." then walked over to his horse. Taking the saddle off Pegasus, he turned it upside down on the ground. The padding there was very thick to protect the horses back from the rough leather. Using his dagger, the young man made a slit along the edge just wide enough to slip the bag containing the book into it. He then took some grass like reeds that grew near by. Weaving them back and forth across the slit, he closed the opening.

When done, he said to Edgar, "Well my friend, no one would ever guess the great treasure I will be sitting on." Both men laughed as Amber put the saddle back on Pegasus.

"Now there is just the matter of coming up with a plan." said Edgar, "We cannot just ride into Galava as big as life. We will have to make sure no one sees us."

"You are wrong." Amber said smiling at the man. "No one has seen your face as you have been hiding in the forest. You will be able to go into the village and keep your ears open for any information about my father and you must find some way to get in touch with Arlo. The sooner my father learns I am alive, the better. I will wait for you in the woods overlooking the valley."

"But it will not be safe for you to be there alone." Edgar said concerned over his master's well being.

"I will not be alone. The men of the hills tribe will protect me. After all, am I not their god?" Amber grinned at the bewildered servant.

Edgar sat thinking things over. "Very well, we will do things your way." he finally said.

When they reached the hill overlooking the village, Amber watched as Edgar rode away. Riding beside him, on Dhin's horse, was the young boy Wallin.

"May the gods look down and keep you both from harm." Amber whispered.

The hills men stood guard over their 'god' while he rested under the trees. It had been a long time since he had slept so soundly. When Amber woke, the sun was high in the heavens. One of the men came over to him with some bread and what was left of the wine. As he sat eating and looking out over the valley, a horse could be seen riding fast towards the hill. As it got closer, he saw it was Wallin.

"Master!" he said to Amber as he jumped from the horse. "Edgar has found the innkeeper to be friendly to our cause. At dusk we are to go on foot down to the village, to the back entrance of the inn. The innkeeper is going to keep you hidden from the Saxon soldiers."

"Did Edgar say if he saw Prince Arlo?" Amber asked.

"He has not seen him yet. But from the talk going around, he learned that the prince usually comes just before meal time to get your father some food. Edgar said he will see him then." the boy explained.

Suddenly Amber was looking at the lad with a startled expression. "You are speaking the language of the Britons!" he said with amazement.

Wallin laughed, "While we were waiting for your return from the fortress of Caw, Edgar said I could serve you better if I knew your language. He is a very good teacher, yes?"

"That he is." smiled Amber with affection, "How lucky I am to have you both in my service."

Wallin sat with Amber and waited for the night to come. It seemed like an eternity before the sun finally went down behind the hills and the moon rose to take its place. The illumination from the golden ball in the black sky gave Amber just enough light to see where he was going as he hurried down the hill with Wallin at his side. Near the village they slowed their pace making sure they were not seen and reached the inn without meeting anyone. Soon they were safe in the back room with Edgar and the innkeeper Hector.

"Master Ambrosius," Hector said as he poured the wine. "it is the greatest pleasure to have you under my roof once again. Edgar has told me of the hardship that your father is suffering. I will do anything in my power to help with his rescue."

"Thank you Hector, but we can do nothing until we talk with Arlo." Turning to Edgar, Amber said, "Have you seen him?"

"Yes, but he could not talk as there were too many eyes watching him." the servant explained, "He did manage slipping a message to the innkeeper, saying that he would be back after the soldiers bedded down for the night."

"I must leave you now." said Hector, moving towards the door. "I will be missed by the Saxons if I stay here too long. When the inn is empty, I will return."

"It will not be much longer." Edgar said to Amber as he handed him a plate of food. "Here is some mutton and cheese. You must be hungry."

Amber took the piece of meat. "All the hills men had was bread and a little wine." he said, "It is good to taste a bit of meat again."

After he felt his hunger satisfied, Amber turned to the boy who had been sitting quietly by the door. "Well, Wallin, how fares your foot?" he asked.

"It has healed nicely, sir." the boy answered, "If it were not for you I would have been a meal for the hungry bears that roam the woods."

"And what bear in his right mind would eat such a scrawny meal as you." laughed Edgar teasing the boy.

Suddenly Wallin stiffened in his chair. "I am sure Edgar meant no harm, lad." said Amber.

But the boy put his finger to his lips, motioning them to be silent. Soon voices were heard in the hall on the other side of the door.

"I tell you, my lord, there is no one in there except a man of the church and his boy servant." came the sound of Hector's voice.

"We will see for ourselves." boomed another voice with a Saxon drawl.

In the time it takes a flash of lightning to reach the earth from its home in the sky, Amber was shoved under the large bed that stood against the wall. As the door flung open the sight before the Saxons was that of a man in a hooded cloak, kneeling on the floor with his hands resting on the bed in prayer. There was a young boy, also kneeling, at his side.

"What is the meaning of this?" Edgar called out as he turned around to meet the intruders. "I have paid you well for this room, landlord. I told you that the boy and I would be in prayer all night and did not wish to be disturbed. I hope you have a good explanation."

"I am sorry my lord." came a voice Amber recognized as Walter's. "We are searching for the son of Lord Dhin and were told the innkeeper might be hiding him. I see it was a great mistake in thinking the fugitive might be here. May I offer you some gold coins to show my apology?"

"A man of the church can take no payment except for work he has done." said Edgar, not being fooled by the Saxon's trick. "But if you wish to make amends, you may give the gold to the lad, who will see that a poor family receives some food bought with them." Edgar then turned his back on the soldiers and returned to his praying. Wallin rose and taking the coins from Walter left the room. Walter and his Saxon soldiers left also.

"They are gone." whispered the servant after hearing the door close behind them.

"I will remain until the lad returns just to be safe." Amber whispered back.

It was not long before Edgar heard the door open again. As he turned he saw the face of Wallin with a grin that stretched from one ear to the other. "It is safe to come out now." he called to Amber as he handed the gold coins to Edgar. After quite a struggle, trying to get out from under the bed, Amber was finally sitting on the floor looking up at Edgar.

"Remind me to find a better hiding place the next time we hear voices in the hall." he laughed, as Wallin and Edgar helped him to his feet.

They sat down in front of the fire and waited for Hector. Soon someone knocked on the door. Two raps, a pause, then one more rap. It was the innkeeper.

"There are no more soldiers left in the inn." said Hector as he came through the door. From behind him came the sound of footsteps and as Amber's hand went to his dagger, the Saxon Prince walked into the room.

"Arlo!" Amber cried, going over to embrace his friend. "It is good to see you again. How is my father?"

"He is well for the time being. Knowing you are alive has lifted his spirits." the prince answered. "But Caw is getting impatient and is thinking that torture will loosen his tongue. We will have to rescue him within the next few days or I fear it will be too late."

As the young man sat with them in front of the fire, Amber told him of his vision and that it could be prevented if Arlo stayed away from Caw.

"That will be impossible." Arlo said, "For I am the only one that can get your father out of the dungeon where Caw is keeping him. I have made friends with the soldier who guards him and feel sure that some gold will buy his help. But I am afraid he will panic if he should see the face of a Briton instead of mine."

"But how can you get Lord Dhin out by yourself?" asked Edgar.

"If you can get some brave men to back us up, we can attack the camp in force. While the soldiers are kept busy, I will free Lord Dhin and hurry him out of the fortress." Arlo explained.

"That is a foolhardy plan." said Amber, "The soldiers will cut us down before we can break in through the main gate."

"There is no need to use the gate." said the prince. "I was exploring the hills behind the fortress and came upon some caves. Deciding I needed some adventure, I went into one of them and found a long tunnel at the back wall. You can imagine my surprise when I discovered it led to the food cellars below the main house. No one else in camp knows about it. The only danger is that the dungeon is under the front part of the house, while the cellar is in the rear and there is no passage way connecting them."

"Then you will have to bring my father into the upper part of the house before you can lead him through the tunnel." Amber said shaking his head. "I do not like that part of the plan. If Caw sees you trying to escape with his prisoner, he will surely kill you and that is what I saw in my vision."

"Do not worry so, for it can be done. We will have all the men enter the courtyard from the cellar where they will be in position to attack the barracks." said the young Saxon. "As long as he sees no one coming towards the main house, Caw will be content to watch from his bed chamber window. During the confusion, I will be able to accomplish my task. When I have Lord Dhin safely in the hills, the fighting men can make their way out the gate which will be open for them."

"I can open the gate." Wallin said excitedly.

"You are too young to get involved in a man's battle." said Amber, ruffling the boy's hair.

"Maybe we should let him." said Arlo, "A small figure such as he could go unnoticed while a larger man would be seen and cut down."

And so they talked on through the night, mostly arguing about the soundness of the plan. Finally Arlo said, "We will have to decide for the sun will soon be up and I will be missed." He looked at Amber for an answer.

"Let us meet when night comes again. That will give Hector and Edgar time to see if there are enough men to follow us." said Amber.

"Very well, until then." Arlo embraced Amber and hurried out the door.

There was time for a rest before Hector would have to open the inn. But none of the men left in the room could find sleep. Shortly Edgar and the innkeeper left Amber to complete their task. Alone with Wallin,

Amber wished he had not been in such a hurry to hide the book. Now would have been a good time for him to read it. He had told the leader of the hills men that above all else, he must be sure to keep Pegasus safe.

Time dragged by as the impatient young man paced the floor waiting for his friends to return. Once or twice he had started for the door only to hear Saxon voices in the hall causing him to reconsider his action. Wallin had curled up on the bed and was fast asleep. His youthful mind at ease as it had no comprehension of the coming danger its body was about to face.

Then, when Amber thought he would go mad with anxiety, there came the familiar rapping on the door. When it opened, all three of his friends came in.

"It is all set Master Ambrosius." said Edgar. "We were able to get fifty men to follow us."

"Fifty men? Are you sure that is enough?" Amber asked.

"If they can surround the barracks, then it shall be enough." said Arlo.

"Then we can go right now, tonight." said Edgar, who was eager to rescue Dhin.

"Not tonight but tomorrow night." answered Arlo. "I will need some time to bribe the guard."

"Very well, we will meet in the hills behind the fortress when the sun goes down tomorrow." said Amber. He sat looking at his friend. All the worry he felt in his heart was seen in his eyes. "You are sure there will be enough men for us to free my father?" he asked.

"It will be all right Ambrosius, you shall see. By this time tomorrow, your father will be free." Arlo leaned over and placed his hand on Amber's shoulder.

"I also fear for your life, my friend." Amber said as the picture of Caw standing over the prince burned his memory.

"You said yourself that the vision can be changed. Do not worry; I will stay well away from my father." Arlo then stood and holding a goblet of wine high in the air said, "To success!"

As they all drank to the next night's adventure, Amber's thoughts were still on his vision.

Ah brave prince, his brain whispered inside his head, *will this be the last time I shall drink wine with you? Can another vision be prevented or are we fooling ourselves?*

Amber sat with tears in his eyes as the young Saxon said good-bye.

CHAPTER 20

Amber and Edgar followed Wallin as he led the way to the hills behind the fortress. Hector was getting the men together and would join them later. Just before the moon went behind a cloud, Amber caught the shape of Arlo waiting for them.

"Is everything set?" he asked the young Saxon.

"A bag of gold bought the guard's silence." smiled the prince. "He will turn the other way while I slip your father out of the dungeon. Caw will think he was taken by surprise and forced to open the cell."

As the moon came out from behind the cloud it showed a large group of men coming up the hill with Hector in the lead. They kept close to the ground and moved silently, not wanting to be seen. As Hector joined the waiting men, Arlo turned to lead them towards the cave.

"You did not tell us we would be following a Saxon." came a voice from the crowd. This started the rest of the men to mumbling also.

Amber stood in front of Arlo, facing the men. "You are following a brave man who wishes to free my father from the hands of a tyrant. Does it matter what blood flows in his veins? He is risking his life the same as you, for Caw will not hesitate to cut down even his own man." The men stood in silence with their eyes on the ground. "Now, do we turn back because a Saxon has showed us a way to free Lord Dhin, or shall we go on and meet the enemy?"

"Go on, go on!" said the men excitedly as they pushed forward, falling into step behind the Saxon prince.

Reaching the cave, they found it to be very large with the same formations Amber had seen some time ago. Arlo lit the torches that were laying in a pile on the floor and handed them to the men.

"From here on, we must speak no words, for once in the tunnel the sound of our voices will carry into the main house." Arlo then turned and walked to the back of the cave where the darkness seemed to melt into the wall like a yawning giant.

A chill ran through Amber as he remembered his adventure in the forest of the fairies. This time though, he was not alone. As they came out of the tunnel and into the cellar, the odor of smoked meat and other food reached Amber's nose. His stomach rumbled, telling him that he had been foolish not to have eaten supper.

"Here is where I leave you." Arlo said in a whisper to Amber as he put out his torch in a pail of water. As the men, one by one, doused their torch they were left in an eerie semi-darkness. The little light that engulfed the area came from a door leading to the outside.

"Take the men out that door to the courtyard." said the prince, "Have them get into position around the barracks. Wait until you have counted five hundred heartbeats, and then attack the men inside. There are only five men patrolling the grounds so if you can get to them before they sound the alarm, you will have the other soldiers trapped." With this Arlo disappeared into the dark shadows.

"Edgar, you will lead the men as I have decided to go with Arlo." Amber said and then hurried to catch up with the Saxon.

Hearing footsteps behind him, Arlo turned to his friend and said, "You do not trust me Ambrosius?" there was the sound of hurt pride in his voice.

"With my very life." Amber answered with deep sincerity. "But you will need help if you should meet anyone in the main hall after freeing my father."

Arlo agreed and led Amber up the wooden stairs to the kitchen. Cautiously they crept through the kitchen and into the hall that led to the stone steps in the front of the house, aware that at any moment they could be confronted. But all was still as the household slept, unaware of the rescue attempt going on. Slowly the young Saxon opened the large door that barred their way.

The cold rancid smell of the dungeon filled Amber's nostrils and he cringed at the thought of his father having to be in that environment. Arlo slowed his step as they reached the bottom of the stairs. Approaching the area where Dhin's cell was, the young Saxon signaled to his friend to stay hidden behind one of the stone pillars.

Meanwhile, outside, Edgar and the men were successful in capturing four of the patrolling guards. This was done quickly and silently with a blade to the throat of the victims. Wallin was sent to hide near the gate, ready to open it when the time came. Aware of the danger, the men positioned themselves around the barracks waiting for a signal from Edgar, who stood like a statue counting his beating heart.

Back in the dungeon, Arlo came to the door of Dhin's cell. The guard was sleeping with his head slumped over the table. The young Saxon was just about to wake him when he took a closer look at the man and found it was not the one he had bribed. The prince stood in shock for a moment trying to decide what to do, when his eyes fell on an empty wine bottle next to the man's hand. Picking it up slowly, he raised the bottle high over his head and came down hard on the sleeping Saxon. The sound of the thud resounded through the hollow dungeon as the man fell to the floor, blood trickling from the gash caused by the bottle. The Saxon prince now hurried to the cell with the keys he had taken from the guard and unlocked the heavy door.

"Arlo!" Dhin cried as he jumped to his feet. "I thought it was Caw, coming to carry out his threat."

"He will not threaten you any longer." said Amber as he appeared behind Arlo.

"My son, how did they catch you?" Dhin had not realized that there was no guard with the two young men.

Suddenly the light dawned in his mind, "You are here to free me?" he was almost afraid to say the words in case his first thought had been right and Amber was also a prisoner.

Amber's eyes filled with tears as he realized his father's confinement had drained much of what was left of the old man's life.

Now he knew why his father had not used magic to escape from Caw. The old age that had settled in his body, left him with only the sight and nothing more.

"We must hurry." Arlo said as he took Dhin's arm and led him out of the cell. "It is almost time for the men to attack. We must be in the cellars before they do or we may run into danger in the main hall."

As the three men climbed the stone steps they heard a moan coming from the guard. Hurrying now, they entered the main hall as shouts of the men told them that Edgar had already started the attack.

"I forgot that a man's heart beats faster when he is going into battle." said Arlo, "We are going to be trapped here unless they have managed to restrain the five patrolling guards."

As his friend spoke, Amber closed the heavy door to the dungeon and pushed the hilt of his sword into its latch to keep it shut. "This will prevent one of them from stopping us." he said.

"We must hurry." Arlo said as he quickened his steps and led the way to the kitchen and their escape.

"Ah, so my treasonable son has tried to free the enemy." said Caw as he suddenly appeared in front of the kitchen door, blocking their departure. He had his sword drawn and behind him was the one guard Edgar had not been able to find.

"You take the guard." Amber called to his friend as he pulled a sword down from its place on the wall.

"No!" cried Arlo as he drew his sword from out the sheath strapped to his waist. "I cannot let you kill my father. I will have to take the sin upon myself." Before Amber could stop him, the Saxon prince stepped forward, shielding Dhin from Caw with his own body.

Amber did not have time to stop him as the guard was now advancing. He could think of nothing else as he fought the Saxon with all the skill he had learned at the court of Arthur. Dhin backed against the wall, still weak from his time spent in the little cell. Arlo would not strike his father but kept Caw's sword from cutting him down.

Sweat poured down Amber's face as the sound of clashing steel resounded through the hall. Back and forth across the room each man tried to defeat his opponent. There were a few times when Arlo and Caw came into Amber's line of vision and he could see his friend holding his own against the Saxon king.

The guard fighting with Amber soon found that he was no match for the almost knighted young man who had once killed a giant. Soon the soldier was laying on the slate floor as his life flowed from the wound in his belly. As the 'Red Warrior' now turned to help Arlo he came face to face with the reality of his prophecy. Standing cold as stone he saw his friend was also laying on the floor. Caw, like in Amber's vision, was positioned over the body with his son's blood staining the sword in his hand.

The Saxon king stood staring at Arlo, frozen with the sudden knowledge that he had killed his own son. Amber, full of angry rage, charged the warlord and drove his sword through the heart of Caw.

"Oh, my foolish friend!" Amber cried as he lifted the young man's body into his arms. "I should not have let you undertake such a dangerous venture. I told you what would happen. Why did you not listen?" he rocked back and forth on his knees, holding Arlo tightly to his chest.

Dhin was now at his side. "You told him?" he asked, "You saw his death?"

Amber looked at his father with tears streaming down his face. "I saw the vision that you spoke of just before your capture, only it showed me who was going to die, Arlo by his father's hand. I told him it could be prevented if he did not return to the fortress but he would not listen. His only thought was in freeing you." Tears flowed freely down the young man's face.

Unexpectedly the young Saxon in Amber's arms moaned as he opened his eyes. "Ambrosius." the words were barely heard as he moved his lips. "You must get out of here. Your men will be making their run for the gate soon." he dropped his head down again as he slipped back into the black world of unconsciousness.

"Father, take my sword." said Amber as he stood up with the young man in his arms. "We will take him with us. While there is still life left in his body, I cannot leave him to the mercy of the Saxons." Going as fast as he could with his heavy burden, Amber led his father to the kitchen, into the cellars, through the tunnel and out the cave.

In the courtyard the last of the fighting men were following Edgar and Hector out the gate. Behind them the area was littered with the bodies of the dead Saxons. Those solders who had not lost their lives were busy trying to put out the fire that had consumed the barracks and was now threatening the larger structures in the compound.

As Dhin, Amber and the wounded prince reached the woods at the bottom of the hill, the men of the village, along with their two leaders, caught up with them. Triumphant in their endeavor they arrived at the inn as the last of the Saxons were hurrying to the fortress over the main road. In the back room at the inn, Amber placed Arlo carefully on the bed and opened the man's tunic. The sword wound went deep into his chest but it was not near the heart. Dhin slumped, exhausted, and into a chair as his son tended the bleeding man.

"It is deep, but I am sure I can stop the flow of blood." he said as Edgar came to his side.

After instructing the servant on what was needed, Amber took his dagger and placed it over the fire in the hearth like he had seen his father once do. Going back to the young Saxon, he placed the red hot blade on the open wound searing the skin shut to stop the bleeding. When this was done he poured some of Hector's best wine over the area, then covered it with the leaves that Edgar had put into the black medicine. When he had wrapped a clean cloth around Arlo's chest, Amber laid a warm cover over his friend and sat by his side waiting for him to regain consciousness. It was then he saw his father sitting in a chair next to the fire. Dhin's face was white and his eyes were closed.

"Father!" cried Amber as he went to the old man. "What is wrong? There is no color in your cheeks."

"Too much has happened to this old body." Dhin replied, "I fear there is not much life left in me." his voice was hollow and he closed his eyes once more.

Amber picked up his father and laid him on the pallet Edgar had used to sleep on. He then took the powder made from the healing plant and put some in a goblet of wine. Holding the cup for his father as he drank, Amber told Edgar to bring over the fur cover from the chest by the door. After placing it over Dhin's chilled body, Amber went back to check Arlo.

This is how the rest of the night progressed as the young man walked back and forth between his father and his friend.

Edgar wanted to help, but Amber would not agree saying, "I am the cause of all this as I was not content to settle into the life of a land owner."

"You must not blame yourself, Master Ambrosius," his servant replied trying to comfort the upset young man. "for your father craved the adventure as much as you did. Otherwise he would not have gone along with this journey. Besides from what you say, it was important to get the book back."

But Amber did not want to think about the book. Not now when his father was ill and his friend lay dying. All he had of value was right here in this room with the gods threatening to take it all away. The hours turned into days as Amber faithfully tended Dhin and Arlo. Edgar was beginning to fear for the young man's health, as he had not slept since the rescue. For three days this went on. Then, on the fourth night, Arlo opened his eyes and spoke.

"Ambrosius." he said weakly.

Amber jumped at the sound of his name, "You are going to be all right, just lay still." he said going to his friend's side. "You are in the back room of the inn. Your wound is healing nicely and the color is again upon your cheeks."

He gave Arlo a sip of wine with the medicine mixed in it and laid the young man back down on the bed.

"You better get some rest, there will be plenty of time to talk later. Right now your body needs sleep so it can build up the blood you have lost."

There were tears on Amber's face as he turned to Edgar and said "Now if only my father would regain his health, then my joy would be complete."

"I am afraid we must face the truth Ambrosius, your father is not getting better. I fear the end is very near." Edgar said with compassion in his voice.

Just then Dhin called out to his son. "You must listen to Edgar, for he speaks the truth."

"No my father, you are not going to die." Cried Amber. "You said so yourself. Did you not say it was not in the stars for you to die yet?"

The young man was besides himself with grief, as he sat by the 'Old one's' side. The thought of losing his father was too much for him to bear.

"Hear me out my son. There is so much I want to tell you and not enough time left." Dhin said taking his son's hand. "The one thing you must know is that you will not be poor for your father is a rich

180

man. Money never had any value for me and all I have gained was put away for my son. You thought the story about the Isle of Mona was just that, a story, but in reality I do own it. The castle on the island holds all my wealth which is now yours, to do with as you please."

His eyes closed, causing Amber to jump to his feet, but Dhin had only paused to catch his breath.

"The one thing I will ask of my son," the old man continued, "is that when the soul flies from this old body, you will bury the remaining shell in the mountains to the west of Meridunum. The gods will lead you to the exact spot where you are to build a tower on top of my grave. A tower that will never tumble to the ground. Promise me you will do this."

When Amber did not answer, Dhin again said, "Promise me Ambrosius, for until you do I will not rest."

"Very well, I promise, but you are not going to die!" the young man said with determination. "Would I have not seen it in a vision? You just need rest that is all."

"The love of a son for his father prevents the mind from facing the truth. I am proud to call you son. Have I ever told you that Ambrosius?" Dhin's mind seemed to be wandering.

"Yes father, many times." Amber answered with tears streaming down his face.

"Well it does not hurt to say it again." Dhin turned his eyes towards the bed where Arlo was sleeping. "He lives?" he asked.

"Just barely." Amber answered, "But he is getting stronger and I have great faith that he will pull through, the same as you will."

"My eyes grow tired, I will rest now." the old man said, not really hearing his son's last words. "Do not worry, my time is not yet up. I have a few more days to spend with my son......" what ever else Dhin was going to say was lost in the clouds of sleep.

Amber could stand the anguish no longer. Putting on his cloak he said to Edgar, "I must get away for a while before my head splits wide open from the pain."

"Let Wallin go with you for there is still danger in the air." his servant said, "The Saxon soldiers are looking for you and your father as well as Arlo."

"No! I must go alone." said Amber as he left the room.

The young man ran from the village, not caring if he was seen. In the forest, the leader of the hills men brought Pegasus to him. Amber mounted the steed and rode like the wind away from the valley. He did not seem to care where he was going. Pegasus, left to decide the course of their journey, headed towards the caves in the mountains of the hills tribe. As man and horse flew over the hazardous terrain they became one with the blackness of the night. Amber was not aware of the land around him as his thoughts were focused on his father.

"He will not die, I will not let him die, and he cannot die!" over and over he said these words into the wind while he pushed Pegasus faster and faster.

But in his head other words kept pounding like his heart itself was in the place of his brain. Words he did not want to hear. *HE IS DYING, MY FATHER IS DYING!*

CHAPTER 21

Somehow Pegasus had found a trail leading to the top of the mountain where Amber found himself sitting on the ledge high above the caves of the hills tribe. He stared up into the blackness above him, trying to gain an answer to the questions that filled his head.

"Why?" he asked, "I have been so long without my father. Now that I have just gotten to know him you are taking him away. Why?" he stood up and shouted into the emptiness.

But no answer came as the stars dotting the heavens blinked noiselessly. They watched the angry young man who was shaking his fists at them, all was still and quiet. Even Pegasus stood without moving as if she were in a hypnotic state.

Amber could contain his grief no longer. Throwing himself down he let all the locked up emotion erupt in great bursts of tears. Once his weeping started, there was no stopping it. His body lay there on the ledge consumed in sorrow, raising and falling with the rhythm of his sobs.

Then, almost as if by instinct, the anguished young man lifted his head to see a column of smoke settling on the ledge in front of him. Amber sat up disbelieving what was happening as he watched a shape starting to form. At first he thought it was the Lady Viviane coming to gloat over his unhappiness. But what he saw was not a woman it was a man. The visor of his helmet covered his face hiding his identity. Then, as he became a solid frame, his hands reached up and took off his headgear. Amber sat like a stone, his eyes transfixed on the specter before him. The man had all the bearing of a noble being and around his head was the same gold ring that had encircled his helmet. The young man's heart beat wildly and he wanted to run from fear but his limbs would not move.

"Ambrosius!" the man spoke. Though his lips moved and formed the words, the sound of his voice seemed to be inside Amber's head.

"Who are you?" the young man's voice trembled as he rose slowly to his feet. Fear was still in his heart but now the knowledge that he had heard that voice before caused him to ask the question.

"I am Uther, of the mighty Pendragons." the apparition answered as he drew his cloak around his shoulders, revealing the emblem of the red dragon sitting on a field of black.

"Uther! My grandfather?" Amber dropped back down on his knees. "It must be a vision." he said softly, then more loudly, "Yes, that is what it is, a vision!"

"This time it is no vision." Now the man's voice was coming from his own lips. "I have told you many times that I would always be with you when you needed me."

"The voice in the tower, and all the other times when I had thought it was my father?" the confused young man asked.

"Yes, it was I not Merlin, helping you to overcome obstacles that barred your way. Now there is an even bigger barrier keeping you from happiness, so I felt my presence was necessary." Uther explained.

"But how can you help? Can you keep the heart of your son and my father beating? Will you be able to breath life back into his failing lungs? Tell me, can you do all this?" all the pain that consumed his body now occupied Amber's voice.

"Only the gods have such power over life and death." his grandfather answered, his voice full of sadness. "When living, I was just a mortal man. Upon my death, the gods chose to teach me the art of helping through words of wisdom."

"Words?" Amber yelled as he rose to his feet no longer afraid of the specter before him. "Words cannot save the life of the one man who means so much to me.

"Maybe not, but it is the wisdom found in words that can ease the pain which fills the heart. It can motivate the mind to endorse what the stars have written. You say you have been so long without your father, that you have just come to know him. But that statement is not entirely true. You met your father when you were but eleven years of age. You knew him as 'Dhin', the 'Old one'. I do not think putting the title of 'Father' on that man would have made you love him more. Your love for him grew as you grew. Strong, faithful, full of confidence. Finding out that he was the one that sired you did not change all that." Uther's voice began to increase in passion as he was determined to move the young man's very soul. "And now that you have the knowledge that Merlin, my son, is your father, your only concern is that he is leaving you. What of him and his desires?"

"He does not want to die." Amber replied boldly. "He has much to live for."

"Are you sure of that?" Uther asked, his eyes burning into his grandson's heart. "Do you know how long he has walked this earth? He has out lived both of his parents and the mother of his son. All the men he has known from the court of my younger son, Arthur, are either dead from battle or old age. Even the king's own death is near at hand. You are the only one he has left. Yet he knows that out of love and loyalty, while he lives, you will remain at his side. You are a young man and as you have shown, crave the excitement that Merlin had in his youth. Your father knows it is unfair for him to keep you from it. But, as you have seen, he is too old to follow you anymore."

Amber stood motionless, his eyes showed all the confusion his grandfather's words had caused. "My father is happy death is near?" he asked, forming the words slowly, not wanting to believe that anyone would really wish to die.

"His only regret is that he must leave you. He knows you have not yet learned the true meaning of your visions or how to use them. The powers that you were born with almost equal that of the gods. If they are used wrongly, you could ruin the lives of those around you as well as your own." Uther's eyes softened as he continued. "Your father is afraid that without his guidance you will use those powers for evil purposes."

Amber looked stunned as he said, "You mean he thinks that I might follow in my mother's footsteps rather than in his?" When he received no answer he went on, "He must realize, being the wise wizard he is, that when he planted the seed of my soul into the Lady Viviane's body, it was a reproduction of himself. She had nothing to do with my being except act as a refuge until the seed had become a child."

"Ah, Ambrosius," his grandfather smiled. "your father did know all that but it was not enough for him to have that knowledge, you needed to know also." tears filled Uther's eyes as he said, "You are truly a man of great wisdom. Your father has no cause to worry for you will be as good a man as he. Read his book well and keep good wisdom in using it. Remember always, being evil is easy for it is bred in the very fiber of mankind. But to do good for your fellow man is the hardest and yet most rewarding of all a mortal's traits."

"The book! Do you mean the one hidden in my saddle?" asked Amber.

Uther did not answer for his body was already turning back into a column of smoke. Just his voice was present and was once more heard only in Amber's head. "Return now to your father. Tell him all that you have learned and make it easier for him to join me, for until he dies you cannot live." The last few words were but a whisper.

Amber jumped as a sound came from behind him. Turning around he saw that it was only Pegasus, pawing the turf beneath her feet. The young man looked back to the spot where he had just seen his grandfather. There was nothing but the stone ledge with blackness surrounding it. He stood for a moment longer, letting their conversation burn into his brain. Then he hurried over to his horse wanting to get back to his father as soon as he could. He had no idea how Pegasus had managed to climb the heights to the ledge so he let the horse have her head and she pushed forward as if the gods were leading her.

In no time at all they were down to the caves and Amber was again riding with the wind to reach his father's side before the old man drew his last breath. As Pegasus galloped towards the valley at the foot of the hills, Uther's words were in Amber's head, *His only regret is that he must leave you.*

"Do not worry my father. I will convince you that you have taught me well. Never shall I fail you." Amber said to the wind as it rushed past him.

When he reached the back of the inn, Wallin was waiting for him, "Master, where have you been?" he cried as he took the horse's reins. "It is almost dawn, the soldiers will soon be in the streets. We have been so worried."

"There was nothing to worry about." said Amber, his voice now stronger and filled with self confidence. "Take Pegasus and hide her well so the soldiers do not find her." he then turned and entered the inn.

"Master Ambrosius." Edgar said as the young man came into the room. Hector had already left and was in the main part of the inn getting ready to feed the hungry soldiers who were soon to come. "I feared the Saxons had caught you." the servant said as he took Amber's cloak and handed him a goblet of wine.

"I had a lot of soul searching to do." Amber answered taking the wine. Looking towards his father he asked, "How is he?"

"He has slept mostly." came the reply, "The few times he opened his eyes and asked for you, I said you were sleeping in the next room. I did not want to cause him worry."

"You did right." Amber said smiling at the man. "And Arlo, have you been watching him too?"

"Yes, he still sleeps but the color comes more and more to his cheeks." the servant said, "I checked his wound and it has stayed sealed with no more bleeding."

"You are a good man Edgar." said Amber clapping his servant on the arm. "Let me tell you now that no matter what happens, I shall want you always by my side."

Edgar's smile showed Amber that the man was nearly dead on his feet from lack of sleep. "You must get some rest now. I cannot do without you if sickness should overcome you too." he said as he led the servant to the door. Edgar was so tired that he could not refuse and left the room.

As Amber sat down next to his father's pallet, the old man opened his eyes. His face brightened up as he saw his son. "Ambrosius," he said softly, "did you have a good rest?"

"Yes father. It has done me more good than you can ever imagine." said Amber as he took the old man's hand in his.

Dhin looked puzzled at the young man, "Your voice. It is so different, as if you have gained much more in years. What has happened?" he asked.

Amber laughed, "I should have known I can keep nothing from my father." He then told Dhin of his ride to the mountain ledge and of all that had occurred there. When he finished he said, "So you see my father, you no longer have to worry about your son. There is none of Lady Viviane's evilness in me, for I am truly your seed, reborn."

Dhin managed to give a weak smile. "As soon as Arlo is well enough for you to leave him, we must return home to Logan Manor." He then closed his eyes and fell back to sleep, holding his son's hand in his own.

Amber gently removed his hand from his father's, pulled the cover up over Dhin's chest and kissed the old man's forehead. He then turned and looked at his friend lying on the other bed. As he bent over Arlo, listening to the steady beat of his heart, the young Saxon opened his eyes.

"Is it still working?" he asked trying to smile.

Amber shook his head, "Here you scare me half to death, thinking you were going to join the gods, and all you can do is joke. If I were in my right mind, I would throw you right out the door." His eyes danced with happiness knowing his friend was going to recover.

He was giving Arlo a drink of wine when the door opened and Hector came bustling into the room. "My lord, good news." he said coming over to the bed. "It seems the Saxon soldiers are not looking for the prince because of the king's death."

"The king is dead?" Arlo broke into the man's words, "My father, was it I who killed him?" he started to get up but Amber gently pushed him back down.

"No Arlo," his friend said with sadness, "I did." When the young Saxon looked at him with horror in his eyes, Amber explained. "I thought he had killed you, and went out of my mind with anger. Before I could think, I ran him through with my sword. Will you ever be able to forgive me?"

"You have saved my life." Arlo said with tears in his eyes. "He was my father. I loved him very much but he was an evil being. How could I not forgive you?"

"There is more." said Hector, reminding them of his presence.

"You are to be crowned king of Galava. The man Walter was killed during the attack on the barracks. The soldiers do not know you were on the enemy's side, or that Lord Dhin was a prisoner. The guard in the dungeon has some how lost his memory and cannot remember why he was down there. The other guards that knew of the plot to get Lord Dhin's treasure are either dead or have run away, fearing for their lives."

"Then all will be well Ambrosius, and you, with your father, will be able to stay here in the court of 'King Arlo'." The young Saxon laughed merrily.

"Hector, will you run and bring the news to the fortress that Prince Arlo is here in our care and will be able to return to the camp by tomorrow." Amber said to the innkeeper, trying not to look at his friend. The young Saxon peered at him with questioning eyes.

When Hector had left, Arlo asked, "What is wrong my friend?" In all the excitement he had not seen Dhin lying on the pallet across the room.

Amber then told him of his father's illness saying, "I must get him home to Logan Manor as soon as I can for he has it in his mind to die where he was born."

"I am truly sorry for the fate that has fallen on Lord Dhin." said Arlo with compassion in his voice. "You know that you will always have a place in my court."

"Right now I cannot think of anything else but my father." Amber replied, "When his soul passes from this earth, I must keep the promise I have made him. After that, if the fates will have it so, we will meet again."

"I will always be grateful that the fates allowed you to change the vision of my death." said the soon to be Saxon king.

"I did not change anything. In my vision I saw your father standing over your body with your blood still wet on his sword. That is just what happened. The wound was not deadly and I was able to stop the bleeding." Amber saw that his friend was growing tired, "You must rest now." he said, "In the morning we will say our good-byes."

That night it was Arlo who could not sleep for he was worried about what his good friend would do after his father's death. Remembering what Amber had told him about the promise, he thought, "But when that is finished, what then? Perhaps he will accept my offer to join the court of my new castle." The young man drifted off with dreams in his head of building his castle high on the hill behind the fortress.

When the sun rose, Amber found that Hector had Dhin and Edgar's horses harnessed to a flat wagon. On the boards was arranged a bed of straw covered with fur hides. Once the old man was laying on them, he was covered with another fur to keep the chill from entering his aged body.

"You will not forget my offer?" Arlo asked as he leaned on Hector for support. He had insisted on coming outside to say good-bye to his friends.

"I will not forget." Amber smiled at the young Saxon, "We will meet again good prince and by then you will have your castle on the hill and be called King." Mounting Pegasus he led the way for the wagon.

Wallin, who's last living relatives had been killed trying to keep Dhin from being captured, was sitting with Edgar on the seat of the wagon. Amber had agreed with the servant that the boy belonged with them. Sitting high on his beautiful black steed Amber looked every bit a king himself. Reaching the top of the hill this handsome warrior looked back down into the valley at the friends he was leaving behind.

"Perhaps some day I will return." he said with sadness in his voice, "Perhaps."

He looked at Dhin who was laying in comfort on the straw. The old man smiled at his son with a faint trace of that familiar gleam in his eyes.

"Someday, my son, you will find your way back to this valley. When you do, I will be with you still." Dhin spoke in a whisper, as he was getting weaker. Then, closing his eyes, he slept.

Amber rode by the side of the cart watching his sleeping father. "How can he believe he will return to Galava with me when he knows he is dying?" He asked the question, not really expecting an answer.

CHAPTER 22

It took longer for the three men to return from their adventure than it did when they first set out. Dhin's life was in the balance and they did not want him to die out in the wilderness. Edgar, with Wallin sitting beside him, guided the horses pulling the wagon with strong determination. He saw every rut and fallen branch laying in their path and maneuvered so the wheels missed every obstacle. In his loving hands the 'Old one' was able to sleep most of the journey.

As they neared the village of Meridunum tears of sorrow welled up in Amber's heart for now his father's time was near at hand. The young man wanted to stop the hands of time right then, right there. Yet when it felt like the pain was going to consume him, his grandfather's voice echoed in his head.

"It's alright to grieve but do not despair. Remember that until he dies, you cannot live." Uther's words were strong and loud. It seemed as if he was standing before his grieving grandson.

"We will soon be at Logan Manor." Edgar said bringing Amber back to reality. "Have you decided what you will tell Jasper? He was also the uncle of Morlan, and brother to Gorfan."

Amber looked at the concerned servant and only shook his head. He had not known Jasper's relationship to their fallen friend. He had been so consumed with his own sorrow that he did not think about anyone else. How selfish of me." he thought as he looked toward the house appearing before him

"It will be bad enough for him to see his dying master and friend." Amber answered, "I do not know how I shall tell him the other sad news."

"When the time comes, you will know what to say." Dhin's halting voice spoke to his son. "You are very wise, my son, just like your father." The old man managed to smile as his eyes showed a glimmer of the old gleam. "Do you know how proud I am to have you for my son?" he whispered.

"Just as proud as I am to have you for my father." his son answered.

Dhin closed his eyes again and the look of peace upon his face made Amber realize his grandfather had been right. His father was happy to be going 'home'. The young man sighed as he tried to accept what the gods had ordained. Hoping beyond all hope that some of his father's contentment would rest in his soul.

When they reached the manor it was evident that Jasper already knew everything that had happened in Galava. He was standing in the courtyard with the rest of the household. The only sounds that could be heard was the clop-clop of the horse's hoofs and the creaking of the wagon wheels. As the horses stopped in front of the servants, Jasper motioned for one of the larger men to carry Dhin to his room.

"Ah it is a sorry sight when a man cannot make his body respond to his brain." said Dhin as he was gently raised from the straw in the back of the wagon. "Jasper my friend, I have missed you and our little talks together." said the old man as he was carried past his friend.

"Lord Dhin." Jasper could hardly get the words out. "I have missed you also. It is good to have you home where you belong."

Dhin smiled and shook his head. There were tears in his failing eyes as he realized the sorrow his servant and friend was going through. He said no more as he was slowly carried to his room.

After the 'Old one' was placed in his bed and tended by his son, Jasper brought some food and wine and placed it on the small table near the hearth. As he was about to leave Amber motioned for him to sit with him. For a while both men just sat looking into the flames, both wanting to say something to comfort the other yet, not knowing what to say.

Finally Jasper broke the silence. "I received word from the hills tribe when you and Lord Dhin first followed the Saxons to Galava. Since then messages came every week. I knew when Gorfan was found and the fate of poor, poor Morlan." he stopped speaking to wipe the tears from his eyes.

After taking a sip of the wine Amber had given him Jasper continued.

"They told me that Caw's torture is what broke him." he said, his eyes on the old man lying still upon his bed. "That being confined in the dungeon without the comfort of any fire caused him to give up hope." The servant looked at the young man sitting next to him.

"The fire in the Golden castle is what kept Lord Dhin going when you were out searching in the forest of the fairies. Starring into the flames, he could watch your every move and therefore have hope. All the years he watched you grow, from birth until you appeared at the temple, he always had hope because the fire was always there. When, in Galava, he could no longer keep you in his sight, he lost the hope that had kept him going long after the gods tried to take him." Jasper let out a long sigh.

"And now, because of my carelessness, the gods have won. They are taking my father away." Amber spoke with all the sadness that was in his heart. "Merlin, once the greatest man in the court of Arthur, is dying, and I have caused it." The young man starred into the flames in the hearth as if he were trying to find a way to keep his father with him.

Jasper knew there was nothing he could say to take the burden of guilt off Amber's shoulders so he quietly left he room.

"My son," Dhin's voice filtered into Amber's thoughts, "come here by my side." Weakly he took the young man's hand in his. "You must stop blaming yourself. There is much that will happen after I depart this earth. I cannot tell you now but you must trust me that when everything I have done comes to pass, you will have all the answers you need. Can you trust me?" the old man asked his son.

Amber looked deep into his father's eyes. It seemed like the blackness was drawing him in. He tried to look away but found it too difficult. All of a sudden the pain that had been like a fire in his heart ceased. In its place was a feeling of contentment that Amber had never known. He laid his head on his father's chest and sighed a deep sigh.

"Yes my father, I can trust you." he said with all the love that was in his heart.

With the deep pain gone Amber could finally let go the tears that were pent up inside him. As he sat there, his head upon his father's chest, unloading all the sorrow in his heart, Dhin soothed his son with words of comfort. Soon both father and son were fast asleep. A sleep that the son would wake from but chances were the father would not.

The next morning the new lord of Logan Manor gathered the sadden household into the main hall. By the tear stained eyes and lowered heads, Amber realized Jasper had relayed the news of his father's passing.

"As you know, Lord Dhin has gone to join the gods." Amber said, "I know you will all miss him as much as I will. You are welcome to remain in my services as I intend to keep his house open and the lands working." the young man looked around the room.

Jasper came over to his side. "As head servant I speak for all." he said, "We agree that as much as we loved Lord Dhin, we also love his son. We will stay and serve you well Lord Ambrosius."

Amber smiled. "Thank you Jasper." he said, overcome with a mixture of emotions. "I would like you, Edgar and Wallin to accompany me to the mountains that are to be my father's final resting place. There, over his grave, we shall build the greatest tower in all the world."

As the servants readied Dhin's body for the journey, Amber collected all the items from his father's room that were going to be put into the tower. As he stood there looking at all the books, charts and bottles of medicines he was amazed at how much the 'Old one' had managed to gather in the short time they were there. His father had been precise in what was to go with him and Amber selected just those things. Soon Edgar and Wallin were once again upon the seat of the wagon ready to follow Amber and Jasper.

They took the west road out of Meridunum and headed for the mountains in the distance. Here and there along the trail were signs to show them the way, just as Dhin had said there would be. A mark on a tree, some stones piled up, or a broken branch to point the way.

They reached the mountains as the last ray of light left the heavens. The next morning when Amber awoke he saw Edgar and Jasper tying his fathers shell onto a makeshift carrier. The path up the mountain was too narrow for the wagon so Pegasus would be used to pull the precious cargo.

When they reached the top Amber marveled at the place Dhin had chosen for his final resting place. The trail ended in a clearing and when Jasper had untied the carrier, the young man rode around the area looking for just the right spot.

"It is amazing!" Amber exclaimed as he returned, "It is as if a giant had ripped off the peak of this mountain. The only trees are the ones that encircle the clearing around the edge thereby hiding this area from view. The land all around is flat, a perfect place to build a tower. We will dig the hole for my father's shell in the very middle of the clearing. But first let us make camp over there by those trees."

Amber had picked a place where the trees were the tallest and they would be sheltered from the elements. It took quite a few more trips down the mountain to unload the wagon and carry its contents to their camp. When they were done Edgar, Jasper and Wallin proceeded to dig Dhin's grave. By the time they were finished the sun had begun its decent and the twilight was revealing its silver stars They then returned to their camp for a quick cold meal after which they bedded down for the night.

As the gray dawn of morning spread across the area three men and a young lad could be seen reverently lowering the wrapped body of their beloved father and friend. Having finished pushing the earth over Dhin's resting place Jasper, Edgar and Wallin stepped back allowing Amber to say his final farewells.

While the rays of the new day's sun beamed down on the grave at the young man's feet, Amber paid homage to his teacher, his friend, his father. Looking like a god himself, with raised hands high above his head, he offered up the spirit of Merlin; Myrddhin Ambrosius; Lord Dhin, to the icons waiting to receive him.

"We must now turn our thoughts towards the building of a tower." said Amber as he turned away from the small mound of dirt. "Jasper take Wallin and return to Logan Manor. There you will gather the materials and men to do the job. Edgar and I will stay here and mark off the land."

As Jasper and Wallin were leaving, Amber and Edgar were bending over a large piece of parchment that was spread out on the ground. On it were laid out the plans Dhin had drawn for his son to follow. The outside of the tower would look just like the one that once stood in Larkwood. Inside stone stairs would circle around the walls until they reached a small landing. There at the end of the landing would be a large oak door with symbols carved into its wood. This would be the entrance to the towers only room.

It took five days for Jasper to return with the materials and the men. In that time Amber and Edgar had managed to haul many of the large rocks that were at the base of the mountain, up to the clearing ready to become the tower's walls. In no time at all their hard work was done and Amber was looking up at the ominous structure standing before him.

"There is nothing else to do here." said Amber, "We must now return to our daily living until one year has passed and I return to read the book that has been such a mystery."

One by one the group of men left the clearing and gathered at the foot of the mountain. Jasper motioned for them to start their journey back home, then settled down to wait for his new master. Soon the noise of Pegasus coming down the path aroused the servant who had been dozing.

"Will the book be safe left in the tower?" he asked Amber as he rode by his side.

"Yes." Amber answered, "There is no one left who might want to gain from it."

Back on top of the mountain an eerie light seemed to glow from the towers window. Layers of white puffy clouds drifted slowly over the structure until it was totally swallowed up. If Amber had looked once more he would have been amazed to find it hidden in the white vapor. He might have caught the sound of a sigh and a voice whispering;

Soon my son, soon. One year will pass very quickly. Then we will be one.

EPILOGUE: THE REBIRTH

Amber sat at the window in the only room of the tower. As he looked out into the distance the beauty of the surrounding area took his breath away. The mountain the structure was built on was high enough to see the blue gray waters of the ocean far over the neighboring hills. The height of the tower made him feel as if he were sitting among the clouds.

Watching two falcons that were circling each other cautiously, Amber became lost in his memories. Thinking back to the day he ran from the evil Lady Viviane and remembering his flight that brought him to the temple of Dusk put a smile on the young man's face. His eyes filled with tears as the past danced before him. He remembered all the days he had spent with the man he later would learn was his father. Amber's thoughts were like pictures in the sky. Back to the court of king Arthur. Back to the forest of the fairies and his grandmother nursing his wounds. Back to the court of Arthur again and the joust with Allon who he now knew was his brother. Back to the killing of the giant of Saint Michael's Mount and their departure to Dhin's birth place. Back to the search for Gorfan and the book and the death of that faithful servant. The meeting of Arlo, Wallin, Hector and the hills tribe drew a sigh from his throat. Then the saddest memory of them all, back to the day, one year ago, when his father had left the world of the living.

It was the same night Dhin had helped his son find some peace even in the face of his father's death. Amber had fallen asleep with his head upon his father's chest. He was awakened by the old man's voice as he tried to speak with the death rattle in his throat.

"Ambrosius, the tower!" he gasped holding tight to his son's arm.

Amber spoke gently as he tried to reassure his father, "I will remember. Your wish will be carried out. The tower shall be built over the grave of your body in the mountains to the west."

"There is something else you must promise." Dhin tried to raise himself up on his elbows, but having no strength he slipped back down again.

"Father, you must not force yourself to talk." Amber said.

"I have no time left and I must ask you one more thing." Dhin took a sip of the wine his son was now offering him. "The book. Where is it?"

With the death of his father so close at hand, the book was the last thing on Amber's mind. "It is still in its hiding place, in Pegasus' saddle." he replied, "Why do you ask?"

"The promise I want of you is that you will not read it until the tower is finished and one year has past from the moment of my death. It is most important that you do this." Dhin's eyes were wide as he waited for his son's answer.

"I will do as you ask, my father." Amber said with lowered head.

In his last moments of life Dhin managed a smile for the young man. "Do you know how proud I am to have you for my son?" he whispered.

"Just as proud as I am to have you for my father." his son answered.

This time his father did not hear the now familiar reply. He had closed his eyes for the last time and there was a smile on his face. Amber remembered the words of his grandfather high on the ledge above the caves of the hills tribe and knew his father was where he wanted to be.

Suddenly the cries of the two falcons locked in combat, brought

Amber back from the past. The sun was near setting and the time to read the book was close at hand. Lighting the candle on the table beside him, Amber picked up the book.

"MERLIN: MYRDDHIN AMBROSIUS." The words jumped out at him, as they had the first time he opened the book in another tower. Turning the page, Amber noticed that the words were still unreadable. His teacher, Gorganis, had taught him many languages but still he could not understand the words. Suddenly, as the sun disappeared into the ocean and a slight breeze caused the candle to flicker, a fine mist seemed to fall around him. As it cleared he saw the writing in the book change into the letters of the old tongue right before his eyes. As last, after almost twenty years he could finally read his father's writings.

Time seemed to stand still as the young man was drawn into the very pages. Beads of sweat were on his brow and his heart beat so wildly it almost jumped out of his chest. When the last word was read, Amber placed the book down on the table and stared out the window into the blackness that had now surrounded the tower.

"I believe I now know what you meant, grandfather, when you said to use the words of my father wisely." He turned back to the book and moved his hand over the cover. "On these pages lie all the wonders of Merlin's magic, everything I will need to accomplish my father's dream."

As he sat there, Amber felt a strange sensation coming over him. Not like when a vision was about to happen, but something entirely different. It filled his body like rippling waves of lightening. There was no fear in him, as he seemed to sense what was happening was his destiny.

Suddenly a voice spoke with the lightness of the wind. "My son, you have followed my wishes well." A column of mist rose from the fire and drifted slowly towards him. The young man stood and stretched out his arms welcoming the spiral apparition. As it settled into his body, Amber could hear the words in his mind. "Now at last I live again, in the soul of my son."

Again, Uther's words rocked the young man's memory. "For until he dies, you cannot live." It seemed like the answers to all the questions his brain had carried were now being answered.

Amber turned and walked to a door in the wall that opened to reveal stairs winding around the outside of the structure. They led to the very top of the tower where a platform had been constructed to resemble a stone ledge. Here on this ledge Amber stood with outstretched arms looking up towards the heavens.

The ebony sky housed millions of celestial lights and he seemed to be reaching to touch them. Suddenly from the motionless void, a wind came rushing around the tower. It caught his red cloak which would have been blown from his shoulders had it not been for the dragon brooch that held it in place.

He spoke now and as he did his voice was no longer that of the unsure young man he had been. It was loud, confidant and resembled the voice of his father.

"Yes! Oh yes!" he said with all the fervor of the emotions that had been locked inside of him. "The father does live again, in the soul of his son." then putting his head back he shouted to the gods. "And now I, Ambrosius Myrddhin, and the great wizard Merlin are one!"

As the moon shed its light on this majestic lord it caught a familiar gleam in his eyes.

The End?
Or just a beginning?

AUTHOR'S NOTE

When Julius Caesar first led the Romans into Britain, he found the people to be warlike, of some mechanical ability and with a slight knowledge of agriculture. Their dominion may be traced by the remains of roads, walls, and villas and by the presence of a few Roman words in the English language. In the year 410, the Romans left and the Britons were at the mercy of the Scots and Picts who came down from the north and northwest.

At the request of the Britons, the Saxons drove away the barbarians and were given the island of Thenet for their home. Before long they found the island too small, so they drove the Britons away from the southeastern corner of the land and took it for themselves. More Saxons came and drove the Britons farther west. These Britons were not cowards and resisted so heroically that it was more than one hundred years before they were conquered.

It was during this time the legend of a king to unite all the kings of the land came into being. This brave and powerful king was Arthur and with his gallant knights he kept England free from the invading Saxons. He had the Castle Camelot built high on a hill where the splendor and brilliance of the court outshone any other. Many tournaments were held where knights in shining armor won the admiration of the fair ladies of the court. There was one man who stayed at King Arthur's side, giving him advice and help in his most difficult tasks. That man was the great and powerful magician known as MERLIN.

The encyclopedia describes this man as; Merlin, or Myrddhin, legendary wizard and bard of Arthurian romance. Was of sixth century Welsh origin and mystic birth, played a part at the court of Vortigern (or, more probably, of Uther Pendragon) and a still more important part at the court of King Arthur, Uther Pendragon's son. It was for the father that (according to one account) Merlin made the famous Round Table. From the twelfth century onward, Merlin was famous as the reputed author of Prophecies (dating to the sixth century) concerning the destinies of England. Merlin figures in Malory's "Le Morte d'Arthur," in Alfred Lord Tennyson's "Idylls of the King" and in many other works including Nemius' "History of the Britons" (in which Merlin appears under the name of AMBROSIUS.)

The legend of Merlin as taken from "The Age of Chivalry" by Thomas Bulfinch, states that Merlin fell in love with Viviane, the Lady of the lake. Being impelled by a fatal destiny, he disclosed to her various important secrets of his art. The lady, not being content with his devotion, chose to use the magic to trap him in the strongest tower in the world. After this event, Merlin was never more known to be seen by mortal man.

There has never been any record of his death and therefore I chose to have him escape from the wicked Viviane, after revenging himself by planting the seed that someday would be his rebirth. Being a myth, it is possible for him to have escaped in the manner I have written and return to the world of the living under an assumed name.

Most of the names of the people in the story are fictitious. Yet here and there the reader may recognize the names of famous figures known to exist during the time of the Arthurian legends.

Consulting maps on England and Wales, I tried to use the names of villages commonly used during the sixth century. The village of Larkwood, of course, never existed.

Even though the story line follows the course of English legend, the tale itself was formed in the author's imagination. The only facts known about the period between the Romans leaving the land and the Saxons total conquest has come down through the centuries in songs and poems recited by the poets, leaving the mind much to dream about.

Knights in shining armor, fighting for their king and land, have always fascinated me. Whenever reading these stories I have put myself right into the pages to feel the wind in my face as I ride by their side.

I hope the reader will enjoy being swept-back into the days when knights roamed the countryside, giants stalked the mountains and nothing was impossible.

Printed in the United States
45848LVS00005B/1-102

9 781424 120345